The Captain and the Cheerleader

The Captain and the Cheerleader

Elaine Cantrell

A Wings ePress, Inc.
Mainstream Novel

Edited by: Jeanne Smith
Copy Edited by: Joan Powell
Senior Editor: Jeanne Smith
Executive Editor: Marilyn Kapp
Cover Artist: Trisha FitzGerald

All rights reserved

Wings ePress Books

Published by Wings ePress, Inc.

Wings ePress Inc.
3000 N. Rock Road
Newton, KS 67114

Dedication

For my sweet grandson, Simon

One

Robin Landford swept into the room and plopped down into an orange plastic chair beside Susan English. "I think Kurt Deveraux is gay."

It was Friday afternoon, but Robin's statement halted the teacher exodus from the faculty lounge.

"Why do you say that, Robin?" Susan asked. Yeah, her voice sounded chilly and a bit snooty, but she couldn't help herself. Robin was fresh out of college and seemed to think she was God's gift to men; she flirted with anything in pants. This annoying little creature had probably made a play for Kurt's attention and been rejected. Of course, in Robin's defense, she'd have to say that not many women could ignore Kurt Deveraux. There might be a man somewhere who had more sex appeal than the blond, blue-eyed coach, but Susan doubted it.

She watched as Robin tossed her hair and pouted. "If I can't get his attention he isn't interested in women."

Several people rolled their eyes. "Oh, I don't think that's the problem at all." Susan smiled her most serene smile at her irritating colleague. "You just don't know how to attract a man like Kurt."

"And you do?" Robin's eyebrows shot straight up. "If that's true why haven't you already gone out with him? Don't tell me you wouldn't be interested. He's hot."

"Until recently I was involved with someone else. I had no desire to see Kurt or any other man socially."

"Well, I think you're full of it," Robin sniffed. "If I couldn't get him to notice me, I know *you* can't."

Around the faculty lounge a murmur of delighted, horrified voices broke out.

Susan finished her soft drink and tossed the can into a nearby recycling bin. "I could make Kurt ask me out if I wanted to."

"Yeah? Prove it. Get him to ask you out. I'll bet you fifty dollars you can't do it," Robin taunted. "All he's interested in is football."

Melissa Taylor, Susan's best friend, cleared her throat. "How long would she have to get the date?"

"Two weeks ought to be enough for an old pro like Susan." Robin snickered as her gaze swept around the lounge. "Would the rest of you like to get a piece of the action?"

All at once a carnival atmosphere permeated the room. They chose Don Brooks who taught art to keep track of the bets, and everyone hurried to put money on his or her favorite.

From the corner of her eye, Susan watched as Robin smirked at everyone in the room. Why did Mr. Dennis hire such an undisciplined, annoying child? It would be a pleasure to give Robin her comeuppance.

Don recorded the last bet on a sheet of copier paper. "It's about fifty-fifty. Sorry, Robin, but my money's on Susan. When she enters a room, men sit up and take notice."

Melissa, who stood near the door, wildly waved her hand to get their attention. "Here comes Kurt now."

Kurt looked surprised to find so many teachers in the lounge. He probably was; on Friday the school usually emptied in a hurry.

"What's up?" Kurt inquired of the room at large as he rounded the corner and turned toward his mailbox. "Why are you all so quiet?"

Susan spoke up before anyone else could answer. "Oh, we were talking about the game tonight. Are we going to beat Middleton?"

Kurt grinned and made Susan's heart pick up a little speed. Bet every other woman in the room had the same reaction. Could any woman alive resist Kurt Deveraux's smile?

Kurt shrugged. "Just between ourselves, we're going to get our butts kicked, but the boys will do their best, so if we lose, we lose. We don't have the talent that Middleton does."

Susan stared straight into those beautiful blue eyes. "You've done everything you can to get them ready. Everyone knows that."

"Thanks for the vote of confidence. I hope we don't let you down." He threw a set of papers into his mailbox and turned toward the football field.

Robin giggled as she grabbed her book bag. "Not too great a beginning. What's wrong, Susan? I thought he'd be falling at your feet."

"It's early days yet," said Don. He picked up his briefcase and waved goodbye while the others collected their belongings, and Melissa turned off the light, leaving the lounge deserted and dark.

Melissa and Susan strolled slowly toward their cars. Who wanted to go home on such a beautiful afternoon? The crisp, cool weather turned the sky a lovely, deep blue, and the trees blazed in shades of scarlet, orange, and gold. The smell of smoke from burning leaves periodically filled the air.

"Good football weather," said Melissa. "Are you going to the game tonight?"

Susan frowned. "I guess I should since I made that stupid bet. I wish I'd never done it, but if I cancel now, Robin will think it's because I can't get him, and she'll never let me live it down."

Melissa nodded. "That's true. Robin's one of the most annoying people I've ever met. Kurt probably ran for his life when she batted her eyelashes at him."

"Well, she might have tossed her hair at him."

Both of them snickered. Robin did toss her hair frequently.

"All I have to do is go out with him once, so maybe it won't be too bad." Susan kicked at a fallen acorn to relieve her feelings.

"I don't get it," Melissa said. "Why does it bother you to go out with him? He's so sexy my knees get weak when he walks into a room."

Susan giggled. "I know what you mean. It doesn't bother me to go out with him, but it does bother me to use him just to put Robin in her place."

Melissa thought about it. "He'll never know, so why worry? If you have a good time you might want to go out with him for real, though. The man is drop dead gorgeous."

"I've noticed." Susan pulled out her cell phone to take a picture of an especially brilliant tree on the edge of the teacher parking lot. "I always notice six foot two, blond Vikings."

"Good description. I'll bet he gets all those muscles working out with the team."

"Wherever he gets them they sure look good." Susan extended her phone so Melissa could see the picture she'd taken.

Susan threw her keys into the basket on the kitchen cabinet and flung her book bag into the closet. It was so much fun putting that thing away on Friday! "Here, kitty, kitty," she called.

An ancient yellow cat with chewed up ears and inscrutable green eyes strolled into the kitchen. Samson was fifteen years old and didn't get around too well anymore, but he had lived with Susan since he was a kitten. She confided in him as she did in no one else. Samson never criticized and always made her feel better.

"Hey, boy," she crooned as she scooped the cat up and scratched his chin. "What did you do today? I got myself into hot water at school with a stupid bet."

Samson purred and offered his own brand of comfort to Susan. "Yes, I know it'll work out okay. It's just that I don't want to hurt his feelings. He seems like a nice man."

A new thought suddenly struck her. "Goodness, Samson. Maybe he really won't be interested in me."

Samson meowed his opinion that Kurt would be interested, so Susan kissed the top of his head to thank him for his support and gave him a can of tuna before she went to get ready for the football game.

If only she hadn't made that horrible bet! Guilt swamped her. *At the moment I don't feel too good about myself. Maybe I should cancel the bet. No! If I do, Robin'll never let me hear the end of it.* Next time she'd refuse to let Robin get her dander up, but this time she intended to show the little witch a thing or two.

Kurt left the faculty lounge and joined the football team for its traditional pre-game meal. He filled his plate from the buffet and sat down beside his longtime friend and fellow coach, Jason Cooper. Jason had been his best friend ever since they were in Mrs. Turner's first grade class at Fairfield Elementary.

"Hey, what's wrong with you?" demanded Jason. He dug his elbow into Kurt's side when Kurt failed to reply to his question about the night's strategy. "You're a million miles away."

"Sorry. I was thinking about what happened in the lounge a minute ago."

"What happened?"

"Susan English gave me a compliment."

Jason laughed. "Did she try to have her way with you?" he teased. "I've got my share of female admirers, buddy, but something about you drives women wild. Even Mrs. Kirby melts when you go through the lunch line, and everyone knows she's as tough as nails."

Kurt grinned. "Susan said she knew I'd tried my best to get the team ready for Middleton."

"Oh, it was a football compliment. Smart girl." Jason leered at him. "You still think she's hot?"

Kurt's fork paused on its way to his mouth. "I never said that, but, yeah, I do. Susan English could put a movie star to shame."

"What about Aleisha Childs?"

"What about her?"

Jason paused to swallow a big drink of his tea and made Kurt smile. Mrs. Kirby always provided the tea for the football team, exactly what he had hoped for when he complimented her on how good it tasted. Everyone at school loved it, and that included the football team.

"We've known Aleisha since we were ten," Jason said. "She's awfully pretty. How many times have you gone out with her now?"

"A few. I like Aleisha, but Susan can put her in the shade. And before you ask, I have no idea if Aleisha and I are serious about each other."

Jason picked up the tea pitcher and refilled Kurt's glass. "You don't have to tell me you like Susan's looks. I've seen the way you stare at her when you think nobody's watching. Especially her legs. You've always noticed a woman's legs."

Kurt cursed his fair skin as his face burned. "I think she's a classy, elegant woman, and you're right about her legs. They're slender and about a mile long."

"Are you thinking of asking her out?" Jason shrugged. "It isn't any of my business, but..."

"You're asking anyway. Yes, I've thought about it. I heard she broke up with that guy, what's his name, Tommy Price, but you'd better keep it to yourself." Kurt frowned at Jason. "I don't see any need for the whole world to know my business."

"Is she coming to the game tonight?"

"She didn't say, and I didn't ask."

"Well, you probably wouldn't have any time for her anyway," Jason said as he picked up his cheeseburger.

They finished their meal and went with the team to the locker room. In the rush Kurt forgot about Susan and her compliment. His team deserved his entire attention when they were facing a formidable opponent like Middleton.

Kurt clenched his teeth and trained his eyes toward the field. The game had gone much better than he had hoped, but the Mavericks were still losing by six points. He winced when his quarterback stumbled and almost went down. This late in the fourth quarter, his players were rapidly running out of steam. Worse still, Middleton's strong defense had frustrated the Mavericks during the entire game.

He had tried some trick plays to gain yardage, but every time his plans had gone awry. If they failed to get a first down on the next play, they'd have to punt and give possession of the ball to the other team. If that happened, Middleton would win.

Shoulders tense with excitement, Kurt jumped when a hand tapped his back. He spun around and snarled at the boy who stood there. "What do you want? Can't you see I'm busy?"

The boy flinched, but he held his ground. "Miss English said to give you this and for you to look at it before the next play."

"Who passes notes at a time like this? What does she think this is, study hall?" He crumpled the note, intending to fling it to the ground, but at the last moment something changed his mind, and he unfolded the paper the boy had handed him. His jaw dropped when he saw the football play Susan had sketched out. *Try this,* he read. *I think it will work.*

It could work. Why not give it a try? At this point, they had nothing to lose. He called his last time out to give instructions to the team. Thank goodness for Ken Banks. The Mavericks had never had a better quarterback. With his guidance they might have a chance of successfully running this thing.

He held his breath as the team lined up on the field and snapped the ball. If he hadn't known better, he would have thought the boys had practiced this play many times because it went as smoothly as clockwork. The Mavericks moved the ball across the goal line almost before the other team could find where it went. The score was tied.

Kurt's fingernails dug into his palms when the team lined up to kick the extra point. The spectators rose to their feet and fell silent until the announcer screamed, "It's good! Mavericks on top twenty-one to twenty." The crowd went wild. With only three seconds remaining on the clock, the band began to play as the cheerleaders led a cheer for their team.

Jason came running from the far end of the field. "What a play! Why'd you keep it a secret?"

"Later," Kurt shouted as his players threw themselves against him in a concentrated group hug.

Pumped with adrenalin, Kurt jogged up the hill toward the locker room with Jason beside him. The football team followed, their cleats clicking against the pavement. He laughed aloud which brought an answering grin from Jason. They'd actually beaten Middleton!

The team overtook Melissa Taylor just as they crested the hill. "Chris!" Kurt yelled, but it was too late. Chris Eades, the Mavericks' kicker and the biggest boy on the team, wasn't looking where he was going and slammed into Melissa who fell to the pavement with a little cry.

Jason got to her first. "Are you okay? That was some hit you took."

"I think so." She pursed her lips. "My knee burns like crazy, but I don't think I'm hurt too bad."

"Chris'll apologize to you on Monday morning," Jason promised. "I know the guys are excited, but there's no excuse for such carelessness." He held out his hand to pull Melissa up.

"Thanks," she said.

Kurt studied her face. "Are you sure you're okay?"

"Yes. I'm fine."

"Jason, you'd better walk her to her car. Getting knocked down sort of shakes you up."

Jason's quick agreement made Kurt smile. Why not help a buddy out? Jason had been watching Melissa for months now. He grinned as he joined the team in the locker room. Who'd have thought he had it in him to be a matchmaker?

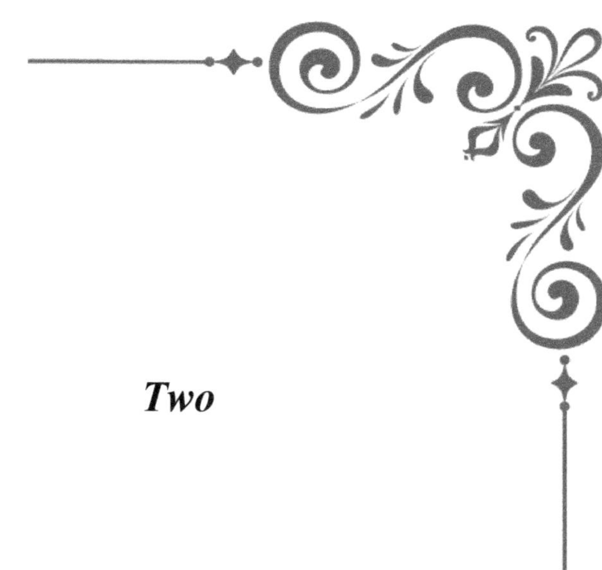

Two

Kurt yawned and turned over to look at the clock. Seven thirty. Dang that barking dog next door. He usually didn't get up until eight thirty or so on Saturday. He squeezed his eyes shut, but he couldn't go back to sleep because he'd started to think of Susan English.

How did a beautiful English teacher come up with such a simple but effective play? *I spend a lot of time creating new plays and devising strategies, but this one strikes me as brilliant. I've never done anything to equal it.* He chuckled. *Hope she doesn't want my job.*

He was in the kitchen making some coffee when the phone rang. A quick glance at the caller ID told him it was Aleisha Childs. "Hi, Aleisha. Did you see the game last night?"

"No, I missed it. I've got strep throat so I guess the party's out too. I'm sorry for the late notice."

Kurt winced. "Oh, that hurts. Don't worry about the party. We'll go to the next one."

"Thanks. I'll talk to you later."

What a shame. He'd looked forward to the party, but going without a date probably wouldn't be as much fun. As he sipped his coffee, he had an idea. Why not ask Susan to go with him? *Aleisha and I aren't engaged or anything, and if Susan went with me I could ask her about that play.*

No, I can't do that. It might make Aleisha mad even though I know she went out with Brent Stephens a couple of weeks ago. Brent made a big point of telling me when I saw him at the football jamboree.

Uh oh. What if he and Susan didn't get along? It might be awkward to work with her if they didn't hit it off.

Okay, he'd wash his car and forget about it. His life suited him just find. Who needed complications? He'd ask Susan about the play the next time he saw her at school.

———— ⚬⚭⚬ ————

Kurt's call came around lunchtime on Saturday. Susan had been waiting since nine, but when she answered the phone she tried to sound surprised to hear from him.

"Susan, it's Kurt Deveraux. I was calling to thank you for your help last night. Without your play we would've lost."

"Oh, you're welcome. I was glad I could do something; I like to see the Mavericks win." Susan bit her lip to keep from laughing. Bet anything she knew where this conversation was going.

"Yeah, I've seen you at a couple of games," he said. "I know it's short notice, but if you aren't busy tonight, I'd really enjoy it if you'd go to a party with me. I've been told there'll be dancing."

"Who's giving a party?"

"You wouldn't know him," Kurt answered. Susan heard the smile in his voice even over the phone.

"Well, I'd love to go anyway. What time will you pick me up? Do you know where I live?"

"I'll pick you up around seven. Be sure to wear something casual. This won't be anything real fancy. Tell me where you live."

Susan gave Kurt directions to her house and went to her closet to see what she had to wear. Maybe her new jeans would be nice with the black sweater she had bought on sale last winter. The jeans fit like a dream, and the sweater always brought out the gold in her hair. Her black boots would look perfect with the outfit and so would some turquoise jewelry she'd bought in Arizona.

Samson meowed piteously and rubbed against her legs. "Do you need a treat?" Susan crooned. Scooping him up, she went to the kitchen for a kitty treat. Guess she might as well call Melissa now too.

"Hi, it's me," she said. "Guess who I'm going out with tonight."

"Not Kurt?" squealed Melissa. "Boy, that was fast work. Robin's going to die."

Susan laughed. "I hope she'll be suitably impressed. How am I going to prove to everyone that I really went out with him?"

"You can thank him for the evening in the lounge in front of everyone. Where's he taking you?"

"Some friend of his is giving a party, and he asked me to go."

Melissa giggled. "Have a good time, but you'd better behave yourself. I saw how you were watching him last night. I think you liked what you saw."

Susan rolled her eyes even though Melissa couldn't see. "Of course, I did. What's not to like? Kurt's absolutely gorgeous."

"I noticed. Whew, this conversation could get out of hand. Behave now, you hear?"

"He invited me to a party for goodness sake." Susan absently stroked Samson who had jumped up on the table. "The worst that can happen is we won't have a good time together."

"I suppose so. Guess what happened to me last night."

"What?" Susan asked as she brushed a cat hair off her nose.

Melissa recounted how Chris had knocked her down. "Jason seemed concerned about me even though I don't know him that well. He's cute, and he has nice hands."

"You've always had a hand fetish," Susan hooted.

"I didn't know you'd noticed. Jason's probably a nice guy, and I do like how strong and shapely his hands are, but he's a coach. No offense to your dad, but most of the coaches I know go around slapping football players on the butt, chewing tobacco, and laughing at dirty jokes. They don't do much teaching either."

"You're stereotyping."

Melissa sighed. "Yeah, I know." Her voice perked up. "I'm sure he'll make Chris apologize to me, and maybe he'll make the kid do a few extra pushups to pay for being so careless."

As Susan hung up the phone, Samson head butted her to get her attention. He always seemed to understand when she wasn't totally focused on him. "I hope we have fun tonight, kitty. Things have been a little stale since Tommy and I broke up."

Samson stared holes through Susan, but the mean look on his face didn't surprise her. "You liked Tommy, didn't you, boy? He always had a treat for you, but that's no excuse for looking daggers at me.

"I feel bad about Tommy too. He's a great guy, but I don't love him the way he loved me. I broke up with him because it wasn't fair to let him hope for something that can never be. Still, I miss him too."

She needed to move on with her life, and going out with Kurt Deveraux seemed like a good way to begin. Maybe this date had come at exactly the right time.

Kurt parked in front of Susan's house and paused for a look before he got out of the car. Her small home was made of red brick just like most of the other houses in the well-maintained neighborhood. Judging by the style, the house had probably been built in the late fifties or early sixties.

But after she admitted him, the interior looked nothing like he had expected. She had removed some interior walls to create an open floor plan, and the back side of the house had big, new windows that would let in lots of light. The skylight was awesome. If you turned off the lights, you'd be able to see the stars shining against the night sky. Susan had decorated the house in soothing neutrals, but splashes of red scattered around the room kept the decor from looking bland.

This open, airy space looked nothing like his small, cramped bachelor apartment furnished with his mother's castoff furniture. "This is a great house, Susan."

She beamed at him. "Thanks. I did most of the design myself, but my brother and my dad helped do the actual remodeling."

"So they live around here?" asked Kurt as Susan indicated he should take a seat on the sofa.

She nodded. "My parents live just outside town on the old Whitaker place. They bought it a few years ago after they moved here from Arizona."

"Did you grow up in Arizona?"

The faint scent of flowers drifted toward Kurt when she sat down beside him. "Yes, but I bragged so much about Fairfield, Mom and Dad decided to pull up stakes and move here themselves. I was thrilled to have them nearby. I wouldn't have left Arizona if I could have found the right job there, but I had a mental picture in mind, and I found it here."

"I'm glad you did," he said. Susan smiled again and made his heart beat a little faster. Man, she was pretty! Her honey blonde hair gleamed under the overhead lights. She wore it short, and it looked so cute with the ends turned under. Was she wearing contacts? If not, she had the most vivid blue eyes he'd ever seen. What word would describe her skin? Maybe velvet would do. Yeah, velvet the color of the palest pink in a seashell. She was tall too, maybe five nine, with great legs and a bottom that had the sexiest curve he had seen in a long time.

He forced himself to stop staring. "I've never had a beautiful woman win a football game for me. How did you know your play would work?"

Susan laughed, a musical sound that made him want to laugh with her. "I wish I could take the credit for it, but I can't. It's one of my dad's plays. He coached high school football for thirty years before he retired."

"No wonder you always enjoy football. You were raised on it. I almost killed your messenger, but I'm glad he stood his ground. Your dad's play won the game."

"Yes, I thought it would."

Susan rose from the sofa and took her jacket off the back of a chair. *My oh my, what a view!* Her entire outfit fit so snugly it might have been painted on, but it didn't look off color or suggestive. Instead, the jeans and sweater looked elegant and classic, just like Susan herself.

A look of chagrin crossed her face when she turned back around. "I think I've been a bad hostess. Would you like a drink before we go, or should we be on our way?"

"I don't really drink. I guess you think it's corny, but I want to set a good example for the kids."

Susan nodded as if his answer pleased her. "I don't think that's corny at all, and I don't drink either. Coffee's about the strongest thing I'm interested in."

"If you're ready, we'll get going."

She smiled at him, and after he helped her with her jacket, she locked the front door.

Jason was right. I've always wanted to go out with her. For a long time I've hoped she'd break up with that guy she was dating. This is my chance, and I don't plan to mess it up.

"Where is this party of yours?" Susan asked as she fastened her seat belt.

"It's out on Bailey Road. Do you know where the old Texaco station used to be? A Hispanic guy by the name of Jose Mendoza bought the property that adjoins the Texaco. He and his family like me because I can speak Spanish. The party will probably be a little on the wild side, though. Jose and his people work hard, but they play hard too."

A stirring of guilt brought a rush of warmth to her face. *I'd give anything if I hadn't made that silly bet. Kurt asked me to go out with him in good faith, knowing nothing about the bet. I feel like a jerk who obtained an invitation through false pretenses. I'll make it up to him, though. I'll do my best to show him a good time.*

"It looks like they're having the party in the barn," Kurt said as they turned off the highway onto Mendoza's driveway. "No wonder. It's bigger than their house."

Mendoza had painted the barn brilliant green. "John Deere colors," Susan said with a laugh.

They parked Kurt's car against a fence and made their way to the barn. "Everything looks great," Susan said. "So clean and spacious." She touched Kurt's arm. "Look. We're having live music. They've set up a stage at the other end of the hallway."

Kurt nodded. "I see it. They put the refreshments down there too. I bet there'll be a lot of spicy stuff and tequila flowing like a river."

Their host saw them come in and ran to greet them. "Kurt, my friend, welcome. Who is this lovely lady on your arm?"

"Jose Mendoza, meet Susan English."

Mendoza took Susan's hand and kissed it. "You are far too beautiful to waste yourself on him, Miss English." Mendoza dug Kurt in the ribs with his elbow and laughed with evident delight.

"Get out," Kurt kidded. He put his arm around her and drew her close.

Susan's knees turned to water the minute their bodies met. *He has muscles in places I don't have places.*

Mendoza grinned at her. "Hmm, maybe I was wrong. Your woman likes your touch, Kurt."

Susan's face burned as Kurt shot a glance at her. "I try to please her in every way."

Mendoza slapped Kurt on the back. "Good job, my friend. Both of you, dance, eat, drink. Enjoy yourselves." With a shout of laughter, Mendoza rejoined the party while Susan took Kurt to task.

"I don't like what you said. I'm sure he thought we were lovers."

Kurt shrugged. "I hope so. If they think you're my woman, the single guys won't be hitting on you." His eyes twinkled. "I want you all to myself tonight with no competition."

Susan thought for a moment. Naturally, she was flattered that he didn't want to share her company with anyone else, but he shouldn't have let Mr. Mendoza believe they were involved with one another. *Oh, it probably doesn't make any difference anyway. I doubt I'll ever see any of the Mendozas after the party ends.*

Kurt cleared his throat. He looked a little uneasy, as well he should. "Would you like to dance?"

Uh oh. Hard to stay mad when he'd said the magic words. "I sure would." Susan grabbed his hand. "I love music and dancing."

A look of approval spread across his face. "So do I."

We're well matched, Susan thought as they spun around the floor. *He knows what he's doing.* By the time the dance ended, both of them were hot, flushed, and laughing.

Susan fanned her face with her hand. "Let's get something to drink."

They made their way to the end of the barn where Mendoza had set up the refreshment table. She handed Kurt a glass of punch and poured one for herself. "This is good," she said as she drained her glass. "I can't identify all of the ingredients, but it tastes good."

Kurt sipped his own drink. "I think it has tequila in it, so be careful."

Tequila? She wouldn't contradict him, but she didn't taste alcohol at all. Alcohol tasted bad, but this punch was so yummy she might have a second glass.

The rest of the evening passed in a blur. Susan couldn't remember when she'd had such a good time. The musicians should try for a recording contract, and the food must have been catered, especially the punch. It was that good. The people were nice too. No telling how many new friends she had made.

The band returned from a break and began a slow, sensuous song. "Danz with me?" Kurt invited. He held out his hand.

Susan giggled when his warm fingers closed around hers. How sweet that he had mispronounced the word dance. He led her to the dance floor where he put his arms around her and pulled her against him.

"You shouldn't hold me so close," Susan sighed. She laid her head on his shoulder and made no effort to move away from him.

Kurt dropped a kiss on her hair. "Mmm, you smell like flowers." A pause. "Why shouldn't I be so close? I like holdin' you."

"Because of the way you make me feel." Susan giggled. "I can't stop laughing."

"I don' see a problem."

When the dance ended, people started to leave. She glanced at her watch. How odd. She couldn't see it very well. "It's late, Kurt, and I hafta go to church ah...tomorrow." She yawned. "I'm a member of the choir."

"Let's say bye to Jose."

Mendoza stood at the door saying goodbye to his departing guests. Just as they reached him and his wife, Kurt stumbled. He fell against Susan and sprawled onto a bale of hay covered with a clean tarp.

Mendoza hauled him to his feet. "I don't think you should be driving tonight, Kurt. Maybe you had a little too much tequila."

"I'll drive," Susan said with a bright smile.

"I think you don't need to drive either," Mendoza demurred. "Let us put you up for the night."

Susan never even thought of calling someone to come and pick them up. She and Kurt allowed Mrs. Mendoza to lead them into her house where she showed them to a bedroom. Like Susan, she too had a hard time speaking around her giggles. "The bathroom is down the hall. If you need anything just call."

When she left them alone, it finally occurred to Susan that she expected them to share a bed. "I can't stand uh, stay here, Kurt. There's only one bed."

"They think we're lovers, remember? We'll just share the bed. It'll be fine."

His reasoning seemed slightly off kilter, but darn it, she couldn't figure out exactly why. "Okay, but I have to go to the bathroom first."

When she got back, Kurt made a trip to the bathroom. By the time he returned Susan had thrown her clothes across a chair and got in bed with the covers pulled up to her chin.

She yawned. "You'd better hurry when you get undressed. It's cold in here."

He turned his back to her and removed his shirt, shoes, and jeans, a process Susan watched with interest. "Golly, you've got great shoulders! I no...no...noticed it when we danced together."

Kurt slid into the bed beside her. "You're shivering."

"I'm freezin'. The room doesn't have any heat."

"Scoot close to me and get warm," he urged.

What a good idea! How nice of him to offer to keep her warm. Susan spooned against him, and after a few minutes of snuggling she felt toasty warm.

"You feel good against me," Kurt muttered. His arm tightened around her as he buried his face in her hair. "Your hair smells like flowers."

"Tha's a nice compliment." She kissed his hand by way of thanks, and Kurt kissed the side of her face.

Susan sighed. "I like that, but I want to kiss your lips." She giggled and turned over and put her arms around him.

When Kurt hugged her back, she kissed him. He was so handsome she couldn't help it. Kurt didn't seem to mind. Judging by the little moan he made, he liked her kisses.

She closed her eyes against a sudden onslaught of feeling as the hugging and kissing intensified. Kurt Deveraux was something else! She made no protest when he cupped her bottom and pulled her intimately against him. At the moment, the tequila was firmly in charge.

Oww, her head was killing her! Susan opened her eyes, winced, and closed one of them. Where the heck was she? She couldn't see much in the dim, early-morning light, but obviously she didn't sleep at home last night. Her stomach lurched. Oh, where was the bathroom? She was about to throw up. *Flu. This feels like the flu.* Her stomach rolled over again, and she swallowed hard.

Hot. So hot. She was drenched in sweat from a furnace pressed against her back. She risked turning her head to see what she lay against and found herself face to face with Kurt Deveraux!

No! No! This can't be! They'd gone to a party, but... inoring the pain in her head, Susan started to cry as memories of the previous evening came to her. How could she! She tried to smother the sound in the pillow, but she had never mastered the art of crying quietly. It came as no surprise when Kurt touched her shoulder.

"What's wrong?"

"Would you please take me home?" Susan tried to get herself under control, but tears kept seeping from her eyes no matter how hard she bit down on her lip. She had done some silly things before, but this horror went beyond silly. *I'm not the kind of woman who drinks too much and falls into bed with a stranger! I'm not! Oh, what have I done?* A bout of shivering shook her. *I don't really know him.*

"Let's get dressed," Kurt whispered.

Susan wiped away her tears long enough to find her clothes, but the darkness made it hard to see much. She started crying again when she bumped her toe on a chair leg.

A gentle tap sounded on the door just as she zipped her jeans. "Kurt? Is everything okay?" came the whisper of their host.

Mr. Mendoza! She couldn't face him! "Go and talk to him," she hissed at Kurt who'd made no move toward the door. She gave him a shove, and he hurriedly buttoned his shirt and stepped outside. He didn't close the door all the way, so she heard their conversation.

"Everything's fine, Jose. Susan's just embarrassed because she had too much to drink and ...and...had to stay the night. To tell you the truth, I'm a little embarrassed myself."

Mendoza's voice sounded kind. "Don't be ashamed. It's better to stay the night than to drive drunk. You had a good time, right? Take the lovely Susan home, and let her sleep it off. By tonight she'll be her old self."

She saw Mr. Mendoza walking down the hall as Kurt came back into the bedroom. "Ready?"

Susan wouldn't look at him. She couldn't for fear of what she'd see in his eyes. Nodding her head, she followed Kurt as they quietly tiptoed out of the Mendoza home.

Susan stopped crying right before they reached her house, but she still refused to look at Kurt. Several times he tried to talk to her, but she only answered in monosyllabic replies. Why wouldn't he leave her alone? Couldn't he guess how humiliated she felt? It was all Robin Landford's fault too! She *hated* Robin.

As the car turned into her driveway, she breathed a prayer of thanks for the early hour. Maybe her neighbors were still asleep and wouldn't see Kurt bringing her home right after daybreak. Mrs. Meyers in particular would just love a piece of juicy gossip to chew on. That was one thing she didn't like about Fairfield. It was so small everyone knew your business as soon as it happened.

"Thanks. I'll see you Monday," she mumbled. She grabbed her purse and prepared to run for the sanctuary of her home. The sooner she got rid of Kurt the better. If she never saw him again it would suit her just fine.

She didn't get far; Kurt grabbed her arm and prevented her from leaving the car. "I'm coming in with you. We have to talk about what happened last night."

"No, we don't."

"Yes, we do."

Kurt let go of her and got out of the car. Short of screaming or running away, there was no way to stop him so she might as well get it over with as quick as she could. He followed her down the walk and unlocked the door for her when he saw how much her hands were shaking.

Once they were inside, she threw her keys in a bowl on the kitchen counter and tossed her jacket toward the sofa. It fell to the floor, but she didn't care. "Go ahead and say what you want. Then I'd like for you to leave because I'm too ashamed to face you. I just want to shower and go to bed."

She chanced a glance Kurt's way. He looked as woozy and bad as she probably did. "I don't blame you for not wanting to talk to me," he said. He ran his hand across the back of his neck. "You don't know me very well, but I promise you I don't make a habit of sleeping with women in no condition to say no. It was just that damned tequila. I already wanted you, and the tequila pushed me over the edge."

"You already wanted me?" She hadn't expected that.

Kurt laughed but he didn't sound amused. "Don't you know when a man asks you for a date he finds you attractive? You're so beautiful that even when I see you at school I.... I wanted to ask you out a long time ago, but I heard you were involved with someone else. When you sent me that play yesterday, I thought it was your way of telling me you were interested too."

"It was."

"Don't you think I'm attractive?"

Susan hung her head. "Yes, you know I do. I...I remember telling you so last night."

Kurt smiled for the first time. "I remember." He took a deep breath. "Don't let this ruin everything. I know we shouldn't have done it, but we did, and we can't undo it. It wasn't just the sex I enjoyed last night. It was everything. I like the way you smile and talk football with me. Dancing with you is fun, and watching you deal with the kids at school is a pleasure. Give us a chance."

The bet! For a minute she had forgotten about the bet. Susan barely resisted the urge to groan out loud. Oh, *why* had she done it? Even though she'd rather die, she had to tell him the truth.

"Before you say anything else, there's something I have to tell you. I'm ashamed of it, but you need to know."

Susan broke off and clapped her hand over her mouth. "I'm going to be sick," she cried. She ran for the bathroom as though wolves chased after her. Yeah, she'd done a lot of humiliating things during the last twelve hours, but she hadn't thrown up in front of another person, and she wanted to keep it that way.

She stayed in the bathroom for a long time even though she knew Kurt was waiting for her. Maybe she'd get lucky and he'd move to Alaska or Africa, anywhere far, far away. He could say anything he wanted, but it didn't change a thing. She had still humiliated herself and done something that appalled her. Oh, imagine what he really thought!

Footsteps sounded in her bedroom. Kurt knocked on the bathroom door and called, "Susan? Are you okay?"

With a big sigh, Susan opened the door.

Kurt studied her face. "You look kind of pale. I know you had something to tell me, but maybe we should wait until you feel better. I'll help you to bed if you like. I think you need to sleep a little while longer."

A reprieve! Putting things off did no good, but that's exactly what she'd do. "Bed sounds good."

Kurt turned back the bedcovers for her and patted the side of the bed. "Sit down and I'll take your boots off."

Susan's stomach quivered at the thought of bending over to tug on her boots. She sat and stuck out her foot.

Kurt wrestled the boots off, and she fell back onto the bed. It felt so soft, and it was blessedly quiet in the room. "Don't go," she mumbled. "I want to talk to you when I wake up."

Kurt watched as Susan's eyes closed. Where did she expect him to stay? With her? Well, why not? They'd already spent a night together. He took off his shoes and shirt and got under the covers with Susan. Before long he too fell asleep, lulled by the soft silence in the room.

Susan stirred and pushed her hair out of her eyes. What was that awful buzzing noise? Why wouldn't it go away and let her sleep? The bed shook, and someone tapped her shoulder. Her eyes popped open. Oh good grief! Kurt lay beside her in the bed. Clenching her teeth, she remembered she had asked him not to leave, but she hadn't meant for him to sleep in the bed with her.

"Door bell," he muttered.

She scrambled out of bed, but she caught her toe in the covers and fell to the floor with a thump that caused her stomach to lurch yet again. Staggering to her feet, she ran for the bathroom, not the door. By the time she got back, the bed was empty.

Oh no, oh no! Kurt had gone to the door! She heard him talking to someone in the living room. Where were her jeans? Flinging clothes all over the room, she searched for her lost jeans, but they were nowhere to be found. Since she couldn't find them she grabbed the first thing she saw in her closet, a pair of pajama pants covered in small, red hearts.

She charged into the living room and barely managed to stifle a gasp; Kurt hadn't bothered to put on his shirt. Melissa sat in the chair beside the fireplace with her lips pursed in disapproval. When she saw Susan she jumped up as if something had bitten her. "This is a bad time, Susan. I'll come back later."

Susan had thought she couldn't feel any more wretched, but she could. Melissa's disapproval scorched and shamed her. If only both of her guests would go and leave her alone. She felt too sick, miserable, and humiliated to cope with them this morning.

Damage control. Okay, I can do this. "No, Melissa, you don't have to leave. Kurt has to go now anyway. Kurt, let me walk you out."

"I need to get my shoes and shirt," Kurt mumbled.

"Of course. Go on and get them." Susan wished the ground would open up and swallow her whole. Oh, *why* did he have to answer the door?

Kurt vanished into Susan's bedroom. When he came back he was fully dressed and had put his jacket on as well. "Bye, Melissa. See you later," he said.

Melissa only waved her hand in reply, which made Susan cringe. Conservative Melissa did not approve of her and Kurt!

She heard Kurt breathe a little sigh of relief once they got out of Melissa's sight. Uh huh. He had felt uncomfortable too.

They paused in the foyer. Susan felt so unutterably miserable that Melissa notwithstanding, she laid her head against his shoulder, and he hugged her. In spite of everything, it did feel so good to be in his arms. "Did you really mean what you said before we went to sleep?" she asked. "Do you really want to see me again?"

"Yeah, I meant every word of it."

Susan sighed. "I still need to talk to you, but it'll keep, I guess.

"Kiss me goodbye?"

For the first time since she woke that morning, Susan smiled. "Haven't you had enough kissing?"

He shook his head as a faint sparkle entered his eyes. "Not nearly enough."

Susan turned her face to his, and Kurt kissed her. "Deveraux, you sure can kiss," she sighed.

"Last night you told me I can do other things well."

"I remember." A ghost of a smile chased across Susan's face. She gave his hand a squeeze, shooed him out the door, and firmly closed it behind him. Now came the harder part. Now, she'd have to talk to Melissa.

Melissa stared at her as she entered the living room.

"Would you like some coffee?" Susan kept her voice breezy and cheerful. Maybe if she acted more or less normally Melissa wouldn't notice anything out of the ordinary. "I'd like a cup myself."

Melissa's voice sounded flat and monotonous. "Yeah, I bet you do. Sit down, and I'll get it. You don't look like you're able to stand, much less make coffee."

So much for not noticing.

Melissa brewed some coffee and brought a cup to Susan who took a sip with a sigh of gratitude. "Ah, you don't know how good that is."

Melissa's bottom lip poked out. "What were you thinking?

"Uh, about what?"

"Oh, don't be silly. It's obvious you slept with Kurt last night. Why'd you do it? You're practically strangers, and sleeping with him certainly wasn't part of that silly bet."

What good would it do to lie about it? "I slept with him because I got drunk," she mumbled. "I got drunk at the party, and so did he."

Melissa frowned. "But you don't drink at all."

"Neither does Kurt, and that's the problem. It didn't take much to get us drunk. We didn't realize how the tequila affected us until it was too late."

Melissa said nothing; she didn't have to. Her sour expression said it all. *I always thought my private life was no one's business but my own, but this time I don't really blame Melissa. No two ways about it, sleeping with a virtual stranger on a first date is bad behavior. I'm no prude, but I'm not promiscuous either.*

Melissa finally deigned to speak. "I don't know what to say. What are you going to do about this mess?"

Now that her coffee had dispelled some of the fog in her head, she didn't know if she had landed herself in a mess or not. True, they shouldn't have had sex, but it was over and done with, and nothing could change it. Besides, she liked Kurt. They'd had a lovely time together. "I haven't made up my mind just yet, Melissa. I hate that it happened, but I'd be a liar if I said I didn't like him. He wants to see me again too. He told me he enjoyed my company, that it wasn't just the...you know."

"Did you tell him about the bet?"

Susan shook her head. "I was going to, but I was so embarrassed when you found us together I just wanted to get him out of here. I'll tell him tomorrow."

Melissa considered the matter. "Please tell me you aren't thinking of having an affair with him. You and Tommy haven't been broken up that long. Rebound relationships never work out."

True, but I do like him. We had a good time at the party, and I don't think the tequila had anything to do with it. Of course, I still have to tell him about the bet. It might make him angry, but I'll be very tactful when I speak to him. He'll understand after I explain about Robin. He probably doesn't like her any more than I do.

<hr>

Kurt almost ran a red light because he couldn't stop thinking about Susan English. He liked her even more than he'd expected to. She was drop dead gorgeous, funny, smart, and had the best legs he'd ever seen. Besides all that, she was obviously a creature of fire, passion, and need. *I wonder what she wanted to tell me? It seemed like something important, but it probably wasn't.*

His face burned when he thought about Melissa. Did she like to spread gossip? As a teacher, it was important to set a good example for the young people who attended Fairfield High. It would hurt him for the boys on the team to find out about that party and what happened after. He had given them many lectures on drinking and sex; if they found out about this, everything he'd ever said would be nothing more than so much hot air.

Did his actions make him a hypocrite? Probably, and wasn't that just great? Besides being a hypocrite, he'd lost control of himself last night. He had been right to lecture the boys about drinking. Just look what happened to him when he had. If he hadn't been drinking he would have taken Susan home instead of taking advantage of her, and yeah, that was probably what he did.

As he drove into his apartment complex, he saw Jason Cooper knocking on his front door. Jason turned around when he heard the sound of a car, and a look of relief spread across his face.

"Where have you been?" demanded Jason as Kurt approached the front door. "I've been trying to call you since last night. I was getting worried about you."

Kurt yawned. "I went to a party last night. Guess I turned my cell phone off." It was always nice to see Jason, but he really wanted a little more sleep. Being hung over felt terrible. Why would anyone routinely drink enough to be in this condition?

Jason studied him as they unlocked the door and went into the apartment. "It must have been some party."

Kurt paused just inside the door and kicked his shoes off. "Why do you say it like that?"

"Like what?"

"Sort of like you're accusing me of something."

Jason let him have it. "You smell like booze and a woman, your eyes are bloodshot, and you need to shower and shave and put on some clean clothes. It looks to me like you're just getting home from your party. If any of the kids at school saw you like this, what kind of an example would it set for them? You know the boys on the team copy everything you do."

"Well, they didn't see me, did they? You're the only one here." This didn't have anything to do with Jason! He and Melissa needed to butt out of other people's business.

Jason scowled at him. "What's wrong with you? I've never seen you behave this way."

Kurt felt his face flush as anger tore through him. "Why is it your business if I have a few drinks and enjoy a woman's company? Does being a coach mean I can't have normal feelings and emotions?"

"Sure you can, but you've told me plenty of times what you think of men who drink too much and sleep around."

Jason had him there.

Kurt raked his hand through his hair and dropped onto the sofa. "I'm sorry. I didn't mean to snap at you, but I don't feel too great. I have a hangover which is bad enough, but I also just got caught in bed with the lady in question."

Jason looked horrified which he probably was. He was a straight arrow if there ever was one. "I can't think of anything...that's ...who caught you?"

"Melissa Taylor."

"Who were you sleeping with anyway?"

If he wasn't like a brother to me, I'd kick his butt out of here. But Jason *was* like a brother and was motivated by true concern, not idle curiosity. He drew a deep breath. "I was sleeping with Susan English."

Jason pursed his lips. "I'm not surprised. You always did want her, didn't you?"

Kurt set his jaw against the disapproval in his best friend's voice. Jason's attitude hurt. "Yes, I always wanted Susan," he admitted.

Jason threw up his arms. "I don't get it. What happened? You barely know her."

In a few quiet words Kurt told Jason about the party.

"So you have to go to school tomorrow and face her," marveled Jason. "You've got guts, buddy. If it were me I'd rather transfer to another school than face Susan."

"That seems a little extreme to me. Sure, I've embarrassed myself, but I want there to be more between Susan and me. I like her a lot. It isn't just the sex, although I...I did enjoy it. I think she and I have a lot in common. I'd like to see where it can go."

"Kurt...man, you've gotten yourself into a mess! Susan's beautiful, no doubt about it, but what kind of woman would..."

"Let it go. It isn't her fault.

Jason treated him to a long, level stare. "If you ask me, Melissa Taylor's twice the woman Susan is. She's got a neat little figure and a pair of pretty brown eyes that sparkle all the time. I don't think she'd have let herself get into the predicament Susan did."

Kurt mentally counted to ten. "Go with Chris when he apologizes to her. You can talk to her then. Ask her out if you like her so much."

Jason brightened. "Yeah, I might do that." He sighed. "Is Susan angry with you?"

"More ashamed than angry. After all, we both drank too much, and I didn't make her do anything she didn't want to do."

"Well, I'm just glad I'm not in your shoes. I don't want any complications in my life." Jason stood up and headed for the door. "I'll see you later when you aren't so hung over and out of sorts."

Three

Susan bounced out of her car with a smile on her face. Usually she dreaded Monday morning, but not today. Today she felt better, and she'd have that talk with Kurt. On the way to her mailbox in the faculty lounge, she mentally rehearsed what she would say when Kurt asked to see her again. Turning the corner into the room, she was greeted by a roomful of teachers, about half of whom clapped and cheered her arrival.

Don Brooks laughed and handed her an envelope. "We've been waiting for you. We hear that you won some money over the weekend."

"I told them you went out with him on Saturday," Melissa explained.

Robin appraised Susan with a gleam in her eyes. "I underestimated you, Susan. How did you do it?"

Susan shrugged. "I let him know I was interested. He did the rest."

"Well, I guess you deserve to win."

Susan handed the envelope back to Don. "I don't want anyone's money. I wish I'd never made that stupid bet, and I don't want any part of it. Just take your money back."

"No, you won it fair and square," insisted Robin. "Take it."

"I won't do that, Robin."

Kurt arrived just in time to hear Susan's answer. "Won't do what?" he asked as he stepped into the lounge and approached her side. He had a nice little smile on his face that made her think he was glad to see her.

The air in the lounge turned positively electric. "Oh, I'll tell you later," Susan replied with a light little laugh, but before she could get Kurt out of the lounge, Robin spoke up.

"Let Susan take you to dinner tonight, Kurt. She can afford it, and she owes it to you big time. After all, you just won her over a hundred dollars."

An expression of surprise flitted across Kurt's face. "How did I do that?"

"Forget it," Don Brooks said. He picked up his briefcase and moved toward the door. "The bell's about to ring and we need to get to class. Susan will tell you later."

Kurt shook his head. "No, I want to know now. Tell me, Robin."

With a triumphant glare Susan's way, Robin said, "Susan bet me fifty dollars she could get you to ask her out. Some of the rest of them got in on it too. They didn't want you to find out, but I think you deserve to know."

"That's what I was going to tell you yesterday when Melissa came over," Susan cried. "I wouldn't take the money because it was an awful thing to do. You know how much fun we had on Saturday. Can you forgive me for being so stupid?"

Kurt's face turned beet red. He laughed. "Why, it's okay, Susan. Why didn't you tell me about it? I'd have been glad to win you the money. Take it. You earned it." With a long, hard look at Susan, he spun around and left the lounge.

"You're a piece of work," Susan spat at Robin. "You wanted to hurt me, but you hurt him too. Don't you ever think about anybody but yourself?"

She ran after Kurt and caught him right in front of his office door. "Please, listen to me. It isn't like Robin's making it out to be."

Kurt stared into her eyes. "You didn't make a bet that you could make me ask you out?"

"Yes, I did, but sleeping with you wasn't a part of the bet. I did that because I wanted to."

"You slept with me because you got drunk, and I was stupid enough to think it might have been something more. Leave me alone. There's nothing else to say."

"Oh, but..."

Kurt slammed his office door in her face. Susan grabbed the door knob, but he'd locked it. "Kurt, please, let's talk."

Kurt refused to answer. Susan waited for a few more minutes, but he still wouldn't let her in, so she finally went to her own room. She hoped Robin Landford would choke on her own poisoned tongue.

* * *

The minute the dismissal bell rang Susan practically ran to Kurt's office in the gym. If he thought she'd give in without a fight, he'd better think again. The door stood open, but the office was empty, so she went in and sat down to wait.

The office looked better than she had expected. Of course it wasn't luxurious, but everything seemed clean, neat, and organized. She saw one large desk that she knew belonged to

Kurt because he had a plaque with his name on it sitting on the desk. A second, smaller desk sat in the corner. The other coaches probably shared it.

Her heart leaped when she heard someone coming, but it wasn't Kurt. Kurt's good friend Jason Cooper stood in the doorway. From the look of surprise on his face, he hadn't expected to see her. "Uh, hi, Susan. Are you looking for Kurt?"

So, Jason knew. He had to; otherwise he would have asked what he could do for her. "Yes, I want to see Kurt," she said, making her voice sound as cool as possible. She had no intention of explaining anything to Jason. If he didn't want her to wait, and she thought he didn't, too bad for him.

"You can wait, but Kurt's in the locker room with the boys. I don't know how long he'll be."

Kurt settled the question by coming into his office with his first string quarterback, Ken Banks. *Oh, good. Ken's presence will give me a little leverage. Kurt won't run because Ken might ask embarrassing questions about his coach's conduct.*

She stood up with her head held high. "Coach, I have something to discuss with you."

"I'll wait outside," Ken said.

Susan appreciated his consideration; she knew why he did it. Lots of teachers would have a little chat with the coach if a boy refused to cooperate. It worked too. Coach Deveraux refused to play any boy who caused trouble or didn't do his work.

She saw Kurt shoot a look at Jason, who said, "Excuse me, and I'll go get the kids started."

He left the office, and Kurt put his desk between himself and Susan. "We have nothing to say to each other. I don't want you bothering me again."

Susan gritted her teeth. "We have plenty to say. I've apologized to you about the bet. I was sorry I did it the minute I opened my mouth, but I didn't take it back because of Robin."

"So it was important to you to get that date."

She nodded. "Yes, but nobody said I had to have a good time or sleep with you. Those things weren't a part of the bet." She took a step toward him. "I had a lot of fun, didn't you?"

His eyes chilled her as he stared at her. "I don't know if I believe you or not, but it doesn't really matter one way or the other. You still humiliated me in front of all my friends. You're beautiful and desirable, and a woman who looks like you can have any man she wants, but that doesn't give you the right to play games with other people.

"No, I think you only slept with me to prove that you could. Or maybe you might have done it because you got drunk. Either way I don't want a woman like you in my life.

"Why don't you go back to that rich lawyer you just broke up with? Rumor has it he wants you back."

Her entire body felt hot and tight. Her eyes prickled. "You're wrong! It wasn't like that. Can't you believe me when I tell you how sorry I am?"

"I don't want to talk about it. If you'll excuse me, I have a practice to do."

He strode toward the door, but Susan grabbed his arm as he went by. "Wait..."

Kurt froze. "Would you please take your hand off my arm?"

Susan jerked her hand back and watched as Kurt jogged away. That certainly didn't go the way she'd planned.

Kurt was on hand that afternoon to hear Chris's apology to Melissa Taylor. "I should have been watching where I was going, Miss Taylor. I'm sorry I knocked you off the sidewalk."

"It's okay, Chris. I appreciate your apology very much."

"Thank you, ma'am."

Chris shot a look at Jason, who nodded his head in dismissal. The adults watched as the boy made his escape.

Jason cleared his throat. "How's your knee? You fell on it pretty hard."

Melissa glanced at her knee. "I skinned it a little, but it's fine."

"Well, I'm glad you weren't hurt."

"One thing's sure," Melissa laughed. "I'm not cut out for football. I didn't like getting hit."

"Oh, we'd put some pads on you so it wouldn't hurt."

Kurt repressed a smile. Oh yeah, Jason was smitten with Melissa. He had an opportunity to talk to her and couldn't think of a single thing to say.

He might as well go on home. Practice was over, and he didn't especially enjoy watching Jason stumble around like a teenager.

Susan shivered as she hurried into her house. Six weeks had passed since her date with Kurt. Since then, the beautiful autumn weather had taken a turn for the worst. It was cold and gray today, and the weatherman predicted snow flurries tonight.

She flung her book bag into the closet and slammed the door. Thank goodness she had taken Friday off! After the week she'd had, she couldn't face school tomorrow. She only prayed that …Never mind; she'd know soon enough.

Samson strolled into the kitchen to greet her. "Hey, boy," Susan crooned. She gently picked him up and scratched his chin for him. "Did you know that you have an idiot for a friend? I've done some pretty silly things lately."

Samson purred his pleasure. As long as she scratched his chin, all was right in his world.

Susan opened a can of food for him and went to change her clothes. Anything to put off what she had to do.

She hung up her school clothes and pulled on her fleecy, winter robe. Her stomach rolled. Now was the time. "Wish me luck, Samson," she whispered as she stepped into the bathroom.

A few minutes later she came out and threw herself across the bed. If only she could die and have it over with.

On Monday Susan got to school thirty minutes before her usual arrival time. She had intended to be one of the first people at school, and judging by the empty parking lot, she was. Using her ID badge, she opened the front door and went inside. The school secretary, Marilyn Hume, wasn't at her desk, but she heard voices coming from the principal's office.

She paused when she heard her own name. Why were Marilyn and Jack Dennis talking about her?

"I don't know what to do about it, Marilyn," Jack said. "Morale is terrible. It's been six weeks now, and the situation isn't getting any better."

"Well, it's partly Kurt's fault. He refuses to be friends with anyone who was involved in the betting. He's nice to them, but it's such a cold courtesy, I think it's worse than outright hostility. Jason Cooper told me Kurt won't go into the teachers' lounge at all, and of course that's where the teachers hang out. He sends a kid to check his mailbox for him, and he always eats lunch in his office in the gym."

Jack coughed and cleared his throat. "Don Brooks told me they donated the money to a local children's home, but that didn't seem to make any difference to Kurt."

"If Don talked to Kurt, he's braver than I am."

"The thing of it is," continued Jack, "I feel sorry for Kurt. They humiliated him in front of the whole faculty, but if he plans on coaching here he has to get over it."

"It's a shame the school is so small. In a larger place it wouldn't get so much attention."

Susan heard the sound of papers rustling. "Do you have the Thanksgiving memo ready for me to sign, Marilyn?"

Ears burning, Susan tiptoed past the office and hurried toward her room. She tossed her book bag behind her desk and headed toward the gym. As she had expected, she found Kurt in his office preparing for the upcoming day. The butterflies in her stomach fluttered something awful, but she knocked anyway. This wouldn't be easy or pleasant, but it had to be done. She took a deep breath and prepared to face the lion in his den.

The look of shock on his face when he turned around and saw her would have amused her under different circumstances. "I'm sorry to bother you because I know you don't want to see me, but I need to talk to you," she said before he could order her out of his office.

Kurt slammed his file cabinet, the sound echoing and bouncing around his office. "There isn't anything to say, okay? I don't want to go into it. Let it alone."

"May I sit down?"

Kurt, who had refused to meet her eyes, finally took a good look at her. *Oh, please don't let him see me trembling! I...I can't steady my nerves this morning.* Her face and eyes burned too, just the way they did when she was overtired or stressed.

A quiver of apprehension passed across his face. He *had* seen. "What do you want to talk to me about?" He waved his hand at a chair beside his desk and indicated that she should sit.

Susan collapsed into the chair. Why couldn't a bolt of lightning strike her or a giant worm swallow her? She drew a deep, shaky breath. "I...I... have to tell you something, but I honest to God don't know how to do it. I'd rather die than be here, but you have a right to know, and if it kills me, I'll tell you."

"Tell me what?"

"I'm six weeks pregnant."

Kurt looked as if a three hundred pound linebacker had tackled him unawares. "Pregnant!"

She nodded. "From the night at Mendoza's house. I did a home pregnancy test on Thursday evening. It was positive so I went to the doctor on Friday, and he confirmed it. I spent the weekend getting up the nerve to tell you."

"I guess I just assumed you were on birth control pills."

Susan heard the slight question in his voice and shook her head. "No."

"I don't mean to offend you, but everyone knows you were involved in a serious relationship right before we went out." He cleared his throat. "Is there any possibility the baby belongs to him?"

At this moment, she wished with all of her heart that the baby did belong to Tommy, but it didn't, and she refused to lie about something so important. "It's your child. If you want a DNA test after the baby is born, we can do one."

The silence in the room almost deafened her, but they'd said it all, right? Susan scrambled to her feet. "I'm sorry. I never meant for any of this to happen. I just wanted to shut Robin Landford's mouth, but that seems awfully mean and childish now. I'm going to tell Mr. Dennis about the baby during my planning hour, but I wanted you to know first."

She practically ran for the door. Kurt wouldn't have to worry that she'd bother him in the future! Telling him about the baby was the right thing to do, but she'd never subject herself to such humiliation again.

Just as she reached the door, she heard Kurt jump up and chase after her. "Susan, wait. Don't we have some plans to make before you leave?"

No, not that she knew of, and who cared what he wanted to talk about? She wanted out of here right now. "I have to go to class. We'll try to talk another time."

"If it's my baby, I want you to marry me. I have no intention of letting a child of mine go through life without a father. I've seen what lack of a father does to a kid."

Susan's chin lifted. "That isn't why I told you. As the baby's father, I thought you had a right to know, but I'm not trying to put any pressure on you. I can take care of myself and my baby just fine."

Kurt frowned at her. "Maybe so, but it's my baby too, and I'll be damned if I get a woman pregnant and then run out on her. Now, will you marry me or not?"

Susan burst into tears.

"Susan! It's okay. Please, don't cry. People are starting to come in now. You don't want the kids to see you crying."

No, she didn't, but how could she not be relieved? It would be so much easier to take care of her baby with a father in the home.

Kurt looked as if she'd turned his entire world upside down, and of course she had, but with a muffled oath, he slammed the door and gingerly took her in his arms, something she'd bet he had vowed never to do again. As he patted her back and made little soothing sounds, her arms closed around him. Knowing she wasn't alone in this mess made the whole ordeal so much easier to bear.

Without warning, Jason burst into the room. "Good morn..." When he saw Susan in Kurt's arms he stammered, "Ex...excuse me. I didn't mean to interrupt." He turned on his heel and hurried away.

Kurt pried her from his chest. "Can you make it to class?"

She couldn't look at Kurt, so she nodded instead. How could she make eye contact with a man who didn't love her after she'd told him she was pregnant?

"I'll tell Mr. Dennis," Kurt volunteered. "You don't have to do it, and if it's okay with you I'll come over tonight about six, and we can make our plans."

"Thank you," Susan mumbled. Giving one final sniff, she hurried to her class. She wished she could go home. If she thought too much about the desperate look on Kurt's face she would literally be sick, but who could help thinking about it? He had manned up and taken responsibility for his actions, but he wasn't any happier about it than she was.

Thank goodness he had volunteered to tell Mr. Dennis! Her fingernails dug into her palms. She hadn't looked forward to it at all. Mr. Dennis probably wouldn't say anything, but it curled her toes to think of sharing such personal news with her boss.

Actually, Kurt had acted decently from the moment she finally got his attention. He hadn't hesitated before asking her to marry him. His proposal had solved a lot of potential problems, but on the other hand, it would probably cause a whole set of new problems.

Now that she no longer dreaded telling him about the baby, her mind shifted to a new aspect of the situation. She was going to be a mother. Somehow, even though she liked children and had expected to have some one day, it didn't seem possible that it would happen to her right now.

For months she had saved her money so she could take a trip to Europe next summer, but there wouldn't be any tour in her future. Next summer she'd be having her baby.

How ironic that her husband-to-be didn't want her. Tommy had desperately wanted to marry her, but Kurt would rather not. Kurt didn't want anything to do with her, but he had decided to do the honorable thing and marry her anyway.

Susan shuddered. She appreciated his willingness to do so, but who wanted to marry a man who didn't want her?

Well, she'd have to make the best of it; she really didn't have any other choice, did she? For the sake of her baby she would need to get along with Kurt. As he had said, a child needed a full time father. Her last parent conference had been with a mother who frankly admitted she couldn't control her son. The boy needed a father to teach him how to be a man, but the father was out of the picture. No, she'd marry Kurt and be glad of the chance to do it. If she could help it, her baby would have a stable home with two loving parents.

Hope surged through her. Nobody had forced Kurt to marry her, and they did have a good time at Mendoza's party. Maybe being his wife wouldn't be so bad.

She'd better make a stop by the bathroom before the kids came in. Her darned eyes wouldn't quit leaking.

Kurt knew Jason would come back any minute, so he hid in the locker room. He sat on one of the benches and buried his head in his hands. Why did doing the right thing make him feel so bad? The world wasn't coming to an end. Susan was beautiful, and he'd always planned on getting married someday.

Someday. Not right now. Right now he didn't want Susan or a baby in his life. He'd rather date Aleisha Childs and focus on being a football coach than be a husband and father.

Too damn bad for him! Whether he regretted it or not, he had gotten Susan pregnant, and after seeing what happened to kids without a father, he'd die before he'd desert his child. He'd be nice to Susan too. She was no more to blame for this mess than he was. If they were getting married they might as well try to get along.

I hope I can forget about the bet soon. It galls me to know that the woman I intend to marry doesn't love me.

Taking a deep breath, he got to his feet. *If only I could say I feel sick and go home.*

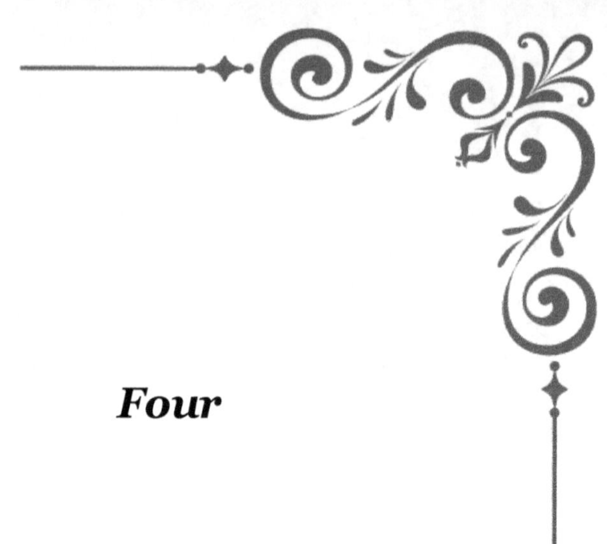

Four

Kurt got to Susan's house a few minutes after six that evening. It was funny how his perception of the house had changed. When he went there the first time, he had thought the house had great curb appeal, but today it reminded him of a red brick prison. He rang the bell anyway and took a deep breath when Susan opened the door.

"Hi, Kurt. Please, come in."

Susan didn't look the same either. Today she had an anxious expression in her eyes. They didn't sparkle and dance the way they had at Mendoza's party. He didn't know why, but she almost seemed afraid of him too. She wouldn't meet his eyes and was taking care not to get too close to him. Great. Just great. Had he acted so badly that she feared to be alone with him?

He followed her into the living room and sat on the sofa, but she took the chair across from him. "Ah, I...spoke to Mr. Dennis today," he began.

Susan's face went scarlet. "What did he say?"

"He said he thought we were doing the right thing and hoped everything turned out okay."

Susan stared at her hands. "Thank you for telling him. I wasn't looking forward to it."

"Yeah, I guess so." *You don't know what embarrassing is until you tell your boss you're getting married because you got a woman pregnant, a woman who only dated you because she wanted to win a bet.*

However, it was in their best interests to get along so he answered in as positive a manner as possible. "No problem. I was glad to tell him."

Susan fidgeted with a button on one of the pillows she had removed from the chair. "Uh, when do you want to do it?"

"Get married?"

Susan nodded.

"I don't see any reason to put it off. How about this coming Saturday?"

She stiffened and swallowed hard before she spoke. "Okay. We'll get married on Saturday."

Kurt had to swallow too. He'd had a huge knot in his stomach ever since Susan told him about the baby, and now it had moved to his throat where it threatened to choke him. After Saturday his life wouldn't be his own anymore. *Don't think about it.* "I assume you don't want a big wedding."

She gasped. "Oh, no I don't! Under the circumstances a small wedding is best. I'll ask my parents and my brother if they want to come, but that's it."

"All right, I'll do the same."

Her eyes swept around the room. "I know you have an apartment but I don't know where it is. Where would you like to live after we're married?"

The South Pole should be far enough away, provided I go alone. "Since I rent the apartment, it would be better to move in here."

Susan nodded. "I think you're right. Do you have someone in mind to do the ceremony?"

"If you have no objections, I'd like Father Duncan to do it. He's been our priest at St. Anne's Episcopal Church for a good many years, and I'd like him to perform the ceremony."

"That's fine." She shrugged. "I guess it doesn't matter who does it. At the moment my biggest worry is finding the best way to break the news to my parents." Curiosity flashed across her face. "Are you telling your folks why we're getting married?"

He nodded. "Yes, I think so."

"Yeah, I guess it's for the best."

A short silence fell on the room. He watched as Susan worried her lower lip with her teeth. "I *am* sorry," she said. "If I hadn't made that stupid bet, none of this would ever have happened. I'm sure you wish you'd never laid eyes on me, and I don't blame you. I...I...wish...things could have been different."

Anger ran through his veins, but Susan wasn't the only one at fault. "I was involved too. I was stupid to let a thing like this happen."

Her eyes were bright with unshed tears. "You let it happen because we were drunk. Oh, why did we have to drink so much that night? We suspected that he put tequila in the punch. I couldn't taste it, though. It just tasted really sweet and good."

"It wasn't just the tequila," Kurt said. "We wanted each other, or at least I wanted you. The booze just relaxed my normal inhibitions."

Susan nodded but made no comment. What was there to say anyway?

Kurt sighed and stood. "I think I'll go and see my parents. I want to get it over with."

"I guess I will too. I hope…I hope they won't be too disappointed in me."

I know exactly what you mean.

⸺ ❦ ⸺

Kurt usually enjoyed visiting his parents, but tonight he got heartburn at the very thought of it. As long as he could remember, both his mother and father had stressed that they expected exemplary behavior from him and his sister, Sheila. He was pretty sure they'd think his behavior was anything but exemplary.

His parents, George and Helen Deveraux, lived on Cherry Street, one of the prettiest streets in Fairfield. The old homes on Cherry Street all looked well-maintained and picturesque. He had always thought of Cherry Street as a white picket fence and red geranium kind of street, and he'd bet a lot of people would agree with him.

Hey! His mother's car wasn't in the drive way. She must be working late. He didn't deserve such a break, but he'd take it. It would be bad enough to confess his lack of judgment to his father, much less his mother.

He went in by the kitchen door and called, "Dad, where are you?"

"In the study."

He found his father working at his computer. George owned a small grocery store just outside town and always kept meticulous records. He jumped up and slapped Kurt on the shoulder. "I haven't seen you in a week, buddy. How're you doing? What brings you out to see your old man?"

The smile left Kurt's face. "I need to talk to you."

"Uh oh. I don't like the expression on your face," Mr. Deveraux said as he took a seat at his desk.

Kurt's stomach rolled as he took the chair opposite his father. "I've...done something I regret. It's hard for me to tell you about it, and I think it'll be hard for you to hear, but nothing can change things. They are what they are."

His father's eyes looked as round and big as an owl's. "What did you do?"

"I got drunk at a party and slept with my date. She's pregnant."

George winced as if he had received a physical blow. "I don't know what I expected, but not that. Son, what were you thinking? You know how to prevent a pregnancy. Didn't you realize..." He paused. "I guess you don't need a lecture at this point, do you? You know you messed up. Are you sure it's your baby?"

Kurt nodded.

"Then what are you going to do about it?"

"We're getting married Saturday morning."

Mr. Deveraux considered the matter. "I am disappointed. I won't try to lie to you about that. You've always had your head on straight and been a great example to your students. I hate to see you make such a life-changing mistake, but I think you're right to marry her. You want your child to have a father, and if you're willing to work at it, I believe you can still have a good marriage. Now, what's her name, and how do you know her?"

"Her name is Susan English. She's a teacher at the school."

"How long have you been seeing her?"

Kurt set his jaw. "It was our first date."

Mr. Deveraux's eyebrows shot upward, but he made no comment.

"English," George mused. "There's a woman at the big grocery store in town whose name tag said English."

"That's probably Susan's mother. She works at Chef's Pantry. Susan said she's the bakery manager and decorates most of the cakes."

His father nodded. "Yes, I think I've spoken to her before. Do you know what her dad does for a living?"

"He's a retired high school coach. He works at Super Mart now. Bill is his name."

Mr. Deveraux absently tapped his desk with a pen. "Do they know yet?"

"Susan's telling them tonight."

His father got up and gave him a hug. "It'll be okay, son, so stop looking like you've lost your best friend. These things usually work themselves out. What time is the wedding? Your mother and I will want to be there."

"It's at eleven." He dropped his eyes. "I was afraid you wouldn't come."

George reproached him with a look. "You know better than that. You're my son. I love you when you've messed up as much as I love you when things are going well. Your mother's working tonight. Do you want me to tell her for you?"

"If you wouldn't mind. I hate to shove it off on you, but I'm ashamed for her...to talk to her..."

George laughed shortly. "I imagine so, but you have enough to worry about. I don't mind telling her."

Kurt almost felt like crying. He had expected his father to have a fit. Instead, George's loving support bolstered his spirits and gave him courage to do what he thought was right. How had he gotten so lucky?

No matter what happens in the future I'll try my best to follow dad's example.

———— ⌘ ————

George told Helen after she got home from work that evening. "Did you have a good night?" he asked as she kicked off her shoes and wiggled out of her slacks.

"It was okay, but we were pretty busy. I'm worn out."

As she sat beside him on the edge of the bed, George rubbed her shoulders. "You're tense, honey."

He massaged her shoulders for a moment. "I've got something to tell you."

"Okay, shoot."

"You aren't going to like it."

Helen turned around to face him. "What's wrong?"

"Kurt came by tonight to see us."

"Well, what did he say?"

George took her hand and squeezed gently. Helen thought the world revolved around both of her children. Kurt's news would hurt her. "He came by to tell us that he got a woman pregnant. They're getting married on Saturday."

"No! It can't be!"

Helen's eyes filled with tears as George took her in his arms and snuggled her against him. "The good part about it is that we're going to have a grandchild," he comforted.

Helen shook her head in quick denial. "No good can come from this horrible situation! What's wrong with Kurt? He should have known how to prevent an unwanted pregnancy." Her lip quivered. "Tell me about it."

Susan arrived at her parents' home just as Mrs. English served dessert. The family had moved into the living room to eat their apple pie and ice cream around the fire.

Her younger brother Tyler saw her first. "Hey, Susan."

"Hi, Tyler. How's school?"

Tyler, who was in his first year of community college, groaned. "Tough."

Mrs. English stood up. "I'll get you some pie, honey."

"Nothing for me, thanks." She took a deep breath. "I came to talk to you and Dad about something."

"What about?" asked her father, as her mother sat back down. "Do you want us to put some walls back in your house?" This was a family joke because Susan had once taken a wall out and had it replaced when she didn't like the result of her modification.

This time the affectionate ribbing brought no answering smile or joke. *Wait a minute. Maybe I shouldn't tell them. Maybe I should marry Kurt with no explanations and let them find out when my pregnancy starts to show.* Her heart leaped at the thought of a reprieve, but no, she couldn't do that.

She drew a deep, quivery breath and came out with it. "I came to see if you would come to my wedding. I'm getting married Saturday morning."

A brief silence fell over the room.

"Susan! Who is it? What's the hurry?" Exclamations suddenly came from all sides, but something in Susan's face dried up the congratulations of her family.

Her mother set down her pie and ice cream. "What's wrong?"

"I'm getting married because I'm expecting a baby."

No one said a word. Her father cleared his throat twice before he finally broke the shocked silence. "Who's the father?"

"Kurt Deveraux."

"He's a great guy," enthused Tyler. "He taught me health last year. You know, Dad. He's the Mavericks' head coach."

Her father's face slowly turned a brilliant red. "You're pregnant by a coach?" he asked. "You let a big, dumb, jock have you? If he teaches health, why didn't he know about birth control?"

"He isn't a big, dumb jock," Susan protested. "If we hadn't been drinking we never would have done it."

If possible, the red in her father's face increased. "So he didn't think to use a condom because he was drunk. You sure can pick 'em, Susan."

"Dad, it isn't the way it sounds! Let me explain."

Except for Tyler who didn't seem to think badly of her and Kurt, the family listened to her story with stony expressions of disapproval. "How could you be so foolish?" Marjorie criticized. "Didn't you realize this young man has feelings too? It worries me that you'd be so cruel."

"Don't blame her for that," Bill shot back. "That bet's no excuse for him to lose control of himself. If a man can't hold his liquor he doesn't need to drink at all, and you can't expect a woman to handle alcohol like a man."

Marjorie let her husband's opinion pass unchallenged. "Doesn't his father own that small grocery store on the edge of town?"

"Yes, and his mother works at the library."

Her dad jumped up and paced around the room. "How could you let yourself be used by a man like Kurt Deveraux? He's a teacher, Susan, a coach. He'll never amount to anything or be anybody. I wanted better for you than that. It was bad enough when you wanted to be a teacher, but I thought it might be okay because you could always marry a man who had a future. What happened between you and Tommy Price? Lawyers make good money, and he loves you."

Susan frowned. He didn't think being a teacher was a good thing? He'd been a teacher himself. "It just didn't work out, Dad. I don't love Tommy the way he loved me, but what's wrong with being a teacher anyway? You always took good care of us."

"Yeah, I sure did." Her father's eyes blazed. "I never had an extra penny for anything. Do you think I wanted my children to wear clothes bought at a discount store? Do you think I enjoyed eating most meals at home? Your mother's a great cook, but I couldn't afford to give her a night off, and I wanted to. I had to scrimp and save for a year just to get the price of that ruby ring she wears. It's not nearly big enough or nice enough for her, but it's the best I could do.

"Do you think I work at Super Mart now because I want to? My retirement isn't enough to live on. It makes me sick to think of him ruining your life." He wiped his face with his hand and drew a deep breath. "You don't have to marry him, you know. That kind of thinking went out years ago. We'll help you with the baby."

"You were a teacher, Dad. You know what lack of a father does to a child."

"Your case would be..."

"That's enough, Bill." Marjorie spoke quietly, but Susan heard a tone in her mother's voice that silenced her father. "You know she's right. A child needs a father, and I don't want to hear another harsh word about him. You're talking about the father of your grandchild. You'll be spending holidays with him, sitting at the same table with him, and babysitting his children for years to come. Besides that, Susan has to live with him. She needs to respect him, but if you run him down this way, I don't think she will."

"Where are you going to live?" asked Tyler whose eyes looked as if they had doubled in size.

Susan realized that her mouth was hanging open and closed it with a pop. "In my house. He lives in an apartment because he's trying to pay off his school loans."

"Great," Bill muttered. "School loans, a mortgage, and now a baby. What a great beginning."

Five

Kurt went to bed at his usual time on Monday, but he tossed and turned all night long. Even though he finally did go to sleep, he had odd, disturbing dreams. When his clock rang, he fumbled around and cut off the snooze alarm. Might as well get up now even though reality bit as much as his dreams had.

Today he'd have to buy Susan a wedding ring. The local jewelry store would be closed by the time practice ended, but he could let Jason handle things until he bought the ring and got back to school.

How much should he tell his staff? Naturally, they'd notice he got married, but should he tell them about the baby or not? It wasn't any of their business, but he did work with them, and they were his friends. *Oh, all right. I'll tell them and get it over with.*

Everyone was waiting for him when he got to school. He and the other coaches always had coffee together before the students arrived, so this was a good time to talk to them. His stomach started to churn as he shut the office door. Taking a deep breath, he jumped in with both feet. "Since we have a minute, I want to tell you all something."

"What's that?" asked Dan Burgess, the newest member of the staff. "You didn't hear about the grant we wrote, did you?"

This was Dan's first job, and Kurt was glad to have found him. Dan was a go-getter, sharp as a tack both on and off the field.

"No, I didn't hear anything about the grant, but we should know something in the next couple of weeks. What I wanted to tell you is that Susan English and I are getting married on Saturday."

Kurt saw a few puzzled frowns as the coaches processed this outlandish statement. He could understand why. For weeks he wouldn't even speak to Susan, and now out of the blue he drops his little bombshell on them. They were all exchanging furtive glances, but nobody said a word.

Dan finally broke the silence. "We know about the bet, Kurt. We also know how you've avoided anyone involved in the betting, especially Susan. What's going on?"

I'd rather eat dirt than tell them, but they'd find out sooner or later anyway. "Susan's pregnant."

They all looked just as surprised as he had thought they would. Worse still, Jason looked as if he felt sorry for him. Gah! Pity! He slapped Jason on the shoulder, perhaps a bit harder than necessary. "Don't look like that. It isn't a funeral."

"I apologize for asking," Dan mumbled. "It's none of my business. In the future I'll keep my mouth shut."

Kurt attempted a smile. "It's okay, Dan. You had a right to wonder. I guess I did overreact a little when I found out about the bet." *Yeah, right.* "I don't want the kids to know about the baby yet, so I'd appreciate it if you all keep quiet."

Dan and Jeff Batson, the other member of the staff, finished their coffee and left the room as soon as possible. They probably didn't know what to say and wanted to escape such an uncomfortable situation.

Jason lingered after Dan and Jeff made their escape. "You need a best man?"

Kurt's heart leaped in his chest. *I feel like an exhausted swimmer who's just been thrown a life preserver.* "If you wouldn't mind, I'd sure appreciate the moral support."

"Yeah, no problem." A startled look came to rest on Jason's face. "Hey, I just thought of something. You're going to be a father. Wow!"

Kurt dropped into his desk chair. "That's what scares me so much. I don't know anything about babies. I'm afraid I'll do something wrong and ruin the kid's life."

Jason sat too. "Why would you think that? You're great with kids."

"Uh huh, but these kids don't belong to me."

"Aw, you'll do fine."

I hope so, but somehow I can't see myself in that role. I don't know anything about raising kids.

Kurt broke into a cold sweat. He'd give anything if he had never taken Susan to Mendoza's party.

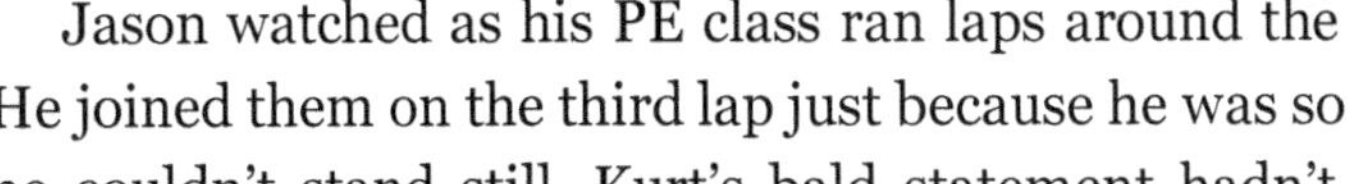

Jason watched as his PE class ran laps around the track. He joined them on the third lap just because he was so angry he couldn't stand still. Kurt's bald statement hadn't really surprised him because Kurt had been watching Susan for a long time, the expression of desire on his face easy to recognize. No, he wasn't surprised by Kurt's revelation, but his own reaction did; he was fighting mad. The two of them had been best friends since elementary school, but when Kurt broke the news this morning, he'd been so furious he'd considered walking out and slamming the door behind him. That one night stand would affect the rest of Kurt's life.

He put on an extra burst of speed. Yeah, he was fighting mad, but he couldn't turn his back on his best friend. Kurt needed support, not condemnation, but no one would ever know what it cost him to offer to attend that wedding.

Why had Kurt done it? Surely he had tasted the tequila in the punch. Did he want Susan so much he used the punch as an excuse to have her?

Aw, it didn't matter how it had come to pass; nothing changed the results of that impulsive evening. Kurt had wanted her, and soon he'd have her for good. Man, what a mess.

Susan unlocked her door and tossed her purse and coat into a chair. With a gasp, she bolted out of the room and ran for the girl's restroom where she heaved her guts out. She hated morning sickness! Footsteps sounded outside the stall, and Melissa called, "Who is it? Can I help?"

Susan flushed the toilet and came out of the stall. "I'm fine, but thanks for asking." She wet a paper towel and pressed it to her forehead.

"I bet you've picked up the stomach virus that's going around," Melissa said. "We've had a lot of absences because of it."

"No, it isn't a virus." Susan wadded up her paper towel and threw it into the trash bin. "The problem is that I'm having morning sickness. I'm pregnant."

Melissa gasped. Her face registered shock and a hint of...something else, but what? "I...I don't know what to say. Is Kurt the father?"

Susan's lips tightened. "Yes, of course he is." *Does she think I'm sleeping with every guy in town?*

"From the party? The one where you got drunk?"

Susan set her jaw. "Yes."

Melissa frowned. "Does Kurt know? Are you going to tell him?"

"I told him yesterday! Do you think I'd keep something so important from him?" Susan bit her lip and counted to ten.

"What did he say?"

The arrival of two students sent Susan and Melissa to Susan's room where they both sat in a student desk.

"Kurt asked me to marry him, and I said yes. We're getting married on Saturday morning."

Melissa's hand flew to her heart. "Oh, that's good. The last thing you need is to be an unwed mother at such a small, conservative school."

Susan shot her a cool look. "What do you think the faculty will do? Pin a big, red A on me?"

Melissa seemed glad to explain it to her. "We live in a small community where the majority of people go to church, feel patriotic, and have old-fashioned values. Everyone knows everyone else. The students' parents might not want an unmarried teacher with a baby teaching their kids. They might say you're setting a bad example. Thank goodness Kurt knows that and is willing to accept responsibility for the baby."

"I see your point." And she did see it, but this was the twenty-first century, not the dark ages. What right did anyone have to judge her?

Melissa cleared her throat. "What about your parents? Have you told them yet?"

Susan barely restrained herself from flinching. "Oh, they know. I told them last night, and I've never seen my dad so angry. I don't want him anywhere near Kurt, but he and Mother are coming to the wedding." She paused. "I do feel bad about disappointing them. My dad had something different, something he thinks is better, in mind for me."

"I can certainly understand that." Melissa's head bobbed. "I'd die if I had to tell my parents I was pregnant, and if that makes me old-fashioned, so be it."

"Yeah, well, I hope you never have to."

"I won't because I don't believe in drinking or premarital sex."

Susan stuck her hands in her pockets. *Wonder what would happen if I slapped that sanctimonious look off her face? She's my friend so I thought she'd support me, not try to make me feel bad.*

Melissa sighed and seemed unaware that she had offended Susan. "Are you asking anyone besides your family to come to the ceremony? I'd like to be there with you if it's okay."

Some of Susan's irritation vanished as a new thought occurred to her. "It would be wonderful if you'd come. Maybe it'll help Dad keep it together if someone besides family is present."

Her ready acceptance seemed to pacify Melissa. "Try not to worry about your dad. Stress isn't good for expectant mothers. He'll come around when he sees that things are going to be okay. They are going to be okay, aren't they? Is having a baby with Kurt really that bad?"

"It's pretty bad," Susan answered with a grimace, "but whether Dad likes it or not, I will marry Kurt on Saturday." She sighed. "I guess I'll buy Kurt a wedding ring after school.

Susan started her class on time, but it was lucky they were watching a video. *How am I supposed to keep my mind on teaching when I've probably ruined my life? I don't want to get married right now, and I especially don't want to be a mother. I want to go to Paris and see the Eiffel Tower and Notre Dame. I want to buy pretty clothes, flirt with cute guys, throw parties, dance and sing, and stay up until dawn.*

Instead, I'm marrying a stranger whose baby I just happen to be carrying. She bit her lip to hold back tears. *It's all my fault.*

And Melissa. I knew she came from a conservative family and would disapprove of premarital sex, but does she think I'm a slut? Did she really have to ask if the baby belonged to Kurt?

I'm surprised she even offered to come to the wedding. That look on her face made we wonder if she still wanted to be my friend. Maybe she's too good to hang out with the likes of me.

Oh well. Add one more person to the list of people who don't like me. I don't blame them; I don't like myself either.

Sheila Deveraux burst through the kitchen door that afternoon just as the phone rang. She slammed the door behind her and yelled, "I'll get it."

Helen winced as the whirlwind that was her daughter swept by. Sheila was only sixteen, eleven years younger than Kurt. After Kurt's birth the doctors had told her she couldn't have any more children, but they had been wrong. Eleven years after Kurt's birth, Sheila had made her appearance into the world. The Deveraux family hadn't been the same since.

Sheila felt things intensely, while Kurt was steady and level-headed. Until this nonsense with that woman he'd never put a foot wrong. He had known what he wanted and had systematically gone about getting it.

Not Sheila. Swayed by any wind that blew, she threw her vast energy into whatever appealed to her at the moment. Loud, vocal, and emotional, she was just the opposite of Kurt. Strangely, she and Kurt were devoted to each other in spite of their differences.

Helen dreaded telling Sheila about the baby, but the longer they put if off the worse it would be. She poured a glass of milk and put two freshly baked peanut butter cookies on a paper towel. Sheila loved peanut butter cookies. Maybe they could sweeten the news a little bit.

Sheila erupted into the kitchen. "Oh, goody. Peanut butter cookies. Thanks, Mom."

"You're welcome. Who was on the phone?"

"Oh, it was Aleisha Childs. She and Kurt had a date on Saturday, but she can't go because her company's sending her out of town. She asked me to tell him."

"Why didn't she leave a voice mail on his phone?"

"She said his mailbox was full."

"I see."

"I like Aleisha," Sheila enthused. "She's pretty. She and Kurt have a lot in common."

Helen drew a deep breath. She'd never have a better time. "Actually, Sheila, Kurt won't be seeing Aleisha anymore."

"Why not? Did they have a fight?"

"He's getting married Saturday morning."

Sheila produced no loud, noisy fireworks, but she did drop her half eaten cookie onto the paper towel. "Getting married? What are you talking about, Mom? Kurt hasn't dated anyone besides Aleisha in months. Who's the bride?"

Helen took the chair beside Sheila. "Susan English. You know her; she's an English teacher at the high school."

Sheila cocked her head and thought for a minute. "Why? He doesn't hang around her at school, and none of the students have mentioned that the two of them are interested in each other."

"Kurt took her to a party a few weeks back."

"So?"

Helen drew a deep breath and crossed her fingers for good luck. "So she told him yesterday she's pregnant."

Sheila made an involuntary gesture of rejection. "Oh, yuck! He had sex with her!"

"Yes, he did."

Sheila's temper flared. Helen could see it in the tensing of her shoulders and the flashing of her eyes. "He's a hypocrite," Sheila cried. "He tells the boys on the football team to behave, and then he goes and does the same things he told them not to do. Was he drunk too?"

"You don't need to know the details."

"In other words, yes." Sheila jumped up so fast that her chair hit the wall and made a small dent. "He should be ashamed of himself. Don't expect me to be at the wedding."

Sheila stormed out of the kitchen, and Helen heard her bedroom door slam. She sighed and threw Sheila's half eaten cookies away. That went pretty much like she had expected.

Sheila splashed some water on her face and scrubbed it with a towel. Too bad crying made you feel so crappy. She threw herself down on her bed and thought about the ugly video she and Harriet Palmer had watched while Harriet's parents went out to dinner.

"It's x rated," Harriet had explained. "My parents don't know I found it."

Sheila had felt both repelled by and drawn to the horrible video. Kurt probably hadn't done all of those things to Miss English, but by golly he'd done some of them, and she had let him.

Miss English always acted so cool and contained at school, but she had taken off her clothes and let Kurt do who knows what to her. How nasty was that? How could her own brother participate in such a disgusting, degrading performance? He had probably even grunted and sweated like the guy in the video. Miss English had his sweat and more all over her. She shuddered and tried to wipe the nasty mental picture from her mind.

She gasped. Maybe all guys were hypocrites like Kurt. Maybe they all said one thing and did another. At school and at church, Kurt preached abstinence to the kids he taught, but he also taught they should be protected if they did have sex. Wasn't that a joke? He sure hadn't had protected sex with Miss English! The baby proved it.

Could it be that she had enticed him? It didn't matter. Even if Miss English had stripped naked in front of him, he could have said no, so it was his fault from start to finish.

What's more, her mother didn't even seem mad about it. She had always favored Kurt, anyway.

Well, from now on she'd do what she wanted, just like Kurt, and if her parents didn't like it, it was just too bad.

Sheila went to school the next morning, but she wished she had pretended to be sick and stayed home. It just killed her to sit in class and work math problems or write stupid essays when her brother had ruined his life.

If she could tell Harriet about it, it might make her feel better, but she couldn't because even saying the words disgusted her. Harriet wouldn't understand anyway. As an only child, she thought it would be wonderful to have a big brother like Kurt. If she told Harriet about the baby, she'd only feel sorry for him.

Her mother had told her father she knew about Kurt, so he had tried to talk to her this morning. He had gone on and on about how Kurt had made a mistake, but he was paying for it, and they had to support him during this stressful time.

Yeah, right. Kurt didn't especially deserve her support. He had humiliated himself with his bad behavior, but he had humiliated her too. Everyone in school knew he was her brother. Nobody ever felt shy of telling her what they thought of him either.

A couple of years ago she had actually gotten into a fight with a kid at school who criticized Kurt. She had been suspended for a day after she punched him. The jerk had said Kurt was the lousiest coach Fairfield High had ever had.

Truthfully, he had been having a bad season that year, but it didn't matter one way or the other to her. She would defend Kurt no matter what. Too bad he hadn't proven worthy of her efforts.

Her eyes narrowed when Miss English entered the cafeteria and got into the lunch line. She looked good, you'd have to give her that. Tall, slender, and elegant. *She seems so perfect I've always hated her. No matter what she wears, she looks like some designer dressed her, and even though she doesn't really need makeup, I've never even seen her with smudged lipstick. Why does she bother with makeup anyway? Her skin is beautiful.*

All of that was plenty of reason to dislike her, but the real problem was her attitude. She acted too darned self-confident and poised. Nothing ever seemed to bother her, at least not until now. Bet Miss English had plenty to bother her now because pretty soon everyone in Fairfield would know what she and Kurt had been up to. Sheila gritted her teeth. Could she stand the shame of it all?

She finished the last bite of her chocolate chip cookie just as Kurt came into the cafeteria. If he was looking for Miss English she'd gag right here at the table. He saw her and Harriet and came over and sat down with them. "Hello, ladies. How's it going?"

Harriet preened which made Sheila long to slap her.

"We're fine," she said, refusing to look at him. "Harriet, are you finished?"

"We still have ten minutes. What's the hurry?"

Sheila shrugged. "I'm finished eating, and it's noisy in here, that's all."

Kurt picked up Sheila and Harriet's trays. "I'd like to talk to you. Come with me to my office."

Sheila froze. "I have to go to class."

His eyes twinkled at her the way they'd always done. "It's important."

"I'll see you in class, Sheila," Harriet said as she hurried away to sit with Bethany Lewis.

"Please come," Kurt coaxed. "I have something to tell you."

All right, she'd talk to him. She'd like to see what he had to say. Kurt returned the trays, and she followed him to his office. "What did you want to talk about?"

"I need a favor," he said.

"That's not what I expected. What favor do you need?"

"Mom told me you know about me and Susan. I wanted you to help me pick out a ring for her."

Sheila shot him a look of disgust. "I don't think so."

Kurt slid his chair closer to her and grabbed her hand. "Why not? Honey, marrying Susan doesn't mean I love you any less."

Sheila laughed and jerked away from him. "So that's what you think the problem is. Gee, Kurt, I thought you were smarter than that."

"Sheila…"

"I'm not interested." She gave him her most ferocious scowl.

"Honey…"

"Oh, be quiet." She spun around and left Kurt fumbling for words. Pick out a ring indeed! She'd rather be drawn and quartered like they did to people in the Middle-Ages. It would be a cold day in July before she did anything for Kurt or his little slut.

Six

Even though they had scheduled the wedding for eleven on Saturday morning, Marjorie awoke around five-thirty. She felt for Bill, but the bed was empty. Even his pillow was cold, so he had been up for some time.

She pulled on her robe and went downstairs to find him. "Hey, you're up early," she said as she followed the morning smell of coffee to the kitchen.

"Yeah, I couldn't sleep."

The look of sheer misery on his face brought her to his side. She put her arms around him and pulled his forehead against hers. "Bill, please don't take it so hard. These things happen; you can't protect your kids forever. They have to live their own lives, and sometimes they'll make mistakes. Now quit worrying and look at what I bought for Susan."

She took the plastic wrap off a pretty, winter white suit hanging in the doorway. "Susan hasn't made any plans at all for the ceremony, so I bought her a suit to wear."

Bill barely glanced at it. "Yeah, it's pretty."

"Susan has nice clothes, but a woman needs something new to wear on her wedding day, especially if she's marrying a handsome man like Kurt Deveraux."

"His looks don't matter," Bill said, his voice cold as he skewered her with a look.

"No, probably not, but when I looked up his picture in Tyler's annual, I liked the expression in his eyes."

Bill's cup hit the table and sent coffee sloshing everywhere. "I can barely stand to go to the ceremony. It's killing me to sit back and watch Susan make the biggest mistake of her life." He glared at her. "Just like you did."

Marjorie dropped the dishrag she had fetched to wipe up the coffee. "What's that supposed to mean?"

"You made a mistake when you married me. A woman with your looks could get any man she wanted, maybe a doctor or lawyer, something like that. Instead you let me talk you into getting married, and you've worked like a dog ever since."

Marjorie picked up the dishrag and put the plastic bag back over the new suit. "Bill, I'm doing a job I love. Besides, without you and the kids, my life wouldn't be worth living. Don't you know how much I love you?"

"Okay," he growled. "You love me, but that doesn't change the fact that you married a loser. Just like Susan's going to."

"But..."

Without waiting to hear what she had to say, he stalked out of the kitchen and slammed the door behind him. Moments later Marjorie heard the water in the bathroom start to run.

Jason sneered at Susan the way she imagined he'd look at a student he'd caught cheating in his class. "You're a piece of work, you know that? What kind of woman sleeps with a guy on their first date?"

Susan grabbed for his arm as he strode toward the door. "Wait. You don't understand…"

"Oh, I understand all right." He jerked away as if her touch had soiled him. "Did you get more than you bargained for when you made the bet, or did you intend to get your hooks into him right from the start?"

Susan sat bolt upright in bed and wiped her sweaty face on her sleeve. What an awful nightmare! It took a minute for her to realize that the knocking she heard was someone pounding on her door. She glanced at the clock. Nine o'clock. In two hours she had to marry Kurt Deveraux.

"Get that look off your face," her mother snapped when Susan opened the door.

"What look?" cried Susan. "I need a little moral support, Mom, not criticism."

"You got yourself into this mess, Susan, so grin and bear it. I don't want your father getting any more upset than he already is. I'm scared for him to see Kurt today, and if you show up looking like you'd rather be dead than alive, there'll be hell to pay." She stepped inside and closed the door. "Let me help you with your hair, and then you can put this on."

She passed a garment bag to Susan.

"What is it?" Probably she deserved her mother's scolding, but she didn't feel upbeat, positive, and happy; she felt terrible! Didn't her mother understand? She had to marry a virtual stranger who didn't love her. She had always longed for a beautiful, fairy tale wedding, not a hurried, semi-secret affair.

"I bought a very nice suit for you," Marjorie said. "It's winter white and very elegant. I want you to look pretty today."

"It doesn't matter how I look."

Her mother's 'I can't believe I'm having to spell this out' expression dried up Susan's bout of self-pity. "You said he was a good guy, Susan. I looked his picture up in the school annual, so I know he's very handsome. Everybody likes him and his family, so you may find marriage isn't so bad. Anyway, he's the father of your baby, and you need to look pretty when you marry him."

Susan's eyes watered, but she allowed her mother to help her. "I guess you're right," she said when her mother finished with her. "Looking good does make things seem brighter."

Marjorie stood back and inspected her work. "Mother knows best. You look wonderful, and I've got a bouquet for you too. Did I tell you I've invited everyone back to our house for lunch and wedding cake after the ceremony?"

"Mom, that's sweet, but it really isn't a festive occasion. Under the circumstances do you think it's wise?"

"I'm making it a festive occasion. Put on your shoes now. It's time to go to the church."

<hr>

"Do you have the ring?" Kurt asked.

Jason sighed. "For the third time, yes, I have the ring."

"Is my tie okay with this suit? I can change if you don't like this one."

"Your tie is fine. Is your suit new?"

Kurt nodded. "Yeah, Dad made me get it. He said he didn't want me to show up looking like a yard dog."

Jason laughed. "You look nice, not at all like a yard dog."

Kurt had picked a well-cut charcoal gray suit that had caused more than one pair of feminine eyes to turn his way when he tried it on in the store.

He pulled his jacket on and studied his reflection in the mirror. "Susan's mother wants everybody to come to her house after the ceremony, and of course I have to go, but I'd rather wrestle alligators than meet Susan's father. Susan told me he isn't too happy about this."

Jason picked a tiny piece of lint from Kurt's shoulder. "You can worry about it later. It's time to leave for the church."

The two families arrived at the church at virtually the same moment. The slamming of car doors sounded like the clanging of cell doors to Kurt. Sure, that was the wrong way to feel, but now that the moment had come, he felt so out of synch and unlike himself he hoped he'd be able to finish the ceremony without falling flat on his face.

No one really said hello to anyone else. A few heads nodded, but Susan never even looked his way. Guess she wouldn't be walking beside him as they made their way into the church. Now that he thought about it, she reminded him of a sleepwalker. She had shown up in body today, but that was it.

Father Duncan waited for them in his office. "Welcome in the name of Christ," he said with a warm smile for everyone. "Maybe we'd better make a few introductions before we get started."

As stiff introductions went around the room, Kurt's shoulders tightened so much he had a stabbing pain radiating down his back. Every single person in the office looked angry or unhappy, especially Sheila and Susan's father. If looks could kill, both he and Susan would be six feet under.

The tension seemed worse, confined as it was to such a small space. He breathed a sigh of relief when Father Duncan suggested that they do the ceremony in the sanctuary. As they filed out of the office, Susan stumbled and bumped his arm. She recoiled as if he'd struck her.

Father Duncan wasted no time getting down to business. "Kurt, Susan, stand right here in front of me. Kurt you stand on my left, and Susan you take the right. Jason and Melissa you stand beside them.

"Ordinarily, I wouldn't speak to a bride and groom the way I'm speaking to you. In most cases I require couples receive pre-marital counseling before I'll marry them, but everyone knows there is some urgency in this case which prevents waiting for the marriage to be solemnized.

"I was disappointed when Kurt called and told me what had happened, but Kurt is a man, not a machine, and sometimes men make mistakes. I think the more of him for trying to right his mistake. He didn't have to marry Susan. He could have left her to raise the child as best she could. Lots of men do that, but instead he chose to live up to his responsibilities and marry the mother of his child. That should tell you, Bill and Marjorie, a lot about his character. I know you're hurt, and I know this isn't what you wanted for Susan, but he'll be good to her and provide for her and your grandchild. Always remember it took two people to make a baby. He didn't do it by himself.

"George and Helen, this probably wasn't the way you always pictured Kurt getting married either. I know you were as disappointed as I was when I heard the news. You don't know Susan yet, but her actions speak about her character too. She could have done what so many young women do and taken the easy way out by quietly disposing of her problem. No one forced her to tell Kurt anything about it, but she did. I believe she'll be a good mother to your grandchild, and always remember this: It took two people to make a baby. She didn't do it by herself.

"This is going to be a stressful time in Kurt and Susan's lives. All of you can help or hurt them by your actions. Be supportive and understanding. Accept the marriage, and give them space to make mistakes and find their way. Resist the temptation to be bitter and to long for what might have been. However it was conceived, the child is a gift from God, and it should be seen as such."

It was time to take their vows. Kurt's voice shook in spite of his heroic efforts to control it. Over the years, he'd heard of grooms who passed out and one who ran away; it would please him to do either one.

Instead he stood there, took his vows, and became Susan English's husband. Susan Deveraux. Unbelievable.

Father Duncan concluded the ceremony in the usual way. "Kurt, you may kiss your bride."

What? Kiss Susan in front of God and everybody? I didn't prepare myself for this.

"Go on, son," Father Duncan urged. "It's customary for the bride and groom to share a kiss at this point."

Kurt placed a chaste kiss on Susan's lips. She let him do it even though he'd bet anything she didn't want to. A faint, light, floral scent swirled in the air when she moved.

"Bravo," Father Duncan applauded. "Marjorie has invited everyone to have lunch at her house, so I suggest we be on our way. I've sampled some of the things she baked at Chef's Pantry, and I don't want to miss a bite." He chuckled. "It's one of the perks of the job. Kurt, Susan, you come with me. I need your signatures on some paperwork. The rest of you can be on your way. This won't take but a minute."

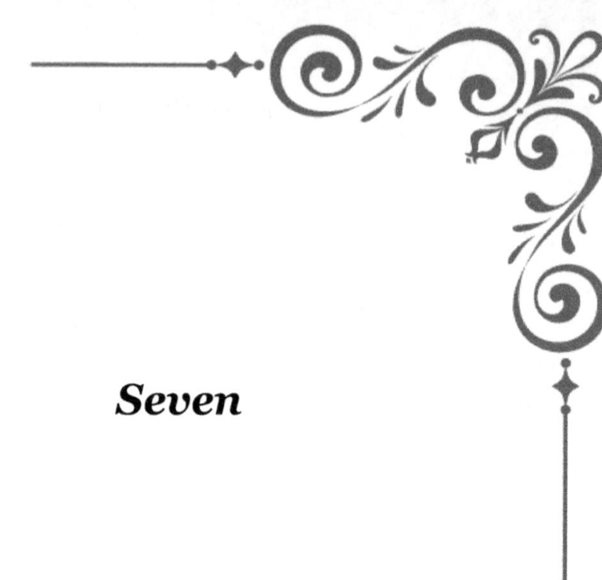

Seven

"Goodness, something smells wonderful," Father Duncan exclaimed as he, Susan, and Kurt walked into the English living room.

Marjorie took his coat and passed it to Susan. "Hang this up, would you, Susan? We're having smoked ham, Father."

"One of my favorites."

As she hung his coat, Susan watched Father Duncan give the English home the once over. From the approving look on his face, she thought he liked her mother's house. No surprise there. Everyone liked it. Her mother had a wonderful sense of color and style.

Father Duncan strolled toward the dining room, which was located at one end of the living room. Susan almost smiled. Such a delicious aroma would tempt anyone. She followed and saw a broccoli casserole, candied sweet potatoes, marinated carrots, and yeast rolls to go along with the ham. A wedding cake sat on a buffet behind the table.

"The cake is beautiful, Marjorie," Father Duncan said, beaming at her mother.

The cake *was* beautiful. It had two layers covered in sugared, edible flowers. Small, sparkling, white wedding bells intertwined with white flowers and pale, pale blue ribbons topped the cake and cascaded over the top layer. Why did her mother bother? No number of cakes could change the way she felt about this marriage.

Her mother called everyone to the table where Father Duncan said grace for them. Then they began to pass the food around, but nobody had much to say. Susan took out a few carrots and caught a glimpse of herself in the mirror that hung on one wall in front of her. She'd seen corpses with better color. Her stomach contracted. No doubt about it, the food looked delicious, but under the circumstances she'd be lucky to eat a bite.

She chanced a quick look at Kurt. He wasn't eating much either. Well, who could blame him? *Daddy doesn't have a kind word for any of them, especially Kurt.*

Father Duncan turned to Jason who sat beside him. "Did you hear the one about the boat God sent?"

"I don't believe so."

Father Duncan told his joke, and even though it wasn't that funny, Jason and Melissa laughed and began to help him.

"Let me tell you what happened in the cafeteria yesterday," Melissa said.

Everyone had started to relax. Her mother chatted with the Deverauxes as if they were old friends, and she treated Kurt with courtesy and respect.

When Susan raised her napkin to her lips, light reflected off her wedding ring and caught her attention. Small diamonds encrusted the ring across the top, giving it a dainty, feminine look. It was one of the prettiest wedding rings she'd ever seen. *I'm ashamed I didn't look at it before.*

He took the time to get a nice ring for me, and I didn't even notice.

Sheila Deveraux was also staring at the ring. "It's pretty, isn't it?" Susan asked as she held out her hand for her new sister-in-law's inspection.

Sheila sneered at her. "It's a wedding ring. They're all the same."

Marjorie shot a look at Sheila and said, "It's time to cut the cake. Susan, you and Kurt come and do it."

Can I get out of this farce? No, probably not. Hmm. Kurt doesn't want to do it either. He looks as if his first string quarterback just quit the team.

"You make the first cut together," Marjorie said. "Then I'll finish it for you."

Susan froze when her mother picked up a camera. "Mom, I hate pictures like this. Why don't we pass on it?"

"You mean those awful things where people smash cake on each other's faces? Don't worry. I don't want you and Kurt to do that. Just let him put his hand on yours, and I'll take the picture."

Like her mom didn't know what she meant. With little choice available, she picked up the knife, and after Kurt put his hand on top of hers they cut the cake. Father Duncan applauded, and everyone except her dad and Sheila joined in. She and Kurt sat down while her mother passed cake to everyone.

"This tastes as good as it looks," Helen Deveraux said.

Wonder how she'd get along with Kurt's mother? Mrs. Deveraux probably thought she was a cheap, tawdry hussy who'd tried to trap a good guy like Kurt into marrying her.

Helen and Marjorie began a discussion about baking while around the table various other conversations broke out.

The dinner ended amicably enough. When everyone left the table, she saw Father Duncan follow her father into the far corner of the living room. He must be a brave man, or maybe not very perceptive. Without speaking a single word, Bill had made it plain how he felt about this marriage.

Father Duncan beamed at her father as if they'd met under better circumstances and found they had a lot in common. "Marjorie told me you have some great pictures of the Grand Canyon hanging on your wall upstairs. I'm a bit of an amateur photographer myself, so I'd sure love to see them."

"Of course. Follow me."

The temptation to eavesdrop almost overcame Susan, but she shrugged and sat in her mother's rocker, letting the wedding luncheon ebb and flow around her.

Father Duncan admired the pictures of the Grand Canyon before he made his confession. "I didn't really get you off up here just to see the pictures."

Bill shrugged. "I thought as much. Let's go into the den to talk."

The den had begun life as a small bedroom, but Bill had equipped it with a desk, computer, television, and a leather loveseat that filled the room with its smell. "Your office is nice," Father Duncan said with a smile. "You've got the type of atmosphere men admire."

"Thank you. Won't you sit down?" If the man thought a compliment or two would make things better, he had another think coming. This stranger could sing Kurt Deveraux's praises until the cows came home, and it wouldn't make any difference.

As they took a seat, Father Duncan asked, "Do you want Susan to be happy?"

Bill tried to keep the scowl off his face and failed. "What kind of question is that? Of course I do."

"Then you have to accept Kurt as her husband."

"You don't understand."

Father Duncan smiled and nodded. "I think I do. She's your little girl, and he got her pregnant out of wedlock. Those of us with daughters naturally want to protect them and keep them safe."

Burning anger swept through Bill's veins. "Yeah, that makes me mad, but I could forgive him for that. I know how it feels to want a woman. What I can't forgive is…"

Father Duncan leaned forward. "Is what?"

So he wanted to know, did he? "Okay, you asked, so I'll tell you. I wanted Susan to have an easier life than I've had, but Kurt's a teacher. He won't make any money. She'll have to struggle just as I've had to."

Father Duncan considered his view. "Material possessions are nice, but I think Kurt has more than that to offer."

"Yeah? What?" He had gripped the arms of his chair so hard his fingers had turned white. It took a moment to make them relax. "School loans, mortgages, babies, and bills?"

Father Duncan laughed. "That's awfully gloomy. I was thinking more along the lines of respect, kindness, emotional support, faithfulness, physical fulfillment, and a good father for her children."

"He's not the only man she could find all that with."

"No, but he's the one she's got." Father Duncan leaned forward. "Think about it, Bill. The time is going to come, maybe not today because they didn't really want to get married, but soon he'll reach for her because she's beautiful, and she's his wife. If she cringes away from him because you've convinced her he isn't good enough for her, how will that make him feel? If she submits to him out of obligation, how will that make her feel?

"What if she approaches him and later is ashamed of wanting her own husband because he isn't good enough for her? It'll be hard for a marriage to last under those conditions. This isn't what you want for Susan. Forgive him. Accept him. You'll be doing your daughter a favor."

Bill's eyes dropped to his hands. He cleared his throat. "I know you've given me good advice, but I had so many hopes and dreams for Susan, and now they're all gone. You want the truth? I'd like to beat him to a pulp."

"It sounds like you think your own life is a failure," Father Duncan said. "Why would you think that? You have a nice home with food on the table and a loving family. It doesn't seem so bad to me."

Bill felt color flood his face. Even his ears burned, and if it weren't for Kurt Deveraux, he wouldn't be having this uncomfortable discussion. Why did everyone want to spill his or her guts to therapists? "I'd rather not talk about it," he said. "I know you mean well, but we've only met, and I don't feel comfortable discussing my failures with a stranger. As far as accepting Kurt goes, I'll try."

Father Duncan stood. "I guess we'd better rejoin the others then. If you ever decide you'd like to talk to me about your own life I'd be happy to discuss it with you."

Don't hold your breath, Bill thought.

———⁂———

Kurt stood on the English deck staring at the back yard. There wasn't much to see, but he needed a break. He heard the sliding glass doors move and turned around to see his father.

George smiled and joined him. "I've been hoping for a minute alone with you. What are you doing after you leave here?"

Kurt blinked. "I don't know."

"You need to take Susan somewhere tonight, overnight, I mean. I was afraid you might not have thought about it, so your mother and I want to give you this. It isn't much, but it's the best I could do on such short notice." He handed Kurt an envelope.

"Thanks, Dad. That's really nice of you and Mom." He opened the gift and found a reservation for a room at the Greenville Hilton and tickets to a concert.

"It'll only take about an hour to get to the city," George said, "so you'll have plenty of time to make the show tonight." He squeezed Kurt's shoulder. "Relax and try to enjoy your wedding day. You're so tense I've got a stiff neck just watching you. Susan's a beautiful woman, and if you try to make your marriage work, I think you can be happy."

Kurt shook his head. "I'm glad *you're* so optimistic. Susan probably doesn't want to go anywhere with me, and it's pretty hard to relax with Mr. English staring at me the way he is."

"Don't worry about Bill. He'll eventually come around. You just tell Susan the trip is a wedding gift, and I think she'll go with you. Let's join the others. I imagine everyone has missed us by now."

Inside, the party was breaking up. Jason approached Kurt and said, "I have to go, Kurt. It was...a...a nice ceremony."

"I'll walk you out."

They didn't say anything until they reached Jason's car. Kurt sighed. "You and Melissa seemed to be having a good time."

"Yeah, we were." Jason smiled as if he had more than had a good time. "Melissa's real pretty. She's interesting too."

"Well, I'm glad you enjoyed yourself." He turned the heavy gold ring on his finger. Susan had probably paid a lot for it.

"It's a nice ring," Jason said.

"Yeah, but it feels funny on my finger, and I don't feel married. Last Saturday night I went to the movies with Aleisha Childs, and today I married Susan. How weird is that?"

Jason chuckled. "Pretty weird, but you'll get used to being married just like you'll get used to the ring. Give it a little time. Did you ask for any days off next week?"

"No, we've still got one more game, and I want to win it." He sighed. "The boys are going to be thrown by this anyway, so I thought I needed to be there."

"If you change your mind and want some time off, just give me a call. Dan, Jeff, and I can handle everything."

Jason opened his car door and gave Kurt a little parting advice. "You look miserable, but you might as well enjoy yourself. Susan's beautiful, and you obviously don't repulse her either. Relax and go with the flow. You may find that getting married isn't so bad."

With an affectionate punch to Kurt's shoulder, Jason slammed the car door and drove away, leaving Kurt to feel slightly abandoned. He'd give anything to get in that car with Jason and leave his problems far behind.

Instead, he went back inside to find everyone waiting for him.

"Better get a move on," George said. "You don't want to be late."

"I guess." He turned to Susan. "Are you ready to go?"

⚬

The detached feeling that had sustained Susan all day abruptly fell apart. *If only I could drop dead on the floor. What will happen to me now?* Every nerve in her body screamed with regret over the loss of her freedom while a knot the size of Texas formed in her stomach.

She blindly hugged and kissed her mother. "Thanks, Mom. I love you."

Her brother came next, but when Susan approached her father, her heart almost broke. Somehow, this was the hardest goodbye of all. "I'll see you later, Dad."

He hugged her close. "Bye, baby. Take care."

She'd guess her father would like to say a lot more, but some, if not most of it was probably best left unspoken.

Setting her jaw, she waited for Kurt to say his goodbyes. What in the world would they do with a whole weekend to muddle through and no one to run interference for them?

Eight

The silence in the car made Susan's strained nerves quiver. She couldn't endure it another second!

"What did your father mean when he warned you not to be late?" Susan asked. *Not that I really care.*

Kurt reached into the inside pocket of his jacket and handed her an envelope. In the process she got a good look at his left hand. She tried not to stare, but the ring she'd bought him gleamed in the afternoon sunshine.

"What are you looking at?" he asked.

"Your wedding ring."

He laughed, but he didn't sound amused. "Looks a little weird, doesn't it?"

Susan flexed her fingers and looked at her own ring. "Mine's pretty. Thank you for that."

"It wasn't any trouble, but even if it had been, it doesn't matter. You're my wife. I expect to take care of you and try to please you when I can."

What a sweet thing for him to say. If circumstances had been different she would have unfastened her seat belt and kissed him. Since that was out, she opened the envelope instead. "That's nice of them."

She really meant it, but she couldn't imagine why they'd bothered. They couldn't like her. Not that she blamed them. At the moment she didn't like herself too much either. Everything that happened to her was her own fault, not Kurt's. He hadn't forced her to do anything against her will.

"Do you want to go?" he asked.

"Sure, why not? It sounds like fun." *I'd hate for him to know how much I appreciate a few more hours before I have to settle him in my house. I don't look forward to that at all. My home is beautiful. It's my own private space, a space I hadn't planned on sharing with anyone for a long time.*

They stopped first at Susan's house for her to pack an overnight bag. Then they swung by Kurt's place. While he packed, she studied his apartment, looking for clues to the personality of the stranger she'd married. As she expected, his scantily decorated bachelor space yielded nothing of interest except a couple of sports' magazines and a set of student papers on the dining room table. The apartment was clean, though. Thank goodness he wasn't a slob.

"The lease is up at the end of the month, which is lucky," Kurt said when he came back into the room. "Jason volunteered to help me move out, but I don't know what to do with most of this stuff. Your house is pretty well furnished."

"Have a yard sale. I love to do them, and so do Melissa and Mom. We usually do ours together."

Kurt paused. "I've never done a yard sale."

"I'll do most of it. You'll just have to move heavy stuff for me."

"Whatever you say. Are you ready?"

Susan was, so they locked the door and left for Greenville. She watched as the scenery flashed by. "It's a good day for a ride," she said. "The sky is a gorgeous blue, and the crisp air makes you glad to be alive."

Kurt laughed. "That's what I was thinking." He glanced her way. "To tell you the truth, I think I feel better because the ceremony is over. My shoulders are finally relaxing."

"My nerves have settled down, which is great because all day I felt like a touch would break me into a thousand pieces."

Kurt started to speak, changed his mind, and finally came out with it. "I meant what I said."

"About what?"

"About me and you. I want to be a good husband."

Susan bit her lip. "I'll try too, Kurt."

"To be a good husband?"

He had made her laugh, and she hadn't expected anything would be funny today. "You know what I mean."

When they arrived at the Hilton, they checked in and went upstairs to their room.

Susan barely stifled a gasp. A huge, king-sized bed dominated the décor. Oh, my gosh! She couldn't take her eyes off it. Was Kurt having as hard a time ignoring that thing as she was? She did *not* want to think of beds and Kurt Deveraux at the same time.

She brushed her hair back and took a deep breath. "What time is the concert?

"Seven."

"Let's change clothes and go shopping. Then we can grab some dinner before we go to the concert."

"Yeah, that sounds fine to me."

He certainly hadn't hesitated before agreeing, so he might be as nervous as she was. Susan grabbed her bag and vanished into the bathroom to change, but she didn't hurry. *The last thing I want to do is barge in there before he changes his clothes.* Her face burned. She had seen him naked before.

They decided to shop at a big mall they had passed on their way to the hotel. Susan paused beside a map that showed the location of the stores in the mall. "Where do you want to start?"

"It's up to you."

"Okay." Susan stared at the map. "I want to go to a lingerie shop."

Kurt cleared his throat as a faint flush spread across his cheekbones. He refused to look her in the eye. "I don't want to go shopping for underwear with you. I feel like a fool tagging along behind women when they're looking at stuff like that."

"Like what?" asked Susan, his masculine reaction bringing a smile to her lips.

"You know, bras and lace stuff." His gaze was focused on some point over her shoulder.

"I hadn't thought about it, but I guess it could be an embarrassing experience. I'll meet you somewhere." Why didn't she think of this earlier? She could look around on her own without Kurt bothering her.

"No, I don't want to do that. I'll go."

Rats.

They soon found a lingerie shop with an extensive selection. Susan sneaked a peek at Kurt whose eyes were trained on the floor, but he could have gone somewhere else if he'd wanted to.

The racks near the door displayed nightwear, so Susan started there. She found a pair of white satin pajamas and held them up to her. "Do you like these, Kurt? I can't make up my mind."

"No, I don't."

"Why not?"

"They look too bulky."

Susan returned them to the rack and kept looking. "How about this?" She held up a form fitting blue satin gown trimmed in ecru lace.

Kurt blushed. "I like that better."

"Good. I've wanted something in blue. Will you hold it for me while I look some more?"

The expression on his face told her he'd rather not, but he tossed it across his arm anyway. Susan hid a smile when she saw him stroke the smooth, blue satin. He almost jumped out of his skin when a saleslady materialized at his elbow and asked, "May I help you, sir?"

"No, ma'am. Thank you, but no. I'm... I'm just following my wife," Kurt stammered.

The sales woman greeted Susan with a smile. "Did you see the new shipment of baby dolls up front?"

"No, but I'll look at them."

"Call me if I can help you. Oh. Your husband likes the blue satin."

Kurt blushed again, which almost made her feel for him. After all, everywhere he looked he could see some type of feminine undergarment or sleepwear. Some of it looked practical and tame, but much of it had been fashioned to appear as seductive as possible.

A feeling of unease washed over her. Maybe Kurt thought she brought him here to tease him. Oh, why didn't she think about his reaction before she dragged him in here?

"I'm finished," she said and made a beeline for the checkout where she got in line behind a woman who looked about nine months pregnant. She pulled out her wallet, but Kurt shook his head and pushed her wallet back into her purse. "That's okay. I'll get it."

"I don't expect you to," Susan protested. She bit back tears. Why was he being so nice?

"I know you don't expect it, but I am anyway."

"Thank you." She couldn't say anything else because she knew she'd cry if she did. Maybe the weepiness was just hormones because of her pregnancy. Her spirits fell. Why had she wanted the gown anyway? Soon she'd be the size of the woman in front of them and wouldn't be able to wear it.

Safely out of the lingerie shop, she started to relax, but Kurt still had a distracted expression on his face. He cleared his throat several times before he finally brought himself to speak. "It was bad enough watching you walk down the hall without thinking about your underwear."

I guess that isn't terribly random, not considering we just left a lingerie shop. "Er, you mean at school?"

Kurt nodded.

Susan came to a halt and allowed the mall traffic to flow around then. "Did you really watch me? You never flirted with me or even talked to me very much."

"I knew you were involved with another guy." He shrugged. "I didn't think you'd care for me to flirt with you."

Susan laughed. "You're probably right, but you are mighty handsome, Kurt Deveraux. It's hard to ignore you."

Kurt blushed again as Susan turned and entered a shop that sold bath and beauty products. "Let's look in here."

In spite of the fact that nobody but women seemed to frequent the store, Kurt looked happier here than he had at the lingerie store. "What are you looking at?" he asked as she opened a jar to look at its contents. "That stuff looks like the byproduct of a dirty manufacturing process."

"It's good for your face. You put it on once a week, let it dry, and then peel it off."

He frowned. "Does it hurt?"

"Of course not." She giggled as doubt flashed across his face.

"I don't think my mom or sister use stuff like this."

"Bet they do." She put the jar into a small shopping bag she'd picked up near the entrance. "Your sister doesn't look much like you."

"No, she took after my mom's side of the family. I look more like Dad."

Susan took the cap off another jar and smelled it, but it was nasty so she returned it to the shelf. "Sheila...didn't seem too happy at the wedding." Actually, that was an understatement. Sheila had looked as angry as a terrorist bent on destruction.

"She was upset," Kurt admitted. "Sheila and I have always been close, and I think she believes I let her down. She'll come around eventually."

"If you say so." Frankly, it didn't matter if Sheila Deveraux liked her or not. She and Kurt were married so Sheila would just have to get over it.

Kurt suddenly chuckled. "Sheila hates her name. She says it's too old-fashioned."

"Your mother must have liked it."

"Yeah, her favorite aunt was named Sheila."

Susan picked up a tube of moisturizer in a sale bin. Great. This was the brand she used. "What did Sheila want to be called?"

"Jennifer or Ashley, something more modern."

They paid for Susan's moisturizer and masque and followed their noses to the food court where they shared a pizza before going to the concert. They talked about it all the way back to the Hilton, but they fell silent when they entered their room. How could anyone not be intimidated by that huge bed?

Kurt walked over to the window. "Look, Susan. The city's beautiful at night."

Susan joined him at the window to admire the view.

"I don't know what I'm supposed to do now," he muttered. "Do you want to make love, or do we wait, or what?"

Susan's face burned. She stared out the window, frozen with no more movement than a statue. "It's not that I don't want you. I... I remember how good it was when we were together at Mendoza's house. I expect us to have a normal marital relationship. It's just that my emotions are all shot, and I....just don't think I'm ready...yet...to be intimate with you."

Relief spread across his face, so she knew he hadn't wanted to any more than she did. "That's fine with me. Why don't we get ready for bed and watch TV until we get sleepy?

We'll take it one day at a time about the other. When we both want it, then we'll make love."

Helen managed not to cry until they got home. Sheila, who had glowered like a thundercloud all day, bolted upstairs to her room the minute they unlocked the door. Good. She didn't feel like coping with Sheila today.

"Oh, George, hold me."

George snuggled her close. "It's been a rough day, hasn't it?"

"It was horrible."

George kissed the top of her head and led her into the living room. "I hate wearing a blamed tie," he complained. He threw the offending tie onto a chair and sat on the sofa beside Helen. "What did you think of Susan?" he asked.

"I couldn't really tell. She was so pale and quiet I couldn't get a feel for her."

He nodded and reached for her hand. "Yeah, that's what I thought. You and Marjorie seemed to hit it off."

"Yes, I liked her because she was nice to Kurt."

"I noticed."

Helen's lips tightened as resentment filled her heart. "Bill sure wasn't nice to him."

"No, but Susan's his little girl, and Kurt's the man who got her pregnant. He'll be okay as soon as he figures out that Kurt's a good husband and father."

"Do you think he will be?" Helen pushed away from him, so she could see his face. "He's been dating Aleisha Childs, and I think he liked her."

"Oh, yeah, he'll be fine." George squeezed her hand. "Kurt knows what his responsibilities are."

"Good old reliable Kurt," Sheila mocked from the living room doorway. "I guess he screwed up this time."

"Sheila, don't start," George warned. "This is serious. We don't need any theatrics on your part."

"Oh, don't worry. Janet called me and wants me to come over to her house. I told her I could."

"You should have asked permission first, but I guess it's okay."

Sheila left without another word or a backward glance. She hated her family!

Kurt was a hypocrite, and so were her parents. They should have reamed him out about getting Miss English pregnant, but no. They were so sickeningly sweet to him it made her want to gag. If she had been the one in trouble, they'd probably have locked her in the basement and starved her to death.

Kurt had tried to suck up to her at lunch, but she'd given him the cold shoulder. She'd die rather than be his friend now, and as far as Susan went, she'd rather eat dirt than be nice to that slut.

She slammed the door behind her so they would know how angry she was. It would serve them right if she never came back.

"Bill! If you don't stop throwing the dishes around I'll need a new set."

"Sorry." He meekly slid a stack of plates back in the cabinet where they belonged and started drying the silverware.

Marjorie picked up the bowl that had held the carrots and started to wash it. "Everything went pretty well, didn't it? I liked the Deverauxes."

"Yeah, it went okay."

She rinsed the bowl and passed it to him. "You don't have much to say."

"What do you want me to say? She's married now, and that's the end of it."

She reached for one leftover glass that had been hidden behind the big bowl. "That sounds a little strange."

Bill opened the drawer where Marjorie kept the silverware. No, not silver. Stainless. Bought with his Super Mart discount of ten lousy percent.

"Bill? Answer me."

"Let it go."

Marjorie rolled her eyes and fixed Bill with a gimlet gaze. "Oh, stop being so silly. What did you mean when you said that's the end of it? The most rewarding part of Susan's life is just beginning."

So she wanted to know, did she? "Okay, I meant Susan's stuck now. No more remodeling her house, no more new clothes, or trips. She can't afford it."

Marjorie passed him another bowl. "Be careful of that bowl. It belonged to my grandmother. As far as remodeling goes, Susan doesn't need anything more done to her house. She may miss her trip to Paris next summer, but there'll be other years to take vacations."

"If they can afford it. You know how much kids cost, and Kurt has school loans to pay off."

She squeezed out the dishcloth and draped it across a rack under the sink. "They'll work it out. You know they will."

Bill scowled. "Like we did, you mean? Look at this stuff," he cried as he brandished a serving fork. "Where'd you get this? Super Mart, right? You've never had any nice silver or china either. What do you call those plates?

"Stoneware, but..."

"But nothing. I'm a failure, and I guess I might as well face it. I wanted to *coach football* for a living! What were you thinking to marry me anyway? Why didn't you listen to your father? Coach football!"

He slammed the fork and drying cloth onto the cabinet and stalked away. Man, he hated Kurt Deveraux!

Nine

Susan opened her eyes and stretched. What a lovely morning. She hadn't felt so relaxed in a long time, mainly because the dreaded wedding ceremony was over, Kurt hadn't put pressure on her to have sex with him, and her father had spoken kindly to her when she and Kurt left yesterday.

She sat up and looked at Kurt lying beside her. He was still asleep, so she quietly slid out of bed and tiptoed into the bathroom. That huge bathtub she'd seen last night was calling her name.

After filling the tub with warm water, she lay back to think. Kurt had been so nice to her yesterday. He had gone lingerie shopping even though he hadn't wanted to, and then he had paid for the things she wanted. It seemed like he wanted their marriage to work, so she'd do everything she could to meet him halfway. If he could forget the way they got together, so could she.

By the time she came out of the bathroom, Kurt had gotten up to read the Sunday paper while he had his morning coffee. He wore a white hotel robe with a golden crest on the pocket. Wasn't that a spectacular sight? If she had to get married, she'd just as soon marry a hunk like Kurt.

He smiled when he saw her. "Would you like some coffee?"

Now that he was aware of her presence she couldn't help feeling a little awkward. He wasn't dressed, and it felt funny to see him in the bathrobe. That was silly because they'd slept in the same bed last night, but she couldn't help it. "I don't want to drink caffeine while I'm pregnant, but thanks anyway," she said.

"It's decaf."

"Then I'd love a cup."

Susan sat on the sofa beside him, and he passed her a cup of coffee.

"I would've ordered breakfast too," he said, "but I didn't know what you wanted. It won't take me long to dress, and then we can get something to eat."

Her head bobbed. "Good idea. I'm so hungry I could eat a horse."

He shot a quick look at her stomach. "Because of the baby, I guess."

Did he find it as hard as she did to believe she carried a child belonging to him?

"I'll hurry," Kurt promised. He swallowed the last of his coffee and vanished into the bathroom. Fifteen minutes later he was dressed and ready to go.

"That isn't fair," complained Susan as he locked the door behind them.

"What isn't?"

"Women have to do so much more than men to get dressed."

His head tilted. "What do you have to do?"

"Well, I shower, shave my legs, do my hair, put on my makeup, select jewelry and accessories to match my outfit, oh, and brush my teeth."

He held the elevator door until she got on. "Uh huh. Whose razor did you use on your legs this morning?"

Susan's guilty expression answered Kurt's question. "I forgot mine, so I used yours."

"That's what I thought. The blade was so dull I cut myself." He turned his head for her to see the nick on the side of his neck.

Susan laughed as the elevator dinged and opened on the first floor. "You're taking it well. Dad always roars like a lion if Mom or I do that."

"Dad bought a bunch of disposables for Mom and Sheila. I could get some for you."

Susan broke into gales of laughter, which made several people smile at them. He sounded so hopeful! "Yes, that would be lovely." Impulsively, she stood on her tiptoes and placed a light kiss over the cut.

Kurt probably hadn't expected her to kiss him, but she didn't think he minded. "That'll make it feel better," she said. With a smile she took his hand, and they walked into the dining room together.

<hr>

"Look. There's Mrs. Myers watching us," Susan whispered to Kurt. "She's the neighborhood gossip. By tonight everybody on the street will know there's a man living with me."

The time Susan had dreaded had finally arrived. Their brief honeymoon had come to an end, and now Kurt would share her home with her. Nosy Mrs. Myers only made this homecoming harder.

Kurt dropped his bag on the ground. "Introduce me to her."

Together they walked over to the old woman who greeted them with a smile. "Hello, Susan. Is your young man moving in with you?"

Kurt answered the question. "Yes, ma'am, I am. My name is Kurt Deveraux, but I'm more than just Susan's young man."

"What do you mean?"

"I'm Susan's husband."

"You're married?" Mrs. Myers looked disappointed that she didn't already know. "Susan, when did this happen? Do your parents know about your marriage?"

"We were married yesterday, Mrs. Myers, and, yes, my parents do know. They were at the wedding."

Mrs. Myers hands fluttered. "My dear, you should have told us. The neighbors would have wanted to do something for you."

"We just decided all at once so there wasn't any time."

They took their leave of their neighbor, and then Kurt hauled his bag into the house. "Where do you want it?"

Oh, she hated this! "There are two closets in the master bedroom. I cleaned out one for you."

She accompanied Kurt as he carried the suitcase into the bedroom and unpacked. It didn't take long because he had left most of his things at his apartment.

"Do you like it?" she asked as his eyes moved around the bedroom.

He nodded. "Very much. It's nice and calm looking just like your living room. Kind of neutral too."

She smiled at his description. "Yes, it is. I don't like things to look cluttered, so I usually avoid lace and ribbons."

"Yeah, I like the neutral look, but the green comforter and those red pillows and prints give it some color."

Susan smiled at him. "I'm glad you like it. Would you like to see the rest of the house?"

"Sure." The smile left his face. "I wasn't in any condition to appreciate it the last time I was here."

Susan indicated the room across the hall, a smaller room painted in the same neutral shade as the rest of the house. "I'm using this room as a storage room at the moment, but how about we make it into a nursery? It's close to us so we can hear the baby when it cries."

"Whatever you think best is fine by me. I don't know much about babies, but I'm willing to learn."

Susan laughed. "Good. That was sure the right answer."

It seemed hard to get settled down. They didn't have anything that had to be done, and there was no place they had to be. *I feel like I have company who've overstayed their welcome, and Kurt looks stiff and unhappy. I bet his shoulders are full of knots.*

The tension built until finally Susan couldn't take it anymore. "This is stupid," she cried. "I don't want to sit here watching golf on TV. I want to call my mother, but I feel responsible for you, and I shouldn't. You're not a guest. This is where you live now. What do you want to do?"

The only word for the expression on his face was hopeful. "If you really want to know, I'd like to find a snack and read a little, but I was afraid you'd think I was being rude."

She felt nothing but relief. "You aren't being rude if you read your book. You know where the kitchen is, and I should have something you'll like. Ice cream is in the freezer, and my mother gave me some chocolate chip cookies. I put them in the red cookie jar on the counter near the microwave. I have some popcorn in the pantry or you can make a ham sandwich for yourself. If you want something you don't find, either go out and get it or make a list and I'll pick it up tomorrow."

Kurt wandered into the kitchen and came back with a large bowl of ice cream. Then, he went into the bedroom and found his book, kicked off his shoes, and stretched out on the bed to read. Susan made a call to her mother, and the rest of the evening passed much more easily.

Ten

"How was the wedding?" Dan asked.

He and Jeff Batson sat with Jason in Kurt's office having their morning coffee. Kurt was running a few minutes late, so his staff had taken advantage of his absence to discuss the wedding.

Jason got up and shut the door. "You could tell Kurt was nervous, but he handled it okay."

"What about Susan?"

Jason's lips thinned. "Susan was as cool as a cucumber."

"Well, did you want her to cry and faint?" demanded Jeff. "She had to do it, so I guess she decided to show a little class. I bet she looked pretty. Say what you like about her, she's hot."

"Oh yeah, Susan always looks good."

Jeff took a sip of his coffee and blew on it. "Burnt my tongue. Kurt may like being married. I think he's wanted her for a long time."

The conversation came to a halt when Kurt walked into the room. "Hey, sorry I'm late. Did you all have a nice weekend?"

"Yeah, pretty good," Dan said. He poured a cup of coffee for Kurt. "Jason said you're a married man now."

"That's right." Kurt held out his hand and showed them his wedding ring.

Dan nodded. "Congratulations."

"Thanks."

Dan looked at Kurt with a gleam in his eye. "I didn't expect to see you today. I figured you'd take Susan on a romantic getaway."

"We went to Greenville after the wedding, but I wanted to be here because of the game on Friday." He smiled at Dan. "A getaway can wait a few weeks."

"When are you going to tell the kids?" Jason asked.

"I haven't thought about it." Kurt shrugged. "Guess I'll just play it by ear."

He threw down the stack of papers he had picked up off his desk. "I left the ones I need in the lounge. I'd better go get them."

Dan broke the brief moment of silence that had fallen on the office. "He seems okay."

"Yeah, he does," Jason answered. "They must have had a good time after the wedding was over."

Dan cracked up. "I hope so."

Annoyance flashed across Jason's face when he realized what Dan meant.

"This is my first year at Fairfield High," Dan continued, "but Kurt made me welcome and paid me the compliment of assuming I knew my job. I owe him for that, so I hope his marriage is a happy one."

Jason nodded. "So do I. Kurt's a good guy. He deserves to be happy."

Kurt did deserve happiness, but no matter how hard he tried, Jason couldn't let go of his anger, but maybe Kurt was too distracted to notice. Where did all this rage come from? Just when he thought he had it pinned down it slipped away from him. Maybe he felt angry because Kurt had disappointed him. Being the high school football coach in a small town meant that Kurt had a high profile job. He'd always been a leader both at school and in his church, but now... *Don't think about it. Just treat him like you've always done and you'll forgive him in no time.*

Susan dropped her book bag on her desk, but before she could sit down, Melissa's head popped around the door.

"Good morning, Mrs. Deveraux."

Susan laughed. "That's hard to get used to. I still feel like Miss English."

Melissa came into the room and sat beside Susan. "You look happier this morning."

She nodded. "I feel happier. Everything was fine after we got away from Mom's house, and it was just the two of us."

"What's it like having him around all the time?" Melissa frowned as she looked at her scarf and retied it.

"So far it's okay." Susan shrugged. "He doesn't make a mess in the bathroom or kitchen, and last night he opened a jar for me."

Melissa laughed. "That's one of the most interesting descriptions of married life I've ever heard. Is it awkward being around him?"

Susan thought for a moment. "Maybe at first, but we actually have a lot to talk about, and I sure don't mind looking at him."

Melissa giggled. "I knew it would work out. You're attracted to Kurt, and he looks at you like he'd love to eat you up."

"Does he really?"

"Sure he does. I noticed it last year, and on Saturday Jason told me that Kurt's wanted to go out with you for a long time."

What a wonderful opportunity to find out more about her husband. "What else did Jason say?"

Melissa hesitated. "Well, Jason's a little upset about what happened. You know he and Kurt are so close. I think it's the bet that bothers him the most."

"Don't remind me." Susan shivered. "I cringe every time I think of it."

"As long as Kurt forgets it you're okay."

———⟡———

Melissa meant every word she'd said. She wanted her best friend to be happy. However, Susan had disappointed her. She'd done something that could never be undone, and her whole life had changed because of it. Thanks to one night of indiscretion, most of Susan's dreams would probably never come to pass. As Susan's friend, it just broke her heart.

———⟡———

The news got out before the first class ended. Kurt had just clicked his mouse and brought up a chart on his interactive white board when one of his football players raised his hand. "Yeah, Benjy, what is it?"

"Coach, what kind of ring are you wearing on your left hand?"

"It's a wedding ring," Kurt said, feeling the ring burn a circle on his finger.

Benjy picked at a scab on his arm. "Why are you wearing that? It isn't yours, is it?"

"Yes, it's mine." He clicked the mouse, wishing he could click this moment away with it.

Benjy ignored the scab in light of his teacher's answer. "But you aren't married."

"I got married on Saturday."

An air of excited anticipation swirled in the totally silent class while Benjy tentatively felt his way through this unexpected development. He looked as if he might have misunderstood Kurt.

"You didn't say you were getting married, Coach."

"That's right. I didn't," Kurt replied.

Benjy stared at Kurt. Two small lines had appeared between his eyebrows. "I don't understand. Why'd you get married?"

This puzzled inquiry broke up the class.

"Why does anybody get married, you idiot?" asked Ken Banks.

"Yeah, Benjy, Coach Deveraux is hot," one of the girls chimed in.

Benjy absently rubbed the scab. "Who did you get married to?"

"Miss English."

An excited buzz ran through the room.

"Our Miss English? The one who teaches here?"

"Yes."

Benjy's scab finally let go and fell to the floor. "But Coach, I never knew you dated her."

"He doesn't clear his social calendar with you, fool," Ken Banks called from the back of the room.

Benjy ignored Ken and refused to give up. "How long have you been dating her?"

"Shut up. That's none of your business," Ken sang out.

"It's okay," Kurt said. "I've been seeing her for a couple of months now."

Conversation broke out all over the class as the students discussed the wedding. Kurt allowed them a few minutes to get it all out of their systems before he began class again, but he knew most of his students were thinking about weddings, not health.

***

"Miss English, is it true?"

"Is what true, Amanda?"

"Did you really marry Coach Deveraux?"

"Yes, I did. On Saturday."

"Was it a big wedding?"

"No, very small and quiet. Just our families."

"He's so cute. You're lucky."

"Yes, I sure am."

How many times had she had that conversation with her students? Thank goodness this awful day was finally over. Her head was killing her. As her last student filed from the room, she sat at her desk and dropped her head into her hands. When Kurt called to her, she jumped and hit her knee on her desk.

He flinched as if he'd been the one who took the hit. "Sorry. I forgot to tell you I have football practice after school today."

She nodded. "Yeah, I thought you would."

Kurt paused and stepped into the room. "Was it bad today?" He gave her a lopsided smile that made her head feel a little better. "I'm ready to kill somebody."

Susan laughed even though this day had been anything but funny. "My head's about to split open, and if one more girl asks me what it's like to be married to you, I may scream."

A thoughtful look crossed his face. "I think the coaching staff wanted to ask something like that, but they were afraid to."

"I bet. Melissa was certainly asking leading questions today."

He gave her an awkward pat on the back. "Just hang in there. I think it'll calm down soon."

"Oh, it will for a while, and then I'll start showing. The gossip and talk will be terrible."

Kurt sighed. "I can't do anything about that, Susan."

Her face burned. *Stupid. What a stupid thing for me to say.* "I've never cooked for you before, Coach," she said, hoping he'd forget her whining comment. "What would you like for dinner?"

"Anything is okay except tuna. I hate tuna."

"Okay, no tuna. What time will you be home?"

"About five thirty."

Why was he still hanging around? She'd bet he had a bunch of football players waiting for him, but instead of starting practice, he was just standing there staring at her. "What is it?" she asked.

Kurt shrugged as his face turned pink. "I'd like to kiss you. That little black dress looks great, and...I wanted to kiss you this morning, but we were late, and you...ah...didn't seem interested."

Susan rose from her desk chair and shut the door. "So, kiss me," she invited. "You look awfully cute in those little gym shorts, Coach."

Kurt didn't argue. As he gently pulled her against him, her arms slipped around his shoulders. Oh my goodness! He felt so good against her! Her eyes fluttered shut, and she tilted her head for his kiss. As her arms tightened around him, Kurt deepened the kiss and slid his hand down her back to her bottom.

The door burst open and startled Susan who jerked out of Kurt's arms with her face burning. Even her eyes felt hot, but she still recognized Benjy, one of Kurt's football players.

Benjy spun around without a word, and she heard him say to whomever had accompanied him, "God, he's kissing her, and his hand is on her butt."

"Guess that'll be all over school by tomorrow," muttered Kurt. "I'd better go. I'll see you at home."

<hr>

"Where's Coach Deveraux?" Jason asked as Benjy slunk into the locker room.

"I don't think he's coming."

Jason frowned. "Why not? Is he sick?"

"He didn't say he wouldn't come, but it looked like he was busy."

Benjy's face flushed, and he refused to meet Jason's eyes.

"What happened, Benjy?"

Kurt answered the question as he hurried into the locker room. "He didn't knock before he opened Miss English, I mean Mrs. Deveraux's, door, and he saw me kissing her."

"I see."

Kurt turned to the boy and prayed he could explain this so the kid would understand. "Benjy, I owe you an apology. I shouldn't have kissed her at school, but I've only been married for two days, and if you want the truth, I got carried away. I guess I should have taken a little time off for a honeymoon, but we have a game on Friday, and I wanted to be here this week. I'm sorry if I upset you."

Benjy cast a reproachful glance Kurt's way. "You're always lecturing us about having respect for girls and not mauling them, but it looked like you were mauling Miss English."

"Her name is Mrs. Deveraux. When you're married it's okay to touch."

Uh oh. Benjy still looked upset. "Is there anything else that's bothering you?"

The boy scowled at him, but with a suddenness that surprised Kurt, he blurted out, "Okay, I'll tell you! It looked to me like you were being rough with her and making her kiss you. I don't think she wanted to."

His toes curled in his shoes. To think he'd have to explain something like this to a student. "Think a minute, Benjy. How was she behaving?"

"What do you mean?"

"Was she trying to get away from me?"

Benjy cocked his head and thought it over. "No, she had her arms around you."

"If I was forcing her to kiss me, would she have been hugging me so tightly?"

Benjy shrugged. "No, I guess not."

"When you're older this'll seem a lot clearer," Kurt said. "For now you just remember what I said about respect for girls, and don't worry about Mrs. Deveraux. I'm not going to hurt her or make her do anything she doesn't want to do."

Benjy grinned, and Kurt saw that he had successfully regained his place in the young student's good graces. "Being an adult looks complicated, Coach. I'm going to the field," he announced as he dashed out of the locker room.

Kurt turned around and saw Jason staring at him with one of the coldest expressions he'd ever seen. "What's wrong with you?"

"Do I have to be afraid now to send a kid to find you?"

Kurt shrugged. "No, you don't, and you know it. Can't you cut me a little slack? I learned my lesson today. I won't be kissing her at school again."

A muscle in Jason's jaw jumped. "Benjy was confused, wasn't he? If he tries out some of what he saw you doing on his girlfriend, you're going to feel pretty bad."

Kurt swallowed his anger as best he could. Was this really any of Jason's business? "I only kissed her, and I had my hand on her backside. That's all."

"Benjy thought you were being rough with her."

His heart had picked up a little speed. "You know I wouldn't do that. Come on... how long have we known each other?"

Jason stared him straight in the eye. "I never thought you'd get drunk and get a woman pregnant either, especially when the woman was in no condition to say no."

Anger sang in his veins, and his control slipped. "I told you how that happened, Jason. I don't appreciate this criticism one bit."

"Yeah, you told me how it happened, but it sounds like a convenient excuse to me." He gave Kurt a look of disgust. "You've wanted to sleep with Susan for a long time, so when you had the chance, you took it."

"So you think I'm an asshole who took advantage of a woman who'd had too much to drink, and now you think I've been roughing her up."

"I didn't say that," Jason came back.

"Yeah, I think you did." Kurt's entire body ached to release the tension flowing through him. "I didn't do a damn thing to deserve a scolding from you. Yeah, I made a mistake, but it's my mistake, and I've done all I can to put it right. What's more, I'll kiss my wife any time I want to."

He'd expected Jason to back off, but Jason was still on the offensive. "I may not be as emotionally involved in this as you are, but we've been buddies since first grade, so I didn't especially like watching what happened to you on Saturday. Now you seem determined to get yourself into even more trouble. Don't you know those kids will tell everybody what they saw? What were you thinking?"

Kurt took a deep breath and tried to get his temper under control. This was not the place for such a discussion. "Let's back off and start over, okay? I'm sorry for what happened with Benjy. I appreciate your support, and I don't want to fight with you. And for the record, I didn't get rough with Susan."

Jason's head dropped. "Aw, Kurt, I'm sorry. Fighting with you won't help anything. It just makes me ashamed of myself. I don't have the right to judge you, and I'm sorry I did. None of this is my business anyway."

"Yeah, some of it is. We're friends."

Jason sighed. "I don't really think you'd take advantage of Susan or hurt her."

"I know."

Jason nodded his head toward the door. "Let's go and get practice started."

Susan waited to leave her room until she had composed herself. Too bad Benjy had interrupted her and Kurt. The feel of his lips on hers and the strength of his arms around her had plunged her into an erotic haze that left her shaking with desire. She remembered some of what had happened when they spent the night with Mendoza, but her pregnancy and the estrangement with Kurt had caused her to forget the strong physical attraction between them.

Now, his kiss and the banked passion she sensed inside him made Susan wonder just what it would be like to greet him at the door of their home wearing something soft and sexy, something that would slide right off with a silken whisper and leave nothing between his hands and her skin except the faintest trace of perfume.

Susan shook her head to clear it. She didn't have time to stand around daydreaming. If she didn't get a move on, Kurt wouldn't have dinner waiting when he got home, and since this was their first home cooked dinner, she wanted it to be nice.

She picked up her purse, locked her room, and went by the faculty workroom to sign out. The room was full of teachers when she got there. All of them took a few moments to congratulate her.

"I'll have to hand it to you," said Don Brooks, "As mad as he was about the bet, I'd have bet he'd never have anything to do with you, much less marry you."

"Let that be a lesson to you, Don. Don't bet."

Amid the laughter that followed her remark, Susan waved and escaped from the school. Thank goodness this particular day had finally ended.

Eleven

Kurt got home that evening at the same time his father drove into Susan's driveway. No big surprise there. His dad had probably been on pins and needles all weekend to find out how things were going between him and Susan.

"Hey, Dad," he called. He locked his car and waited for his father to join him. "I was going to call you tonight."

George shrugged. "I couldn't wait. I had to know if you were okay. Your mother and I spent the weekend worrying about you."

Kurt hung his head. He'd figured as much, but he hated to hear the truth confirmed. "Aw, I don't want you worrying about me. You and Mom have your hands full with Sheila. I'm fine. Everything went better than I ever expected. Going away overnight was a great idea. I guess it sort of broke the ice between us. You'll never know how much I appreciate it."

Mr. Deveraux smiled. "Parents never stop worrying about their children. You're a grown man with a wife and a baby on the way, but I'm as concerned about your happiness now as much as I was when you were a child. Are you sure you're okay? Tell me the truth."

"Yes, sir, I'm fine."

His dad breathed an audible sigh of relief. "I'm glad to hear it. I think there's a good chance things will work out with you and Susan, and of course the baby gives both of you plenty of motivation to make your marriage work. If you're all right, I'll go on home and let you spend the evening with Susan. You don't need your father keeping you company so soon."

Kurt hesitated. "Uh, Dad, I'd like to talk to you about something. Can you stay just a minute?"

"Sure. If it's important to you I can."

Kurt used the key Susan had given him only that morning to unlock the front door. "Susan?"

"I'm in the kitchen. Who's that with you?"

"Dad."

Susan came out of the kitchen wiping her hands on a paper towel. "Hi, Mr. Deveraux. Can you stay for dinner?"

"Please, call me George. I'm not going to butt in, Susan. I just came by to see Kurt for a minute."

"Well, stay if you can. I'm a pretty good cook. You two go and talk and I'll finish things up in the kitchen."

She vanished into the kitchen while George sat on the sofa with Kurt. His eyes darted around the room. "This is a nice place."

Kurt nodded "Yeah, Susan did a good job."

"What did you want to talk to me about?"

Kurt's face flushed; he cleared his throat. How did you ask something like he was going to? Well, it was either talk to his father or suffer in silence, and hadn't he suffered enough lately? He marshaled his thoughts and said, "Do you think there's anything wrong with me? Susan and I have been married for two nights now, and we haven't, you know, made love yet. We held hands Sunday morning, and I kissed her today. I liked it...a lot, but I haven't wanted to make love to her yet. I got to thinking about it today, and it worried me."

Compassion spread across his father's face. "There's nothing wrong with you. Some men are okay with the idea of sleeping with a virtual stranger, but a lot of guys aren't."

"Dad, she's pregnant by me. We sure aren't strangers."

"You are in the ways that matter." His father sat back on the sofa, removing a decorative pillow that Kurt wouldn't have touched with a ten foot pole for fear of messing it up. "The two of you have had some major emotional blows to weather, so why wouldn't you want to take it slow and get to know each other before you sleep together? Holding hands and stealing kisses is about where you ought to be right now."

Well, that was good news. Kurt's spirits lightened. "How long do you think I should wait before I do anything?"

George laughed as if something amused him. "There's no timeline for a thing like this. It'll probably happen sooner rather than later because you're married, and it's okay for you to be intimate with Susan, but if it's a week or a month or whatever, it doesn't matter. Are the two of you sleeping in the same bed?"

"Yes."

"Good. That'll make it easier." George reached over and patted his son's knee. "Don't worry so much about it. One night you'll both know the time is right, and everything will work out just fine."

"Dinner's ready," Susan called as she entered the living room, "and, George, I set a place for you. Kurt already mentioned that his mom works late on Monday."

"Come on, Dad. Susan's invited you."

"If you sure that it's no trouble, I'd be delighted," George returned.

Kurt thought the evening went well. Susan was a thoughtful hostess, and dinner was good, but more importantly she'd gone out of her way to make him and his father feel at ease and enjoy themselves. She even deferred to him a couple of times when his dad was talking with her about decorating a nursery. In fact, she acted as if it pleased her to be his wife. And he knew he hadn't imagined that she was tentatively flirtatious with him.

Maybe his father was right. Maybe he and Susan would have a happy marriage just like his folks did.

Helen was waiting for George when he got home. She took his coat and hung it in the closet. "Where've you been?"

"I stopped to see Kurt tonight."

Anxiety filled her face. "Are they okay?"

"Yes, they are. I was very pleased to see how well they're getting along. I really think things are going to work out for them."

"I hope so. That baby is our grandchild."

Sheila came out of the kitchen in time to hear her mother's lament. "If I'd have done what Kurt did, you would have killed me," she dramatically announced. "Why aren't you mad at him?"

"Sheila, we are upset about this situation. Don't you understand how serious this is? Kurt and Susan are having a baby." Helen doubted Sheila even listened to her. She had a positive genius for seeing only what she wanted to.

Sheila tossed her hair at her mother. "Kurt was always your favorite child, wasn't he? He never did anything wrong, and I never did anything right."

"Sheila, that's enough," Mr. Deveraux said softly. "This is a tense situation, and I expect you to be a little more mature about it. Kurt made a big mistake, a mistake he's having to pay for. Try to be a little more understanding."

"It doesn't sound to me like he's paying for anything," Sheila scoffed. "You and Mom didn't even fuss at him, and you can't wait for his baby to be born. If I get pregnant are you going to treat me the same way?"

"Go to your room," Helen snapped.

Sheila obeyed. With a sniff she spun on her heel and ran up the stairs.

Helen started up the steps, but George laid a restraining hand on her arm.

"Don't, Helen. Let her calm down a little."

"This is all Kurt's fault," Helen cried. "If he'd acted like a decent man, none of this would have happened." And Helen also bolted up the stairs.

Mr. Deveraux sighed as he locked the doors and turned off all the lights. Life used to be so much easier.

- ❧ -

The rest of the week passed pleasantly enough. Things at school did settle down, and both Kurt and Susan fell into an everyday routine that worked for them. Mrs. Deveraux and Mrs. English made contact with their children, but Bill still refused to see either his daughter or son-in-law.

Marjorie chided him for his stubbornness after her return from Susan's house. "You're being silly. Why didn't you come with me and get it over with? You have to see them sooner or later. The longer you put it off the harder it'll be."

Bill's coffee cup thumped as it hit the table and spilt coffee over Marjorie's clean placemat. "I know you're probably right, but I'm still too mad to see either one of them. I can't stand the thought of him living there with her, much less the idea of him having sex with her."

Marjorie giggled. "I doubt they'd have talked to you about their sex life, but whether you like it or not, they will sleep together. They're young, healthy, and attractive, and they are married."

Bill got up and rinsed the coffee from the placemat. "I wanted better than a high school football coach for her."

"I think he's going to be a fine husband and father. I believe Father Duncan was right about his character. I can tell he's been good to her so far because she doesn't act at all uneasy or afraid around him. They're comfortable together."

"If he knows what's good for him, he'll never give her cause to be afraid of him. If he ever lays a hand on her in anger, he'll have me to deal with."

"Why are you so willing to think the worst of him?" Marjorie sat beside him and touched his arm. "I just told you he's kind to her."

"I'm just telling you."

"Go and see her if you don't believe me when I tell you that so far everything is okay. You blame him for what happened, but Susan admits she was as much at fault as he was."

Bill rolled his eyes before draining his coffee cup. "Susan is being kind and trying to make the best of a bad situation."

Marjorie stared at him without speaking for a moment. He *hated* it when she did that. Whenever it happened, she usually had something to say he'd rather not hear. "What are you going to do when the baby comes?" she asked.

He frowned. "I have no idea what you're talking about."

"Do you plan on rejecting Susan's child, your grandchild, just because Kurt Deveraux is the baby's father?"

"Frankly, I haven't got that far in my thinking, but no, I don't plan to reject Susan's child."

"Then you'd better make your peace with Kurt. He knows exactly how you feel about him."

"Okay, okay. You've made your point. Now can we have our dinner?"

***

The bell above the door tinkled as Father Duncan entered George Deveraux's grocery store on the Thursday after Kurt and Susan's marriage. "George, Kurt, how are you?" he called.

George and Kurt both nodded to Father Duncan. "We're fine. Just talking a little. Can I help you?" asked Mr. Deveraux.

"I came by for some of that New York cheesecake you stock."

"I have some in the back. Hang on just a minute and I'll get you one."

As George took himself off to the storage room, Father Duncan smiled at Kurt. "How's married life? Have your nerves settled down yet?"

Kurt laughed, although he could clearly remember the intolerable stress of that day and hoped never to repeat it.

"Yes, things are a lot calmer now, and the food is a heck of a lot better now that Susan's cooking for me."

Father Duncan laughed as he'd intended. "I'm glad to hear it. I want you to know if you need somebody to talk to, you can always call me. You and Susan had a rocky start to your marriage, and if problems crop up you don't have to face them alone."

Ever since Susan had told him she was pregnant, he'd had moments of sadness that felt awful. This turned out to be one of those times. "Thank you. I appreciate it more than I can say. I...don't really deserve having you so concerned about me."

The look of shock on Father Duncan's face almost made him feel better. "Why would you think you don't deserve my help?"

"Well, you know, I'm not proud of losing control of myself, and I've caused a lot of hurt feelings in my family and Susan'.and think of the awful example I've set for my students."

Father Duncan pursed his lips. "Nobody's perfect, even you. We all make mistakes, but that doesn't make you a bad person."

"I appreciate your saying so, but..."

"You still feel guilty," Father Duncan said, finishing his sentence for him. "You've got to let that go. Susan's a lovely woman. If you work on it, I think the two of you will have a happy marriage."

Kurt sighed. "I'm sure trying, and so is Susan."

"Good. The three of you are going to be a happy family; wait and see.

"I hope so." He absently reached for a soft drink in the cooler behind him and took a big swallow. "Lots of my students come from one parent families, so I know exactly how much a stable home with two loving parents means to a child. I want to make a go of my marriage for my child if not for myself."

He said goodbye to his dad and Father Duncan and hurried home. Susan was waiting, and they needed to spend time bonding with each other.

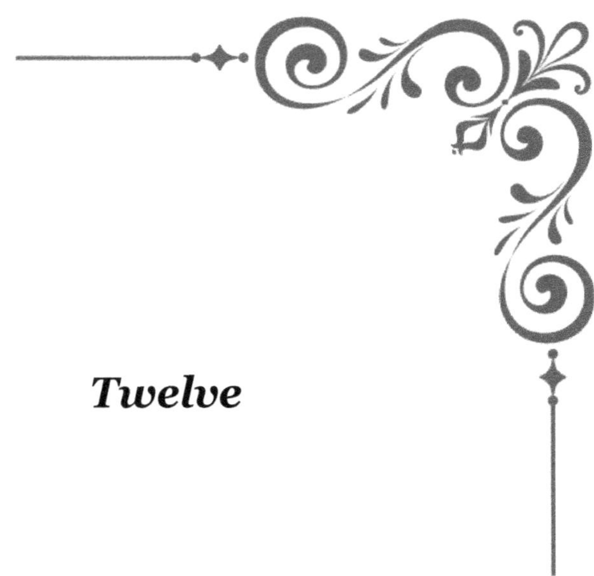

Twelve

The next day, Friday, was the last regularly scheduled football game of the year. Even though the team had had a winning season, and the remaining game looked to be a sure win, the Mavericks weren't advancing to the state playoffs.

Kurt rinsed his razor and replaced it in the medicine cabinet in the master bath. *I'm disappointed, but it's what I expected. Our team doesn't have as much talent as some of the other teams in the district.*

He went into the kitchen and found Susan dishing up a bowl of oatmeal. "Here," she said as she passed it to him. "Will I see you before the game is over?"

"No, not unless you need me for something. After school, the coaches have dinner with the team, and then we get ready for the game."

"That's the way that my father did it too."

Kurt ate his oatmeal and wondered if Susan planned on coming to the game. He wanted her to be there because he felt he would win, and even though he'd die rather than say so, he wanted to show off for her. *But how can a man tell his wife to come to a game so he can show off for her?*

Susan tasted her oatmeal and got up to add a little more sugar. "I hope it won't be too cold tonight. I guess I'd better wear some thermal underwear."

"Oh, so you're going to the game?"

She laughed. "Yes, of course I'm going. How would it look if the coach's wife wasn't there? You don't mind my going do you?"

Kurt felt his face flush as he made his confession. "I wanted you to come, but I wouldn't ask because I didn't want you to feel obligated if you had something you'd rather do."

"That's so sweet!"

Lord, that smile dazzles me every time I see it. He almost lost his breath when she jumped up and seated herself on his lap.

"You get a big hug, Coach."

"What did I do to deserve this?" He had to fight the sudden desire to kiss Susan's throat as his arms encircled the enticing, soft, female body pressed against his own.

Susan laughed and kissed the tip of his nose. "You can be very...endearing." She rubbed his shoulders for him before going back to finish her own breakfast.

He appreciated the attention, but the last thing he needed to think about on game day was the way she felt in his lap. And the scent of her! If they had time, he'd like to do some things he'd really enjoy. His stomach quivered at the thought of Susan melting against him, her lips parted for his kiss. *No, stop thinking about it!*

One thing he'd learned for sure since his marriage; he couldn't ignore Susan English Deveraux

By this time, Susan had crossed the gym and unknowingly distracted every boy in the room. She greeted the coaches with a big, cheerful smile. "Hey, coaches. Where's Kurt? I need him."

"I bet he'll be glad to hear it," Dan said with a smile.

Jason cringed when she narrowed her eyes at Dan. She looked scary. "He's over there in the corner with those kids."

"Thanks."

Susan strolled to the far side of the gym in search of Kurt, who was teaching a group of young men to climb a rope. One of the students with Kurt saw her coming. "Coach, your wife is here."

Guilt struck Kurt. Oh, the thoughts he'd had this morning! Aw, that was stupid. Susan was his wife.

"You guys keep practicing," he commanded as he went to meet Susan. "Hey, Mrs. Deveraux. We don't see you in this part of the school too often."

"I have more motivation to be here now. Mr. Dennis sent you a message, and it's big."

"What is it?" Why in the name of goodness had she worn this sweater to school? He couldn't keep his eyes off her and would bet every other young male in the vicinity felt the same way. What had she meant about having motivation to come to the gym? Maybe *he* was her motivation and not Mr. Dennis's message.

"Mr. Dennis said to tell you Middleton won't be going to state playoffs because they were playing some boy illegally. That means if you win tonight, the Mavericks will have a shot at a championship."

Euphoria burned through his veins. "Is he sure?"

"Yes, he is." She laughed. "I thought you'd be pretty happy about it, and you are."

"You'd better believe it! I've got to tell the guys."

"Well, go on and tell them. I've got to go to class."

Susan walked away, but in spite of his excitement, Kurt took the time to watch her. He'd swear under oath she strutted her cute little bottom out of the gym just to capture his attention. He saw Jason and Dan in the door watching him and dragged his eyes from his retreating wife. He jogged across the gym and slid to a stop in front of the other coaches. "You'll never believe what Susan just told me!"

"Hey, did you hear about Middleton?"

The news spread like wildfire around the school. Both students and teachers alike knew that if the Mavericks wanted a shot at the championship they had to win the game that night. Advance ticket sales jumped as many people changed their plans in order to attend the game. The principal scheduled an impromptu pep rally for the last class period. By the time it began, the students hummed with enthusiasm and school spirit.

As if they didn't already know, Mr. Dennis told everyone the reason for the pep rally, and then he turned the program over to Kurt who gave a short motivational speech to the student body. Since he was a popular teacher, the students greeted him with applause and cheers. He was the last speaker on the program, but before he could turn the floor over to the cheerleaders, Ken Banks walked up to the microphone.

"Coach Deveraux, could you hold on a minute?"

Kurt paused and cocked his head toward Ken. Ken grinned at him and winked. "Coach, you've brought us a long way this year. Nobody thought we'd have a winning season, but we did, and now we've got a chance to go to the playoffs." Ken paused as the gym erupted into thunderous cheers. "The guys on the team want you to know we've decided to dedicate our victory tonight to the newest member of the Deveraux family, your wife, Susan Deveraux."

Ken had to pause again and wait for the cheers to die away before he could continue. "In honor of your marriage, the team would like to invite Mrs. Deveraux to have dinner with us before the game."

The applause and screaming almost deafened him. He looked around the gym and located Susan who sat across the room with the other teachers. He sprinted across the floor to the teachers' section and pulled her to her feet. With the whole student body watching, he kissed Susan's cheek, and the crowd went wild. The noise sounded so loud Susan flinched.

"You'll come, won't you?" Kurt shouted.

Susan nodded, but when she would have rejoined the teachers, he kept hold of her hand and led her back to sit with him and the varsity football team, a maneuver which pleased the team very much indeed.

They had dinner in the school cafeteria. Ken had put Susan at the front of the buffet line with Kurt right behind her. The coaches always let the boys go first, but tonight the guests of honor took the lead. Earlier, Susan had attempted to thank the team, but her voice had started to shake, and Kurt had realized she was about to cry. He had casually moved to stand by her side, and she finished her speech leaning on his arm. It warmed his heart for her to take comfort from him.

"Hormones," Susan sniffed.

They sat down at the head of a long table of football players where Kurt's staff soon joined them. Kurt thought being around the coaches made Susan feel awkward because he had told her the coaching staff knew about her pregnancy.

He didn't feel awkward at all. Susan's presence and his kiss on her cheek would motivate the team as no pep talk could ever have done. It was also nice to have a few extra minutes to spend with her.

He smiled to himself. Spending time with Susan had turned out to be a pleasure, and to tell the truth, he still wanted to show off for her. Come to think of it, he'd enjoyed the entire week, and of course that was totally due to the way Susan treated him.

He'd never liked getting up in the morning, but somehow it wasn't so bad if someone else was there to eat breakfast and listen to the radio with. She had a droll take on some of the news stories that cracked him up. And so far she was content with the disposable razors and had left his alone, even though she constantly threatened to use it.

She had a way of looking over her shoulder at him and smiling just the tiniest bit. When she did that, she'd never tell him what she was thinking, so he'd spent a lot of time trying to figure out what she might have meant.

He had seen that the coaching staff too saw the motivational benefits of Susan's presence, but mostly they seemed curious about her. Except for Jason no one knew too much about the events surrounding his marriage other than he'd gotten her pregnant on their one and only date.

From the little frowns on their faces and the expressions in their eyes, he didn't think they wanted to like her, but the more they observed him and Susan together, the more they had relaxed with her.

"Hey, Susan," called Jeff. "Is he hard to live with?"

Susan smiled sweetly at Jeff. "Not as hard as you would be, Jeff."

Dan joined in as the laughter at Jeff's expense died away. "Oh, come on. Don't tell me he doesn't leave his socks and dirty dishes everywhere. The man's a coach, a pig."

Kurt pretended to be outraged. "I never leave dirty dishes! Samson licks them clean for me."

"Who's Samson?" asked Jason.

"Susan's cat."

The look of horror on Susan's face made the coaches roar. She looked into Kurt's eyes with desperate hope. "You aren't really letting that cat lick the dishes, are you?"

"Just the ice cream bowl. Samson and I have ice cream every night."

Susan saw he was teasing and laughed along with the coaches. "Thank goodness. I love Samson, but I really don't want to eat cat slobber."

They didn't linger over dinner because they had a lot to do before the game. The other coaches left for the field house, but Kurt stayed behind to talk to Susan. "Thanks for coming. The kids appreciate it." He reached for her hand. "I do too."

"You know I didn't mind."

"Would you mind if I kissed you? For good luck."

She took a step backwards. "Maybe not right now. If you win tonight, I'll give you a kiss."

He stepped with her. "What if I lose?"

"You won't lose, but if it should happen, I'll kiss you to comfort you."

"But I need a little motivation now."

He took another step, and their bodies melded together. Susan didn't say yes or no about that kiss, but her eyes fluttered shut, and her head obligingly tilted. Good answer. As he kissed her slowly and deeply, his head started to spin. No one, absolutely no one, could kiss like Susan Deveraux.

He lifted his face and pulled her head against his shoulder. "I've got a confession to make," he whispered. "I haven't been able to concentrate all day for thinking about you sitting on my lap this morning."

Heat flared in her cheeks. He had to listen closely to hear her reply. "I've had a few concentration problems myself."

He bent his head to kiss her again, but this time she pushed him away. "Remember what happened with Benjy. You'd better get to the field house."

Kurt's head dropped. He rested his face against her hair and breathed in the apple scent of her shampoo. "I think about you all the time. You feel so soft snuggled up to me at night, and you smell just like a woman ought to smell. Today in the gym I thought I'd need a cold shower before I could get focused again." He smiled at her as he admitted this fault. "I should have been focused after what you told me." He took a deep breath, bathing his senses in the feminine scent that surrounded him. "I hate to leave you."

"I don't want you to leave either."

He tilted her chin up so he could see her eyes. "Will you keep your promise about that kiss?"

"You can count on it, Coach."

With a flashing grin, he pulled away from his wife and went to do his job.

Sheila sullenly joined the line of kids who were waiting to get on the bus. She hated riding the darn thing, but today nobody could pick her up because her mother had to work.

Just as she was boarding the bus, her best friend, Harriet Palmer, yelled to her, "Wait for me!"

Sheila let the boy behind her get on the bus and waited for Harriet. "I almost missed the bus," Harriet gasped. Since she was slightly on the heavy side, running had taken her breath away.

"Why were you late?"

"Miss English was helping me with an assignment, and after I left her room I had to stop by the office to turn in an excuse."

Sheila's lip pooched out. "You mean Mrs. Deveraux, don't you?"

"Yeah, I do. I've been meaning to ask you why you didn't tell me she and your brother were seeing each other?"

"I didn't know myself." She thought of telling Harriet about the baby, but she couldn't bring herself to do it. Heat flooded her face. Harriet had seen that video too. Like her, Harriet would imagine Kurt and Miss English doing nasty things together before they got married.

Harriet chatted away, but Sheila didn't pay much attention to her. She was thinking of how rude she acted this afternoon when she met Miss English after lunch. Both of them had been late, so they were the only two people in the hallway.

Miss English had spoken first, and she'd been really nice. "Hi, Sheila."

She had forced herself to speak to her sluttish sister-in-law. "Hello," she'd mumbled.

"Would you like me to write you a pass so you aren't tardy?"

"No."

"I really don't mind." Miss English had smiled as if the two of them were best pals. "We Deverauxes have to stick together, right?"

It had made her so mad! "Don't flatter yourself. Nobody really wants you in the family. Your last name may be Deveraux now, but you'll never be one of us."

It gave Sheila savage pleasure to remember the hurt expression on Miss English's face, but it also made her slightly uneasy. She'd probably tattle to Kurt who might not like her speaking so rudely to his wife.

Well, what if he didn't? He should have behaved himself to start with. He was as bad as Miss English if you got right down to it.

She snapped out of her dark thoughts when Randy Poser moved into the seat behind her and Harriet. Randy looked great, no doubt about that, but his behavior was awful.

He lived in the trashy, low-class part of Fairfield and had been trouble since he started kindergarten. Today was his first day back at school after being suspended for drinking. Huh! Kurt was the one who busted him.

Randy poked Sheila in the back. "Why'd a babe like Miss English marry your tight ass brother? Doesn't she know he's a stupid jock?"

"Why don't you ask her?" Sheila retorted, making her voice as cold as possible.

"I'm asking you."

Fresh anger surged in her veins. If it weren't for Kurt she wouldn't have to endure this hateful conversation. She turned around to scowl at Randy, but she changed her mind when she noticed afresh how handsome he looked. "If you want to talk about Kurt, you'll have to go out with me."

Harriet gasped. "She's only kidding, right, Sheila?"

"No, I'm not kidding."

Sheila thought he intended to refuse, but he said, "Sure. How about tonight?"

"Cool."

Sheila sat back with a smile on her face. Wait until Kurt got wind of this.

Randy watched as Sheila got off the bus. He had intended to turn her down, but he had changed his mind when it occurred to him how upset Coach Deveraux would be if Sheila went out with him. Jeremy Thatcher distracted him by moving up to sit beside him.

"I heard what Sheila said to you. You really going out with her?"

"Yeah, why?"

Jeremy shrugged. "No reason. She just doesn't seem like your type."

"She isn't, but think how mad this'll make her brother."

Jeremy laughed. "I thought you didn't care if you missed school or not."

"I don't, but Deveraux's got no right messing around in my business."

"Well, this oughta piss him off."

"Yep, it sure should."

That afternoon Susan opened a can of cat food for Samson before she dressed for the game. He purred and attacked the food as if he hadn't been fed in days. "You old faker, you," she teased. "You had a huge breakfast." She sighed and sat in a kitchen chair to talk to him. "Kurt threw me when he kissed me in the gym, Samson, but I'm glad he isn't ashamed of me. It's nice that the team accepts me too, but I've got to wonder how they'll feel when they find out I'm pregnant. They seem to respect Kurt, so maybe they won't be too quick to judge us. I'm not sure about Jason and the rest of the staff, though. I could see they feel sorry for him and blame me for what happened."

She paused her commentary to Samson who had finished his dinner and was rubbing against her ankles. Scooping him up, she and her furry companion went to the sofa for a nice cuddle.

"I think Kurt will want me soon," she continued as she rubbed the old cat's ears. "In fact, he might want me tonight. What he said to me in the cafeteria makes me think he's ready to be a husband to me, and to be honest, I'm ready to be a wife to him."

She hid her face in Samson's fur. "I remember how it was at Mendoza's house. He knows how to please a woman." Her face burned. "I remember how his body felt against me. He likes my body too, but I'm worried that when the baby starts to show he might not be attracted to me."

Samson purred and seemed to say, "Nonsense."

"Oh, kitty, I hope you're right! It's his child so he shouldn't complain, but he might. I don't know Kurt well enough to say, but I guess I'll find out soon enough."

If she intended to go to the game she'd better get a move on. She kissed Samson between his ears and went to change clothes.

Thirteen

The football team's good news spread rapidly through the town, carried by students and staff alike. Bill English heard the news as he clocked out of his job at Super Mart. He thought about the game all the way home, and when he and Marjorie sat down to dinner he shared the news with her.

"It's a shame you don't like Kurt," she said as she set his plate in front of him. "It would be fun to go to the game and see what kind of a coach he is."

Bill would rather have died than admit it, but he had wondered if Kurt did a good job or not. He had heard comments from various individuals, some of whom knew what they were talking about, and most people seemed to think Kurt had done a good job in spite of the fact that he had a small, inexperienced team.

"Why don't we go?" asked Marjorie. "It would be fun."

Bill grumbled, but he allowed himself to be persuaded, so eight o'clock found them seated in the bleachers wrapped in blankets and drinking coffee to keep warm.

"Look, Bill. There's Susan over there in the teachers' section. Do you want to join them?"

"You go ahead. I want to watch the game."

"Yeah, I know. I'll be back in a few minutes."

Left alone, he watched the Mavericks take the field. They looked fired up about the game, but it was a controlled excitement that would later be channeled into constructive action.

While the team's behavior spoke well of their coach's training, Kurt himself seemed nervous. He couldn't stop pacing up and down and Bill would bet he was giving excessive directions to his quarterback.

If he doesn't relax a little he's going to make them nervous. He couldn't help smiling when he remembered his own coaching days. Nothing could match the thrill of a good football game, and if you were the winning coach it was that much sweeter.

Almost as if he had heard his father-in-law's voice, Kurt slapped the boy on his shoulder and sent him on his way. Jason Cooper jogged up to Kurt, and the two started to confer.

"Hi, Bill, how are you?"

Bill looked around to see who had spoken. "Mind if I sit with you?" asked George Deveraux.

"No, have a seat," replied Bill, cursing himself for having manners enough to let the man sit with him. He didn't want to see Kurt's father any more than he wanted to see Kurt. Hell would freeze over before he got cozy with any of the Deverauxes, including George.

"Kurt thinks they'll win tonight," George said as he took his seat beside Bill.

"Hope so, but it's a football game, and you can't ever tell."

George nodded. "That's true. He has to win tonight if he wants to go to the playoffs. I hope nobody gets hurt. We don't have much depth."

Bill glanced at the program. "He's had a winning season."

"Yeah, but he needs a few big linebackers. He has speed but no muscle or size."

"How's he putting points on the board?"

Pride came to rest on George's face. "Passing and some trick plays you'd have to see to believe."

Bill sighed. He'd rather have eaten dirt than praise Kurt, but he couldn't argue with the team stats. "Well, his record here in the program is pretty good."

"Coming from a coach, that means a lot." George beamed at him as if they'd suddenly become best buds. "You can understand all the work and effort that goes into a winning season."

"Yeah, I guess."

George shivered and turned up his coat collar. "It's cold tonight. Susan gave me a good dinner on Monday. Who taught her to cook like that? If Kurt isn't careful he'll get fat."

That's just great. She's cooking for the Deverauxes now. "Marjorie taught her. They both like to cook."

"They seem to be getting along with each other."

"Susan and Kurt?" Bill shrugged. I" wouldn't know."

George's eyebrows shot straight up. "You haven't seen them since the wedding?"

"No, I haven't." He tore his eyes off the field and looked at George. "To be frank, I'm too mad to want to see either one of them. I didn't raise Susan to play with a man's emotions or sleep with him without the benefit of marriage. I hope this doesn't hurt your feelings, but Kurt isn't what I'd hoped for in a son-in-law either. I guess I'm too damn old-fashioned because I'm grateful to him for giving the baby a name, but I still can't stand to think of my Susan married to him."

"She could do a lot worse than Kurt," replied George, whose face had started to turn an interesting shade of red.

"Yeah, she could, but he's not what I wanted for her."

George's face was tight, his eyes cold. "Just what's wrong with Kurt?"

"He doesn't make enough money."

George jumped up and fired a parting shot. "He might not be good enough for you, but he was good enough for Susan, wasn't he, and whether you like it or not, he's the father of her baby."

Bill sighed as George stalked away. That was the whole trouble in a nutshell; Kurt was the father of that baby.

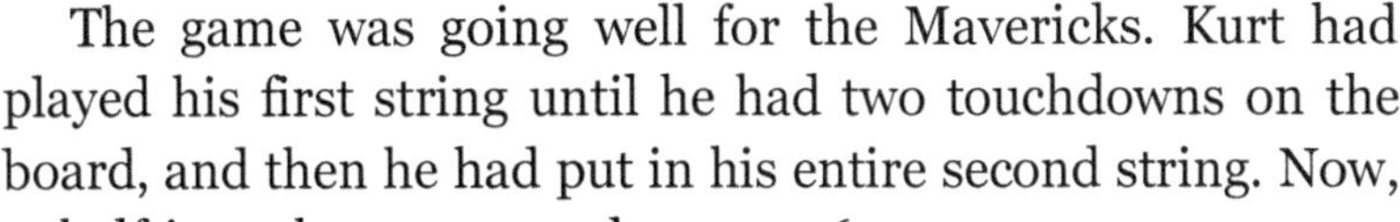

The game was going well for the Mavericks. Kurt had played his first string until he had two touchdowns on the board, and then he had put in his entire second string. Now, at halftime, the score stood at 20 to 6.

Marjorie nudged Bill with her elbow. "Why don't you go get us some popcorn?"

"Okay, but it'll probably take forever," he grumbled. *Crap. It isn't Marjorie's fault that George upset me. I shouldn't be so grouchy with her.* "Sorry. I'll get your popcorn."

He made his way to the concession stand and got in the line, which as he had expected, stretched a long way. Without meaning to in the least, he overheard the conversation of the two ladies standing in the line ahead of him.

"They say Coach Deveraux got married last weekend. Who'd he marry?"

A short woman with burgundy-red hair answered, "It was a teacher he works with, but I can't remember her name."

The first woman laughed. "I can't remember either. Anna came home from school telling how the team invited her to eat dinner with them and dedicated their win tonight to her."

"Did she tell you Coach Deveraux kissed his wife in front of the whole student body?"

"No, she didn't."

The burgundy-haired woman's face took on a look of importance. "Well, it was just a peck on the cheek they say, but Benjy came home Monday with quite a different story to tell."

"Oh? What about?"

"It seems he went into this woman's room without knocking and surprised the coach being romantic with his wife."

The first woman frowned. "Wait a minute. I'm not sure he ought to be doing stuff like that at school."

The red-haired woman nodded and sent burgundy curls flopping into her eyes. "Benjy got the impression the coach was forcing his wife to kiss him. You know Benjy thinks the world of Coach Deveraux, so he got pretty upset about it. He talked to the coach, and the coach apologized. He convinced Benjy he wasn't forcing her to kiss him, which I feel like is the truth. She probably knew it was a bad idea to be kissing at school and was trying to calm him down a little."

The two women continued their conversation, but Bill's anger drowned out their voices. If Kurt thought he could get away with mistreating Susan, he had another think coming.

"Marge, I think we'll go by Susan's house after the game," Bill said as he returned with her popcorn. "Kurt's doing a good job tonight, and I want to talk to him." He hated to lie to her, but if he told her the truth she'd refuse to go.

"You're doing the right thing. If you'll let yourself, you'll like Kurt. The two of you have a lot in common."

Resentment flooded Bill. Yeah, she was right in one way. Both he and Kurt were football coaches with limited incomes, but that's where they parted company. He was nothing like Kurt Deveraux. Nothing.

Susan's eyes widened when she opened the door and saw him and Marjorie standing there. "Mom, Dad, come in. It's wonderful to see you. I thought Kurt had forgotten his key. What are you doing out so late?"

Marjorie giggled. "It's only ten-thirty, Susan. We went to the game and decided to stop and see you and Kurt on the way home. Believe it or not, we don't turn into pumpkins at nine o'clock."

Susan smiled at him. "You went to the game, Daddy? Did you think Kurt did a good job tonight?"

Bill nodded. "Yes, he did. He was smart to use the second string. The experience will come in handy if he needs them in the playoffs." It tugged at his heart to see the warmth in her eyes. Kurt Deveraux didn't deserve her, and he never would.

"Maybe if he asks, you could give him a few tips for the playoffs, Daddy. You've won a lot of championships."

Bill laughed. "I'm sure he has things under control. It looks like he's a good coach. He wouldn't appreciate his father-in-law telling him what to do."

"I guess you're right." She smiled at him. "Have a seat, and I'll get us some cake and coffee."

Sitting around the fire with Marjorie and Susan, Bill forgot for a few moments how Kurt had ruined Susan's life, but he remembered why he had come here when he heard Kurt's car in the driveway. The tricky part would be to get him away from Susan and Marjorie. Kurt deserved what he was going to get, but he didn't want to do it in front of the women. It would make them angry, and besides that, he might not like Kurt, but he didn't want to shame him in front of Susan. A man needed to be able to hold up his head in front of his wife.

Susan heard Kurt's car too and jumped up and ran to meet him. Bill watched as she gave him a brief hug. "Congratulations, Coach," she cried. "You're going to a playoff."

Kurt's face lit up as he smiled from ear to ear. "I was nervous about it."

Hmm. Kurt felt proud of his team. It probably pleased him to show his father-in-law he knew his business.

Susan took Kurt's hand when they joined her parents in front of the fire. She sat on the hearth beside his chair and absolutely beamed at him. "Would you like some cake and coffee?"

"Sounds good."

He started to get up, but Susan laughed and pushed him back into the chair. "Not tonight, Coach. Tonight you get the royal treatment for winning the game. I'll get it for you."

Bill stared as Kurt cleared his throat and shifted in his chair. It was making him nervous to be alone with the in-laws. *Bet he'd rather have gotten the cake himself. Guess I'll get the conversational ball rolling.* "That Banks kid is good."

Susan returned with Kurt's cake and coffee, and when she saw that he and Kurt were talking civilly to each other, her eyes misted over. As Kurt set his plate and cup aside, Bill said, "Ladies, I'd like to talk with Kurt in private for a few minutes if you don't mind."

Susan instantly moved to protect Kurt. "Daddy, anything you have to say to him you can say in front of me."

"Bill, what's this all about?" chimed in Marjorie.

Bill scowled. "You women seem to think I'm going to hurt him. I think Kurt's man enough to have a talk with me."

"It's okay," Kurt answered. "Why don't you two go into the kitchen for some more coffee or something?"

When Susan and Marjorie reluctantly obeyed, Kurt faced him with a wary expression. "What's this all about?"

"I came over here to belt you one."

"Why?" Kurt asked. "Because of the baby?"

"No, but you deserve it for that if nothing else. Drunk or sober you should have thought to use a condom, but this is because of something I heard at the game tonight."

Kurt's calm manner irritated Bill. "I guess it made you mad if you're planning to belt me one. Why don't we go outside to do it? I don't want Susan watching."

He has guts; I'll give him that. "You know a kid named Benjy?"

"Yeah, he's second string quarterback."

"He went home and told an interesting story to his mother, who repeated it tonight to her friend. I just happened to overhear it."

Kurt sighed. "I thought I'd gotten that all cleared up."

"Oh, you did. They're giving you the benefit of the doubt, which is more than I was prepared to do. If you get rough with my daughter, especially when she's pregnant with your child, you'll have me to deal with."

Kurt flushed. "Mr. English, I was kissing Susan. All I did was put one hand on the back of her neck and the other on her hip to pull her close to me. Benjy's probably never seen anything like that except maybe in movies, so he mistook eagerness for force. That's all it was. Ask Susan if you don't believe me."

"In a manner of speaking, I already have. I've decided to give you the benefit of the doubt because I saw that Susan was glad to see you when you came in. If you were being rough with her, she wouldn't have been, but know this: I'm keeping an eye on you, and you'd better toe the line. I won't tolerate any kind of mistreatment."

Kurt's lips tightened. "Why do you always want to think the worst of me? I'd never hurt Susan. I know I made a mistake with her, but are you going to hold it against me forever? I'd like for us to try to get along." Kurt's stiff, rigid posture told Bill how he felt, but he seemed to be in control of himself.

He didn't bother to answer Kurt's question. All Kurt needed to do was listen up. If he thought that the two of them would ever be friends, he had another think coming. "I think we should keep this conversation between the two of us, agreed? And you'd better not take any of the anger I see in you out on Susan. She's proud of you and has no idea what I came here about."

He rose from the couch and called, "Marjorie, it's late. Let's go."

Susan and her mother hurried from the kitchen. *Gah, look at the worried expressions on their faces. Why do they feel so protective of Kurt*? "See, he's fine. You didn't have to be so worried about him."

Susan shot an anxious look Kurt's way and slid her arm around his waist. "Is everything okay?"

He put his arm across her shoulders and smiled. "Don't worry. Everything's fine."

The rest of the evening seemed anticlimactic to Susan. After Bill and Marjorie left, she and Kurt got ready for bed. She wondered if Kurt would remember her promise of a kiss and his hint of wanting even more from her, but he seemed distracted and tired and went to sleep after giving her only a perfunctory kiss on the cheek.

Kurt sighed and tried to relax enough to sleep. What right did Bill have to come into his home and interfere in his life? He would like to have told Susan the whole nasty story, but Bill had been right about one thing anyway. Susan didn't need to know anything about this mess. Was the man really going to hold a grudge forever? Well, let him. He was sick and tired of worrying about Bill English.

Randy handed Sheila another bottle of beer. "Drink up."

Sheila took the bottle and set it on the table. She wasn't having too good a time and wanted to go home.

"What's wrong with the beer?" Randy asked.

"Nothing. My head's just spinning around, that's all."

"So what? Don't you like getting a buzz?"

"I have to go home now. Do you want my mother to kill me?"

Randy hooted. "Aw, anybody could fool your mother. She took me for a nice Sunday School kid."

"Yeah, she sure did. She'd die if she knew I was hanging out at The Fuzzie Dice."

She knew teenagers had no business hanging out at The Dice. It attracted a rough crowd. They weren't too particular about checking anyone's ID either. They had asked Randy how old he and she were, and when he said eighteen, the bouncer waved them in.

Bet anything Kurt had never come here. Or had he? She wouldn't have thought he'd get drunk and get Miss English pregnant either. Maybe she didn't know him as well as she thought she did. He might be a regular visitor to The Dice.

Randy grabbed her arm. "Let's play pool."

Sheila had played before, but she wasn't any good. She followed Randy to a table, and as she had expected she lost big time.

"Not too good at it, are you?" Randy laughed.

Sheila scowled at him. "Never you mind," she cried. "I may not be a good pool player, but I can do other things just fine."

"Oh yeah? What?"

Sheila giggled. "That's for me to know and you to find out."

"I like a challenge." He took a step closer and stroked her cheek. "You're not much like your brother, you know. You're cool. I can see some good times in our future. This has turned out all right."

Fourteen

Susan and Kurt slept late the next morning, and over breakfast Kurt announced his intention of cleaning out the gutters on the house.

Susan yawned and smeared strawberry jam on a piece of toast. "Will it take long?"

"Not too long. Why?"

"The bathroom faucet is dripping, and there are some light bulbs that need replacing."

"You mentioned that you thought the dishwasher was leaking too," Kurt remembered.

It took him the rest of the morning and part of the afternoon to complete his work. Susan helped him when she could, but in some cases he refused her help saying that pregnant ladies didn't need to be doing this or that.

She teased him to tell her what her father had wanted to talk to him about, but he refused, saying only that her father had asked him to keep their conversation private. When it became clear he wouldn't give in and tell her, Susan finally gave up.

"You're being stubborn about it," she said, exasperation written on her face. "I know he upset you, and he had no right to do that."

Kurt grinned. "It almost sounds like you're taking my side."

"I am. You're my husband, and Dad has to realize it and accept you."

"I wouldn't hold my breath." He laughed. "Your dad doesn't like me."

"Oh, Kurt…"

"Let's go out to dinner and see a movie. We both need a break."

Susan flashed a smile his way. "I'll get the paper so we can find out what's playing. I love movies." Going to the movies was cool because it almost seemed like a date. She and Kurt hadn't had a normal courtship and romance, and of course they couldn't go back and pretend they weren't married, but going out together could be a way to help normalize their relationship.

⸺ ❧ ⸺

Kurt stood up and whistled when Susan entered the living room. "You're looking especially well this evening, Mrs. Deveraux."

"Why thank you, Mr. Deveraux. I tried."

"You certainly succeeded," Kurt answered as he escorted her to the car and opened the door.

He got into the car himself, and Susan asked, "Where are we going for dinner?"

"It's one of my favorite restaurants, a place called Darnell's. Have you ever eaten there?"

"No, but I've heard it's pretty good.

When they arrived at the restaurant, Kurt helped her choose from the menu. "If you've never eaten Thai, you may need a little help."

"Then it's lucky you're here with me."

Kurt's heart warmed. He was trying to show her a good time in hopes she'd realize being married to him wasn't so bad. She'd been mildly flirting with him ever since they got in the car, which had made him feel kinda good, like maybe she didn't think he was a big loser for his bad judgment at Mendoza's house.

She was in the middle of a football joke when he leaned over the table and kissed her. His heart leaped when he saw how her eyes were sparkling. "That's a nice surprise, Mr. Deveraux."

"I like kissing my wife. Is it okay?"

"Yes." She looked at him with a sexy little smile curving her lips. "I like your kisses."

"What do you like about them?"

She pretended to think about it. "The shape of your mouth is pleasing, for one thing."

"Is that all?"

She shook her head. "No, I like the way your lips feel."

Her hand had somehow come to rest on the table and was well within his reach so he took it. "How do they feel?"

"Well, they're firm, but soft too, and they're just the right size."

"Is my technique any good?"

She glanced at him from under lowered lashes and seemed to promise all manner of delights. "On a scale of one to ten I'd give you a ten."

"How does it make you feel when I kiss you?"

Heat flared in her eyes and caused him to tighten his hold on her hand.

"When you kiss me," she said, "it gives me an empty, longing feeling down deep inside, and I know the only cure for the emptiness is more kisses."

Kurt took a deep, steadying breath. "Do you want more than just a kiss from me? I know other ways to make the emptiness go away."

Susan's face and eyes gave him the answer her words never formed. Before she could speak, Jason Cooper and Melissa Taylor stopped beside their table.

"Hey, buddy, have you come down to earth yet after last night?" asked Jason. He grinned from ear to ear as he slapped Kurt on the back.

I'd like to kill him, thought Kurt, but he answered, "Not yet. How about you?"

"Melissa and I are out celebrating too. You guys want any company?"

What could he say? He didn't appreciate the interruption, but he didn't feel like explaining why, and he doubted Susan did either.

Susan slid her chair closer to his to give Melissa a little more elbowroom. "We'd love the company," she said. "Now come clean and tell us; is this a date?"

Melissa and Jason both laughed and looked a little sheepish. "I guess it is," Melissa said. "We really enjoyed each other's company at your wedding, so here we are."

Kurt grinned at Jason. He had seen this one coming.

The conversation turned general, and when the meal ended Susan invited Jason and Melissa to go to the movie with them.

"What are you seeing?" asked Melissa.

Susan drained her glass of water before she answered. "It's a love story. Something called *Late Last Night*."

Melissa frowned. "Why would you want to see that?"

"It was either that or a kung fu movie, and I can't stand those things."

Kurt didn't think Jason wanted to go either, but in the end all four decided to see the movie.

Kurt quickly realized why Melissa had questioned Susan's choice. The movie revolved around a woman who conceived an unwanted baby whose father left her to raise the child alone when the demands of pregnancy and home life became too much for him. Why hadn't Jason pulled him aside and warned him? His stomach churned. What if he turned out to be like the guy in the movie? It could happen. He prayed the awful movie wouldn't upset Susan, but judging how still and stiff she looked, it had.

He was right. In spite of the fact that she tried not to, Susan had begun to identify with the heroine. After all, Kurt had only married her because of the baby. What if he did leave her? He might, and if he did, what would become of her? *It scares me to think of raising a child with no help. Women do it all the time, but I don't want that for myself.*

After one appalling scene, her fingers clenched reflexively. She'd had all she could take! "Kurt, I have to go to the restroom," she whispered. "It may take me awhile, so don't worry about me."

She lingered as long as she could in the bathroom, but eventually she had to go back. When she entered the lobby, she saw Kurt waiting for her. A look of relief spread over his face. "Are you all right?"

"Sure. I'm fine." She bit her lip. "I...I guess I don't like the movie too much. If it's okay with you, I'd like to go home."

"It's fine by me." Kurt reached for her hand, but before they could make their getaway, Jason found them.

"I was getting worried about you two."

"Yeah, well, the movie's upsetting Susan," Kurt replied when Susan made no answer. She couldn't. If she tried to speak she'd cry. Jason didn't much like her anyway, and now this awful movie would remind him and Melissa of the bet.

"Let me get Melissa, and we'll leave too," he said. "We could stop by the Dairy Queen for some ice cream."

"Don't do that," Susan croaked, taking a chance on her voice. "It's a good movie unless you happen to be in the same boat as the characters."

She saw the look of amazement on Jason's face. "Why would you say such a thing? Neither of you is in the same predicament as those people in the movie. Susan, he isn't going to leave you, and Kurt you can handle the responsibilities of marriage and fatherhood just fine. Why did the two of you want to see this anyway?"

"We didn't know what it was about," Kurt said.

"Please, Kurt." She tugged on his arm. "Can we go now? I need to go home."

"Sure, baby." Kurt put his arm around her shoulders, waved to Jason, and they almost ran from the theater. This had to be one of the worst dates in the history of the world.

They didn't have much to say on the way home. If only he knew how to break the silence, to say something, anything, that would reassure Susan, but for the life of him he couldn't think of a single thing that would sound like anything more than empty promises. Jason's words in the theater lobby had helped, but the similarities between the movie and real life were just too great to ignore.

As soon as they got home, Susan fed Samson. Then she called a goodnight to him. "I'm going to bed. See you in the morning."

"Good night." Enveloped in a cloud of misery, Kurt sat to watch the late news. The newscaster didn't get one whole story done before he heard Susan crying. She was trying to be quiet about it, but he had learned that when Susan cried, you knew about it.

Susan couldn't have stopped crying for a million dollars, but the movie was only a part of it. She cried for being so careless with another person's feelings that she would make a silly bet. She cried for the lies of omission she told at Mendoza's house. She cried for all the tequila she drank, and she cried for shame over having sex with a strange man.

Her heart broke when she recalled the torment of realizing her period was late, and she shuddered over the memory of the positive reading on the pregnancy test.

She dabbed at her eyes to staunch the flow of tears, but she remembered how horrible it felt when she told Kurt about the baby and cried even harder. She cried for the disappointment of her family and friends as well as the loss of the beautiful wedding she had always dreamed of. She cried because she had had no romantic honeymoon and because there was embarrassment yet to come when the baby began to show.

But most of all, she cried because crying wouldn't do any good anymore. Her freedom and all the choices belonging to it were gone forever. Like it or not, she had a husband and would soon give birth to his baby.

She didn't know Kurt had entered the bedroom until she felt his weight on the bed. He slid his arms around her and pulled her against him. How ironic that he should be trying to comfort her when part of her tears were because of their marriage.

Gradually, her sobs tapered off, and finally she lay quietly in his arms. Kurt gently pushed her tumbled hair back from her face. "Would you like a glass of water and a cool cloth for your face?"

"Yes, thank you," Susan answered, her voice thick with tears.

Kurt kissed her forehead and returned in a moment with a glass of ice water, which she gulped down. He took the cool washcloth and ran it over her face, and then he folded it and laid it across her red, swollen eyes.

"Thank you," Susan sniffed. "Not many men would be as understanding. I don't really think you'd leave me."

"I know. It's everything."

Kurt stood and unbuttoned his shirt. "Do you need to go to the bathroom before we get some sleep? Things'll look better in the morning."

Susan didn't expect to get much rest, but emotional turmoil had worn her out. Her eyes closed as Kurt pulled her against him, and she drifted right off.

When Susan got up on Sunday morning she seemed like a different person to Kurt. She didn't busy herself with breakfast or chatter to him over things she heard on the radio or read in the paper. Nor did she threaten to use his razor on her legs that morning. All she did was sit on the sofa and stare at the television, but he knew she wasn't watching it. He tried to get her to eat, but she refused his offer of breakfast, saying all of that crying had taken her appetite away. His stomach clenched. Was something wrong with her? Susan usually ate even more than he did.

No, probably not. She was still upset over the movie, so he wouldn't press her. Missing one meal wouldn't hurt either her or the baby.

Maybe she'd feel better now that she'd had a good cry. It was possible she didn't want breakfast because she was trying to make sense out of and find meaning in what had happened to them.

Around noon she said she wanted to take a nap and vanished into the bedroom. A little later he looked in on her and found that she had indeed gone to sleep.

Kurt was trying to decide whether or not to call her mother when the doorbell rang. Peeking through the window, he saw his parents standing on the porch; he'd never felt happier to see them. *And as much as I hate to admit it, I'm glad Sheila didn't come with them. I feel too bad today to cope with her.*

"We thought you and Susan might be at church today," said Helen Deveraux as she gave Kurt a hug. Fleetingly, he remembered a time in his life when his mother's hug could fix anything.

"I haven't thought about church at all, but since you bring it up, I'm not sure I want to go anymore," Kurt said as he escorted his family into the living room.

"Why would you say a thing like that?" exclaimed Helen.

Kurt felt hot blood flood his face. "I'm too ashamed of myself to go to church. I've known most of those people since I was a baby, and I bet they've all figured out why Susan and I had such a quick wedding. Anyway, you've told your friends, haven't you?"

"Son, you can't keep a thing like a baby a secret," George protested. "You and Susan aren't the first couple to have an early baby. Nobody's going to say anything to you or make you feel uncomfortable, and if you're afraid we've told them details, we haven't. All they know is that Susan is pregnant." He looked toward the kitchen. "Where is she?"

"She's asleep."

"You must have gotten up early," guessed Helen.

Kurt shook his head. "No, we didn't. We had a bad night, and now Susan's acting weird."

Helen's eyes widened. "How do you mean? Is it the baby?"

Kurt gladly told them. Maybe they could think of something to do. They listened to his story in silence; then his mother smiled and patted his knee. "You handled it well, Kurt. Holding her while she cried was the best thing you could have done."

"Maybe, but it hurt my feelings." He stared at his clenched hands. "She was crying over having to marry me, I guess."

"Don't take it that way," Helen said. "I think crying was Susan's way of coming to terms with the things that have happened to her. Holding her while she cried will bond her to you. The movie just brought everything to a head, which may be a good thing. With all of the regrets out of the way, the two of you can move forward."

George gave Kurt an encouraging smile. "If she hasn't already, it's only a matter of time before Susan realizes what a prize she snared when she married you. Any woman should be proud to be your wife, and that includes Susan."

Mr. and Mrs. Deveraux stayed with Kurt for about an hour, but Susan showed no signs of waking, so they left after making him promise to call if he needed them. Kurt stayed awake until around three-thirty. Then, since he had worn himself out worrying about Susan, he fell asleep on the couch.

Susan stretched and yawned, amazed at how much better she felt. As usual, Samson lay curled up beside her. She stroked the old cat and yawned again. "I feel as weak as a kitten, Samson. I've been in bed too long. Have you seen Kurt?"

Samson answered in the negative, so Susan went to find him. When she saw him on the sofa, a wave of tenderness washed over her. *He's worn out. I guess I've given him a hard time this weekend. I'll get dinner while he sleeps.*

He looked cold so she took the afghan from the back of the sofa and threw it over him. *Now, what can I find for dinner?*

Kurt awoke to the delicious aroma of baking bread and decided to get up and find something to eat. He followed his nose into the kitchen where Susan was putting the finishing touches on their dinner.

"Hey, there," she said. "Can you eat yet or do you need awhile to wake up?"

"I'm hungry now. Susan?"

"What?"

"Are you feeling better? You don't look so...dull and desperate."

She smiled, a smile that reached her eyes and soothed his worry. "Yes, I'm feeling much better,"

"When I woke up I had an afghan over me. Did you do it?" he asked.

"Yes, you were curled up like you were cold. Why?"

"I just wondered. Can I help you finish dinner?"

"No, everything is ready."

As Susan walked by him to get some butter from the refrigerator, he pulled her to him. With a smile, she snuggled close and laid her head on his chest.

"I'm sorry about the movie," he said.

"I picked it too, Kurt, but don't worry. I'm fine now. I don't think you'll be a jerk like the character in the movie either. It was just... everything. It's been pretty rough the last few weeks, you know."

"You got that right." He gave her a hug. "Let's eat. I'm starving to death."

Fifteen

On Saturday the weather took a turn for the worse. A polar front sweeping down through Canada caused all the weather forecasters to predict an ice storm. Bill got home from work around three-thirty and found Marjorie baking a cake. "You're just in time to lick the bowl," she said.

He ran a spoon around the bowl. "It's good. Do you think I should call Susan to find out if Kurt is ready for the storm?"

"You can if you want to, but I'm sure he is."

"Good. If there's one thing I don't want to do, it's talk to Kurt Deveraux."

Marjorie rolled her eyes at him as he headed to the living room. He turned on his favorite news program and tried to concentrate, but he finally gave up. Seeing to Susan was a long ingrained habit that he had no intention of breaking. Thank goodness Susan answered instead of Kurt.

Her voice sounded cheerful and perky. "I'm so glad you called, Daddy. How'd you know I was in the mood for a nice chat?"

"Sorry, honey, but I ain't psychic. I'm getting ready for the storm. Has Kurt got everything under control?"

"I think so. He checked the emergency heaters and got fuel for them, so if the power goes out we should be okay. I have a good supply of candles, flashlights and batteries too." She giggled. "I even have milk, bread, and ham so we won't starve if I can't cook."

Bill laughed with her. She'd always been able to make him laugh. Well, except where her ...Kurt was concerned. "You need to tell Kurt about the thermostat."

"What about the thermostat?"

He began an explanation, but Susan soon interrupted. "Daddy, I don't understand a word you're saying. If you think Kurt needs to know this, you'll have to tell him yourself."

"Okay, put him on."

In the background, he heard Susan call Kurt and mention the thermostat. He came on the phone and said, "What is it about the thermostat?"

Bill laughed. "Right to business, huh? Okay, listen up." He explained to Kurt about the thermostat. "So you know what to do if the thing doesn't kick on to keep the house warm?"

"Yes, I got it. I'll replace it as soon as the storm passes and I can get to town."

"Yeah, I meant to, but I just didn't get around to it." Bill paused. "Is Susan feeling all right?"

"Yes, sir, she is. She doesn't have morning sickness anymore, and even though she's eating enough to feed two babies, she's keeping her weight where the doctor wants it. He said the baby looks healthy so far too."

Bill scowled at the wall even though Kurt's answers were exactly what he wanted to hear. "Are you treating her right like I told you to?"

"Yes, sir."

"Okay. Put Susan back on for a minute."

Bill finished his conversation with his daughter and hung up, but in spite of Kurt's respectful behavior, in his heart he still felt a burning resentment of Kurt Deveraux and all that he stood for.

Susan called Kurt to dinner shortly afterward. "I hope you like meatloaf," she said. "This hamburger needed to be used before it went bad."

"Yeah, I like it fine."

"The storm isn't supposed to get here until the wee hours of the morning, right?"

"That's what they said."

"Then I think I'll run to Super Mart after we eat. I saw some red towels in their sale paper this week that would look beautiful in the guest bath." Super Mart was the local discount store.

Kurt hesitated. "I'd kind of planned on watching the game on channel fifteen."

"You sound like Daddy." Susan flashed him a smile. "You can watch your game. I don't mind going alone."

"Are you sure?"

"Yeah, I'm sure." A mischievous expression filled her face. "But you can do the dishes while I'm gone if you want to."

Kurt laughed. "That sounds like revenge to me, but I guess I could do them for you."

When they finished their meal, Susan put on her coat and got ready to go. "I won't be long," she promised. "Do you need anything?"

"Yeah, I'm almost out of shaving cream."

"Anything else?"

"No, that's it."

Susan gave him a quick kiss and drove to Super Mart. The store usually had a large crowd, but tonight the parking lot seemed almost empty. People had probably stayed home because of the weather. She looked at the towels first and liked them. After selecting the ones she wanted, she found Kurt's shaving cream. The doctor had warned her to keep her weight down, but Super Mart sold a delicious brand of Swiss chocolate, so maybe just one bar wouldn't hurt.

She had to pass the baby department on the way to the candy aisle. Her step slowed, and she came to a stop. *So far the baby doesn't seem too real to me. Of course I've noticed some slight changes in my body, but nothing major. The baby hasn't moved yet either. Kurt and I don't talk about it, but sooner or later we'll have to.*

Oh, look at those cribs over there. They only have two different styles, but good grief they're were expensive. Well, it didn't matter how much the crib cost. They'd have to buy one.

How amazing! I had no idea babies needed so many things. The store sold thermometers, bathtubs, blankets, sleepers, burp pads, crib sheets, bottles, mobiles, banks, hooded towels, strollers, swings, bouncy seats, bibs, and a thousand other things. *It's so weird to think that soon Kurt and I will have all this baby stuff in our house.*

One cute thing caught her eye. A little white bathrobe with a yellow duck embroidered on the front pocket hung on a tiny hanger right in front of her. The robe came with a tiny pair of booties that had ducks on them. She had to have this.

"Shopping for your baby?" a familiar voice acidly inquired.

Susan turned around and held out the little robe for Sheila to see. "Isn't it precious? I thought I might buy it because either a girl or boy could use it."

Sheila rolled her eyes. "Oh, it's precious all right. You're pretty smart, aren't you?"

"I don't know what you mean."

"You trapped Kurt into marrying you, and now you're buying cute little things to remind him why he has to stay with you. What's wrong? Is he getting restless?"

Susan clenched her hands around the buggy push bar in case she either choked Sheila or at least slapped her. "I don't care for your attitude," she replied, her voice dripping icicles. "I didn't trap Kurt into marrying me, and for your information, I'll be buying a lot of things for our baby. This has nothing to do with obligation."

Sheila ignored her. "You're lucky Kurt decided to marry you. If he hadn't your baby would be illegitimate, wouldn't it?"

"But he did marry me."

"Yeah, he did. I guess when he found you, he sank to his proper level."

Susan's face burned. The color of her face probably matched her new towels. "Why don't you grow up, Sheila? This isn't about you, and it never was. You're rude, verbally abusive, and totally unpleasant, and I for one have had enough of you."

She hurled the little robe into her shopping cart and strode away. At that moment, she hated Sheila Deveraux!

She hurried to the checkout line and saw Sheila leave the store with a young man. He looked a little scruffy, but lots of kids did these days. When the boy turned around to look at her, she identified Randy Poser.

Of all the boys in school, why did it have to be Randy Poser? She couldn't think of a single good thing to say about him. A young girl like Sheila had no business hanging around with a boy like Randy.

Guess she'd have to tell Kurt about it. Unless she missed her guess, he wouldn't like this at all.

Kurt was standing on the steps checking the weather when Susan turned into her driveway. "I was getting worried about you," he called. "The storm's getting here faster than they thought it would."

"So far it's just rain."

As soon as she reached the porch, Kurt took her packages and opened the door. His heart sank when he saw her angry face. "I'm sorry I didn't go with you, but I did get the dishes done."

Susan's eyes narrowed. "That's not the trouble."

"Then..."

"The trouble is your sister." She glared at him. "I met her at Super Mart where she reminded me that you had to marry me, and if you hadn't my baby would be illegitimate. Like I care if it is or not. This isn't the dark ages."

Kurt tossed her bag onto a chair and took her hand. "I'm so sorry. She's upset about us getting married, but she has no right to talk to you that way. I'd like to turn her over my knee and tan her backside for her."

"Oh, that's par for the course. I saw her in the hall at school, and she told me I'd never be a part of the Deveraux family."

He pulled her stiff body into his arms. "I'll have a talk with her," he promised. "She's way out of line. What's more, she's wrong about everything."

"Wrong about everything?"

"You are a member of the Deveraux family. You're my wife and the mother of my child. You're as much a part of the family as Sheila is."

Susan dropped her eyes. "But you did have to marry me."

Kurt stroked her hair and kissed the top of her head. "No, I didn't. I could have given you some money from time to time and left it at that, but I wanted us to be a family. That's why I married you. You don't have to worry about Mom or Dad not liking you either. They do."

"Well..." As he had hoped Susan was calming down.

"I respect you and care for you and plan on doing my best to be a good father," he continued.

"There is one more thing." She sighed as she snuggled into him.

"What?"

"Sheila was with Randy Poser."

"Good grief!" Kurt exclaimed. "Are you sure it was Randy?"

"No doubt whatsoever."

"Crap. I'll have to talk to her."

Susan shook her head. "Tell your parents and let them do it."

"Yeah, that's better. She's too mad at me to listen to a thing I have to say." Eager to change the subject he asked, "What did you buy?"

Susan showed him the towels. "I like them," he said.

"Yes, I thought they'd be perfect for the guest bath." She hesitated for a moment. "I...got something for the baby."

Kurt's head came up. "What did you buy?"

Susan took the little robe from the bag and passed it to him. He touched the yellow duck and stuck his finger inside one of the booties. "It's pretty small, isn't it?"

"Very small."

He felt so strange. A new, unusual emotion poured into his chest and constricted it. The more he stared at the robe, the more intense the sensation became.

He had known the baby would be small and that he and Susan would have to take care of it, but seeing this little robe made the child's coming a reality. He didn't know exactly why his chest felt so tight, but he knew it had something to do with that little white robe.

"I guess we should start buying things. For the baby I mean," he finally said.

"Let's start looking for cribs. I didn't much like the ones they had at Super Mart, though."

"I'll start cleaning out the bedroom tomorrow," Kurt promised.

Susan slid across the sofa and put her arms around him. "Hold me."

Kurt knew a good idea when he heard it; he needed a hug too.

<hr>

Kurt woke up right before dawn on Sunday morning. The room felt icy cold, so the thermostat had failed, or the power had gone off. He turned his head to look at the clock and tried not to disturb Susan who had snuggled close beside him with only the tip of her nose stuck out from under the covers. The clock still worked so the power was on.

It must be the thermostat. I need to get up and work on it.

But somehow that seemed awfully hard to do. The rain, sleet, and wind lashed the trees outside and beat on the roof and against the windows, but he felt toasty warm under the covers with Susan nestled against him. Truly, having somebody to help you warm the bed was one of the best things about marriage. Without Susan he'd probably need another blanket.

In just a minute. Rolling over, he threw an arm across her and buried his face in her hair. Even her hair smelled good. His body's reaction was so powerful it almost took his breath away. He wanted her. Biting his lip, he tried to divert his thoughts into more appropriate channels.

The pipes might freeze if he didn't get up, but so what? He'd fix them. What if he lost the playoff and gave Bill English another reason to scorn him. Yeah? Who cared? Of course Bill would like to give him a beating, but at the moment it didn't seem important. In fact, nothing seemed to make the slightest bit of difference. He wanted to make love to Susan, and for the life of him he didn't know how to get out of that bed without doing it.

Well, why not? She's my wife, and we've got to do it sometime. Why not now? It's part of being married. She was ready a week ago, and so was I.

Kurt's heart raced and the blood pounded in his ears as he made his decision. He ran his hand across Susan's stomach, noticing that it seemed a little bigger, not quite so flat. Susan's breathing changed, so he knew she was awake.

She wiggled against him, and the feel of her soft skin under his hand sent a shiver of warm, sparkly tingles up and down his backbone. His heart took off at a mad gallop. Finally, he'd find out if they were as good together as he remembered, and this time there was no alcohol to cloud his mind. Susan rolled over and put her arms around him. Oh, she did feel so good!

<hr>

"Kurt, let me up. I have to go to the bathroom."

"I don't want to. I'd rather we stayed close."

"Kurt."

"Okay."

The minute he let her go, she ran for the bathroom. She didn't stay there too long which didn't surprise him at all. It was too cold in the house not to be under the covers.

In the faint gray light of early dawn, Kurt saw her hunting for her pajamas. She couldn't seem to find them, so she gave up and dived under the covers. She stayed on her own side of the bed, the stiffness of her posture making his heart sink. "What did I do wrong?" he asked.

"Nothing."

"Sure I did. If everything was okay you'd be snuggling with me. Instead you don't want me to touch you. You acted like I pleased you, so what's wrong?"

Susan shifted in the bed. "We just consummated our marriage," she replied, speaking so low he barely heard her.

Kurt nodded. "I know. Is there something wrong with that? I thought we were both ready."

"No, that isn't what I meant!"

Jaw clenched, Kurt threw back the covers and searched for his own clothes. "That's what it sounds like to me," he snapped. "I've got to fix the thermostat. I won't bother you again."

"Wait. Let me explain."

Kurt ignored her and stalked out of the room, and Susan flung herself down in the bed and cried.

Susan sighed. Was he going to pout forever? She hadn't meant to hurt his feelings, but no matter how she tried to smooth things over he stayed mad. Of course, it didn't help that every time she tried to explain the words came out wrong. At this point she was out of excuses.

"You're my husband," she said, trying not to let her frustration spill over into her voice. "I expect us to make love just like any other married couple. I liked being intimate with you. You know I did. I was just feeling a little strange, and I expressed it poorly. I wish you'd stop making a federal case out of it. I'm trying to make up with you, but you won't let me."

Kurt subjected her to the cool scrutiny she'd seen him use a time or two on a student. "There's nothing to make up. You can't help that you hate having to marry me. I'm sorry I misread the situation and bothered you. It won't happen again."

Susan took a deep breath and tried one more time. "Please don't act so cold and hateful. I know I hurt your feelings, but I didn't mean to. Can't you just chalk it up to nerves and forgive me? From now on I want a normal marital relationship with you." She smiled at him. "I wouldn't mind having a little afternoon nap right now. Don't you want to love me again, sweetheart?"

Kurt shook his head. "Let's not discuss it, okay?"

Fine! She was sick and tired of groveling in front of him. *Let him stay mad if he wants to.* Grabbing a set of English essays from the coffee table, she stalked into the bedroom. Let him be that way; she didn't care.

Sixteen

"What was the fight about?" asked Jason as he rummaged in the storage closet for another basketball.

Kurt threw down his pen and turned around to talk to Jason. He was grateful for the interruption. This morning's ride to school with Susan had been uncomfortable at best, and he hadn't gotten a lick of work done all morning.

He had tried so hard to be a model husband in spite of the fact they had to get married. Couldn't Susan meet him halfway? Did she want a platonic marriage forever? He sure didn't.

His reaction to the consummation of his marriage had surprised him. He had enjoyed the sexual release, but he had also felt emotionally connected to Susan, exactly the way a man should feel after intimacy with his wife.

He'd spent the morning wondering if he'd pushed Susan before she was ready. He wasn't in the habit of forcing women to sleep with him, and the thought that he might have done so with his own wife shamed him. Susan hadn't seemed at all reluctant to make love to him, but afterwards...

"Who was fighting?" he hastily asked.

"I don't mean here at school. I mean you and Susan."

Great, just great. Could the whole world tell they'd had a fight? "Who said anything was wrong?"

"Nobody had to," Jason said, giving him an impudent grin. "The way you've been acting today I expect you and Susan had your first argument."

"Is it really that obvious?"

"Yep. Sure is."

Kurt sighed. "I was so mad. I still think Susan's in the wrong, but since our marriage didn't start like most marriages, I've tried to make some allowances and overlook a few things. Well, I forgot all about that when she hurt my feelings. She tried to apologize and make it up to me, but I wouldn't let her." He shrugged. "I'm still ticked off at her."

Jason locked the closet door and sat down beside him. "Unless she came at you with a knife or gun, you probably should accept her apology." He snickered. "I can't imagine Susan doing either one no matter what you did to provoke her."

"Yeah, guess you're right." Holding grudges and pouting would only make matters worse. He should make up with Susan as quickly as possible. Hopefully, if he apologized to her they'd be able to talk about what happened without hurting each other.

He grabbed his pen and a sheet of paper and wrote a note. "How do you think this sounds?" he asked as he slid the paper to Jason.

Jason picked it up and read, *Susan, I'm sorry for the way I acted yesterday. Can I take you to dinner tonight to make it up to you? Love, Kurt*

Jason nodded. "That's good, but you need to do a little more. Buy her some flowers or perfume. You know, something romantic."

"I know just the thing." Kurt turned around and picked up the phone.

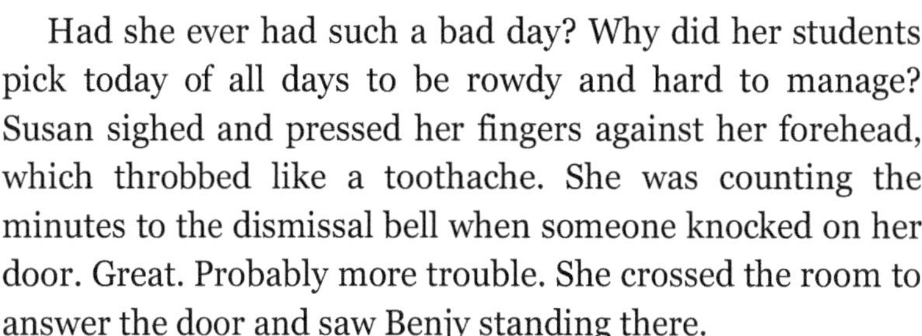

Had she ever had such a bad day? Why did her students pick today of all days to be rowdy and hard to manage? Susan sighed and pressed her fingers against her forehead, which throbbed like a toothache. She was counting the minutes to the dismissal bell when someone knocked on her door. Great. Probably more trouble. She crossed the room to answer the door and saw Benjy standing there.

"Hi, Mrs. Deveraux. This is for you." Benjy handed Susan an envelope and a bouquet of daisies complete with a yellow helium balloon covered in pink hearts. "They're from Coach Deveraux."

Susan set the bouquet on her desk and read her note. She couldn't help smiling. At the chorus of ohs and how sweets that came from her class she blushed furiously.

She smiled at Benjy, distracting him from his flirtation with Candace Holliday who sat on the front row. "Tell him the answer is 'yes'."

Benjy frowned. "Is that it? Isn't there anything more you want to tell him?"

"Such as?"

"Well, you know. You could tell him you love him or something," Benjy mumbled. "That's what they always do in the movies."

Susan shivered at the idea of sending such a message by a student. "He knows how I feel about him, Benjy. You just tell him 'yes'."

It came to Susan like an unexpected bolt out of the blue. *No, he doesn't know how I feel. All he knows is the hurtful stuff I said to him on Sunday morning yet he's still trying to please me.*

"Benjy, wait," she called. "There is something else. Tell him it's a lot more than just making the best of a bad situation. He'll know what that means."

"Got it," replied Benjy. "That's some sort of romantic thing between you and the Coach, right?"

"Benjy, that is entirely too personal for me to answer."

Benjy nodded. He winked at Candace, but as he reached the door he abruptly backtracked. "Mrs. Deveraux, I forgot to tell you. He said he'd be about an hour late today, so you go on home by yourself. Coach Cooper will bring him home."

"Okay, thanks."

The dismissal bell finally sounded. Susan exhaled loudly and collapsed into her chair. The kids had acted like demons today, but of course she felt so horrible because of the way she'd treated Kurt. It had nothing to do with the kids.

She cringed to think of the things she'd said to him. No wonder he thought she didn't want him! She had wanted him plenty; she was glad they had consummated their marriage, but at the same time it did make her realize just how much her life had changed.

Was it a bad change? She enjoyed Kurt's company and didn't mind living with him. Did she love him? Probably not, but truthfully, she didn't know how she felt about him. Her emotions had been in a tailspin ever since the night at Mendoza's house.

Well, no use to worry about it. It wouldn't do any good anyhow. Kurt wanted some ice cream, so she'd stop at the grocery store before they went out to dinner. She'd do her part that evening; fighting with each other served no purpose. They had a baby to consider, and for the sake of their child, they had to get along.

Susan frowned as she brought her car to a stop in her driveway and stepped out. Icky rain. How was she supposed to get all of her things into the house without making two trips and getting soaked? Oops. Kurt's ice cream just landed in the mud. Okay, two trips. No big deal. She carried the ice cream and her flowers into the house and found her umbrella. Then she went back to her car for her briefcase and the rest of the groceries.

A horn sounded behind her as a champagne-colored Lexus pulled into her driveway. A tall, well-dressed man with a handsome face got out of the car and waved to her.

Oh, how nice! She hadn't seen him in ages. "Tommy Price, you old thing you! Come and give me a hug."

Tommy grinned and gave Susan a hug and a quick kiss. "Susan, you're as pretty as ever. Why'd you have to break my heart? I'm not over you yet."

"Oh, yes, you are. I can tell by the gleam in your eye."

Tommy laughed. "I'm telling you the truth. You just don't want to believe me."

"Come on in. It's too cold and rainy to talk out here. Anyway," she whispered, "Mrs. Myers is probably watching." Tommy reached for the grocery bag, and they went into the house.

"I remember Mrs. Meyers very well," he said as he set Susan's grocery bag on the kitchen table. "It's a shame her nosiness caused us to spend most of our time at my house instead of here. You've made a showplace out of this space."

He went into the living room where he seated himself by the fire and made himself at home.

Susan turned on the gas logs and sat beside him on the couch. "Maybe I should be an interior decorator."

"You should, but you won't. For some obscure reason you want to teach. I'd kill somebody in a week."

"Yes, you probably would." She laughed as she slid closer to him and squeezed his shoulder. "I'm so glad to see you, Tommy. I've missed you."

Tommy smiled and looked pleased. "Good. I'm glad you missed me. Now offer me something to drink."

"How about some hot chocolate?"

"You never change, Susan. Don't you have any decent, adult beverages in the house?"

"Coffee?"

Tommy surrendered. "Okay, hot chocolate. I tried to educate you on the merits of fine wines and other beverages, but you thwarted me at every turn."

"I'll get your hot chocolate," Susan answered with a grin. Using her microwave to heat the water, she fixed some hot chocolate for both of them and rejoined Tommy in the living room. He had removed his suit jacket and loosened his tie. Some official-looking papers were spread out on the coffee table.

She sat the cup on the end-table beside him. "What's that you have there?"

"Divorce papers."

"Who's getting divorced?"

"I hope you are."

Susan set her cup down as laughter and happiness drained from her heart. "How did you know I got married?"

"I saw your dad downtown. He told me you'd married a man you work with, but the guy isn't much account. Why, Susan? Why'd you get married so soon after we broke up? We've got such a lot in common. I know you said it wouldn't work out between us, but I think it would. I was going to give you a few months to come to your senses and maybe miss me a little bit, and then I was going to propose again. Are you in love with this man?"

Without thinking, Susan answered honestly. "No, I'm not in love with Kurt."

"Then divorce him." He winked at her. "I'm a good attorney, you know. I can get you your freedom, and it won't cost you a dime. As a matter of fact, I'll throw in an engagement ring for you too if you want it."

Her eyes filled with tears. For a moment, it had seemed like old times. Oh, how it hurt to think she had no carefree, independent days in her future.

Her tears had made Tommy angry. He slid forward and pulled her against him. "Shh, it's okay. Don't cry." He stroked her hair and settled her more firmly against his shoulder. "I can fix it. What's wrong with him? Is he abusive? Because if he is..."

"No," sobbed Susan as she clenched the back of his white shirt. "He's kind and sweet, but I didn't want to marry him. Seeing you just reminds me of all the freedom I lost."

"If you didn't want to marry him, why did you do it? If you regretted breaking up with me all you had to do was call. You know that."

"I'm a fool," cried Susan as she scrubbed at her eyes. "He took me to a party, and I got drunk and slept with him. I'm pregnant."

Tommy fell so quiet Susan self-consciously pulled away from him. In his presence she had briefly forgotten her troubles, but she had married another man. If Kurt saw her hugging Tommy he'd throw a fit, especially in light of their quarrel.

"A baby complicates things," Tommy finally said. He rubbed the bridge of his nose as Susan had often seen him do when faced with a complicated legal problem.

"Tell me about it."

"When is the baby due?"

After she told him, Tommy stood and paced the length of the living room with a thoughtful expression on his face. Presently, he turned to her and said, "It doesn't make any difference. If you aren't in love, you should divorce him."

"I can't, Tommy. He's the father of my baby. I sleep with him. I can't just divorce him for no reason."

A brief flicker of annoyance crossed his handsome face. "You can if you want to. I'll always be there for you, Susan, and that offer of a ring still stands."

Susan never answered because she heard the sound of a car in the driveway. "Quick, put away the papers! Promise me you won't say a word of this to Kurt! Promise!"

"Okay, okay," muttered Tommy.

Susan heard Kurt's key in the door and saw the surprise on his face when he saw Tommy. All at once she remembered she had been crying and hoped her eyes didn't look red and puffy. She shot a quick glance at Kurt. Oh, he had noticed all right.

"Hey, Kurt," she called. "Come and meet a friend of mine, Tommy Price. Tommy, this is my husband, Kurt Deveraux."

"Hello," Kurt responded while Tommy nodded coolly. Neither man offered to shake the other's hand. When Kurt kissed Susan's cheek, the tension in the room ratcheted up another notch or two.

Susan could barely breathe. Almost everyone in Fairfield had heard of Tommy Price, so Kurt probably knew who he was. Tommy's family lived on James Street, the most exclusive residential area in Fairfield, and had more money than they knew what to do with. Tommy was an attorney who'd won quite a reputation for himself. He didn't like to lose and didn't mind going the extra mile for his clients.

Kurt took a seat across from the sofa on which Susan and Tommy sat. "So, are you two catching up on old times?"

"Yes, we are," Tommy answered.

Susan cringed and bit her lip. Both of them sounded so...confrontational.

"Is that right?" Kurt asked. His voice was polite but cold.

"Yes, it is. We've been catching up on old times and exchanging news. Susan was telling me she's expecting a baby."

"Yes, we are." Nobody missed Kurt's slight emphasis on the word we.

A short, tense moment of silence fell in the room. Miserably uncomfortable, Susan prayed the two of them wouldn't start a fight. They reminded her of two teenage boys puffing out their chests and strutting around to see who got the girl.

Tommy stood up. "I'd better be going, Susan. If you need anything call me."

The angry look on Kurt's face told Susan he didn't like the idea of his wife needing anything from another man. "Thanks for coming by, Tommy. I'll walk you out."

Tommy paused on the front porch. "Is it okay to leave you alone with him? Don't be brave about it, Susan. If he's going to act ugly I'll stay, or you can come with me. I could take you to your dad's house too if that's where you'd rather go."

If only she could have fallen in love with Tommy! "I'll be fine. He isn't like that. I told you; he's kind."

Susan said her goodbye to Tommy and promised to call if she needed him. Then, she took a deep breath and went back inside to confront Kurt. She'd bet the farm they were about to have another fight.

The best defense was a good offense, so Susan went on the offensive the minute she went back into the living room. "I didn't know he was coming here, Kurt. He pulled into the driveway right behind me. I didn't invite him."

"You must have been glad to see him. He had your lipstick on his mouth."

How vexing! She hadn't meant anything bad by that kiss. She and Tommy had always greeted each other with a kiss. It hadn't occurred to her that since she got married she probably shouldn't do it.

"I did kiss him," she cried. "So what? We've known each other a lot longer than you and I have. He's still my friend, and I was glad to see him. Neither his visit nor that kiss has anything to do with us."

Kurt's lips pursed. "Uh-huh. Why don't you tell me the truth? A blind man could see he's in love with you, and since you've been kissing him and crying on his shoulder, I guess you want him too. I must have been right all along. You really do agree with your father about me."

He shrugged briefly. "No wonder your dad was so disappointed when we got married. Tommy Price could have given you a life of privilege and comfort, and I can't. Do you regret breaking up with him?"

He laughed harshly. "And to think I believed some flowers and a dinner would help solve our problems."

"You're wrong," she retorted, struggling to hold on to her temper. "I'm married to you because *I want to be.* I broke up with Tommy before you ever came along. I'm not in love with him! His visit has nothing to do with us."

Kurt's rock-hard, determined expression almost scared her. "Why did he really come here? Don't lie to me. I mean to know if I have to see him myself. I'd rather hear it from you, though. It might be less humiliating."

Humiliating? She hadn't thought about Tommy's visit in those terms. One thing was sure though; Kurt meant what he'd said, and she didn't want the two of them anywhere near each other. In his present mood, who could say what Kurt might do?

It would be best to tell him everything and hope for the best. "Tommy's a lawyer." She sank down on the couch across from Kurt who hadn't moved a muscle since Tommy left. "He saw my dad downtown today, and Dad told him I'd made a bad marriage. Tommy drew up some divorce papers and brought them over hoping I'd sign them."

Kurt jumped up and started to pace around the room. "Who the hell do they think they are? You're pregnant with my baby. We were married by a minister. Doesn't that count for anything at all? Well? Did you sign the papers?" he barked. "Do I need to find a new place to live?"

"No! I have absolutely no plans to divorce you! Not now, not ever."

Kurt's anger abruptly subsided. He shrugged. "It doesn't matter anyway. You never pretended to love me, and you sure didn't want to marry me. I had hoped once we got to know each other everything would work out between us, but I guess that was pretty stupid, huh?"

He walked over to the window and stared outside. Why was he so quiet? Did he plan to leave her? No! She didn't want him to go. Joining him at the window, she gently touched his shoulder. "Please, look at me."

Her heart raced the moment she saw his face. He looked so beaten and defeated, and his expression was as cold as winter. What had she done? She'd never planned to leave him or hurt him, but, plainly, she had done both.

"You're my husband," she said, taking both of his hands in hers. "As far as I'm concerned, our marriage is forever. We're going to have a baby together and hopefully another one after that. Tommy can bring over all the papers he wants to. It doesn't make any difference. Do you understand me, Kurt? It makes no difference to us. I'm your wife, and it's going to stay that way."

He shrugged. "Okay, I believe you, but you know what does make a difference?"

"What?"

He gently pulled his hands out of hers. "You may stay married to me, but I'm not who or what you wanted. You *are* trying to make the best of a bad situation. I feel like a fool for being so damn needy, but I wanted you to fall in love with me. I thought maybe if I pleased you in bed it would help, but once the passion is over you still regret being my wife."

Kurt paused and dropped his head. "I even wonder if my babies are good enough for you."

Sheer, primitive rage flooded Susan. "Don't you dare say a thing like that, Kurt Deveraux! This baby is mine and yours, and they don't come any finer! If I *ever* hear you say a thing like that again, I'll... I'll... well, you'll regret it."

She spun around and strode toward the door where she paused to yank her coat and purse out of the closet. Mints, tissues, and red pens scattered across the floor as she fished for her keys.

"Where the hell do you think you're going?" Kurt growled.

"To see my father. This is all his fault."

"Wait a ..."

The door slammed behind her, and a moment later her car wheeled out of the driveway and sped down the road.

Seventeen

Susan parked in her father's driveway and sprang from her car. How could her father have done this to her! She slammed the car door as hard as she could and burst into the house where she almost bumped into her mother who carried a pot of tea and some gingerbread.

"Hello, Susan. Sit down. Are you okay? Kurt called and said you were on your way here." Mrs. English's soothing, quiet voice and the air of repose about her calmed Susan a little.

"Kurt called?"

"Yes, he did. He said you were upset with your father, but he wouldn't say why. He's worried because he said you were driving too fast. Call him now, and tell him you're okay. I'll pour you some tea and cut the gingerbread while you do it."

"I want to talk to Dad, not Kurt."

Her mother gave her the look she'd always given her and her brother when they had done something to displease her. "You do what I tell you. Call Kurt now."

She hadn't come here to argue with her mother, so she picked up the phone and called Kurt who answered on the first ring. "Kurt, it's me. I'm at Mother's house. I'm okay."

She heard Kurt exhale loudly. "Thank God for that! I was afraid you'd smash the car into a tree or hit somebody. Are you too upset to drive home? I can come pick you up."

"No, I'm all right. Don't come out here. I'll be home soon."

"Are you sure, Susan? I've never seen you so upset."

"Yes, I'm sure. Talk to you soon."

Susan hung up and joined her mother who had just poured both of them a cup of tea. "You didn't tell him you love him," Marjorie said.

"I don't know that I do love him," Susan flashed back as she took a seat across from Marjorie. "Why should I say I do?"

"Because if you say it often enough, and if you act as if it were true, it will come true."

Susan scowled and ignored the tantalizing odor of the gingerbread. "Why does everybody think I have to love him? He told me he wanted me to fall in love with him. We're married, for goodness sake. I'm going to have his baby. I must have loved him sometime!"

Her voice rose toward the end of her speech, a fact her mother overlooked. "Life is a whole lot easier if you're in love with your husband. Anyway, from all that I can see, Kurt is falling in love with you. Why shouldn't you return his feelings?"

Susan reached for a piece of gingerbread and considered her mother's point of view. Marjorie sometimes saw things others missed. Was Kurt really falling in love with her? "I'm trying to return his feelings, Mom, and half of the time I think I do love him."

"What about the other half?"

"The other half I think about being tied down and missing out on so many things I want to do," Susan muttered. "Like my trip to Paris, for instance. Do you really think I'll ever get there now? Like Daddy said, babies are expensive, and so are school loans, groceries, and house payments."

Marjorie laughed. "Well, it is true that husbands and babies have to be taken care of, but they do offer a lot in return. Haven't you enjoyed having him around?"

"Sometimes, well, most of the time."

Her mother took a sip of her tea and looked into her eyes. "Can I ask you something personal?"

"What?"

"Do you sleep with him?"

Susan blushed to the roots of her hair. "Mother!"

"It isn't a hard question, honey. Either you have sex with him or you don't."

"We did it for the first time on Sunday morning," answered Susan. Who'd ever have dreamed she'd be having this conversation with her mother, of all people.

"Did he please you?" Her mother poured herself another cup of tea as if she hadn't said something so outrageous.

"I can't believe I'm having this conversation with you," cried Susan. "I didn't come here to talk about my sex life or about whether I should try to love Kurt. I came to talk to Dad and to tell him to butt out of my business."

"If you don't want to talk about Kurt, maybe you'd better tell me what your father did to make you so angry."

Susan's ears burned. "Where is Dad?"

"I sent him to the grocery store after I spoke to Kurt. I wanted to talk to you first. We've had enough trouble in the family already, and we don't need any more. If your father has done something he shouldn't have, it needs to be handled properly, and it will be. Now, tell me about it."

"Okay, I will, and since you're so curious, I'll tell you about Sunday morning too."

"Okay, let me see if I have this straight," Marjorie said when Susan finished her story. "You wanted to consummate your marriage, but afterward you cringed away from Kurt and pretty well trashed his self-esteem. Then, to make you feel better, he offers you dinner and flowers, but when he gets home you've been kissing and crying on the shoulder of an old boyfriend. Have I got it right?"

Shame flooded Susan. How could she have been so mean and awful to Kurt? "Yes, that's about it," she said.

"Your father is at fault in a big way, and he'll be told so in no uncertain terms, but first you have to make things right with Kurt."

Susan's cup clattered into her saucer. "I don't know how. Every time we start to get close something bad happens. I'm still mad at Dad too. Tommy would never have drawn up those divorce papers if it weren't for Dad."

"True, but if you hadn't been crying and kissing Tommy, Kurt wouldn't have thought anything out of the ordinary was going on and never would have known about the divorce papers."

Mrs. English paused for a moment, and almost as if it were an afterthought, she asked, "Why did it upset you so much for Kurt's feelings to be hurt over the divorce papers?"

"Because he's my husband. I'd never hurt him on purpose. He's been nothing but kind and good since we got married."

"Hmm, you're very protective of him, Susan. I wonder if your feelings for him are deeper than you think."

Susan thought for a moment. "I don't know how I feel. I know it terrified me when I heard the car in the drive way, not because I was afraid of Kurt, but because it seemed important that he not know about the divorce papers."

"Maybe it was because you were afraid he might leave you. Would you be sorry if you didn't see him every day?"

A ghost of a smile chased across Susan's face. "I like being with Kurt in the morning. We eat breakfast together while we read the paper. Usually, we share things we find interesting. I tease him about letting Samson sample his oatmeal before he gets it.

"In the evenings I like knowing he's in the house. It's fun to argue with him over what we'll watch on TV, and I love to tease him about using his razor on my legs. So, yes, I would miss him if he weren't there."

Marjorie smiled and patted her arm. "Oh, Susan, don't you know you're in love with him?"

"I'm just not sure." She bit her lip. "You've given me a lot to think about, but I'm not sure anything I've said means I love him."

"You'll see that I'm right, but now we have to fix the mess Tommy and your father got you into."

Susan sighed. "How? Kurt's really upset."

Marjorie laughed. "That's easy. Go home and be sweet to him. Flatter him, stroke his ego, and flirt like crazy. Be very provocative, and make him want you so much he forgets about Tommy and your father and takes you to bed. When he does, be loving and responsive, and for goodness sake let him please you. Be sure he knows you enjoyed yourself too. If you do this consistently and make a real effort to fall in love with him, everything will be fine."

"What about Dad?"

"I told you I'd see to your father. Now, you finish your tea and get home to Kurt."

Susan finished her tea in one long swallow. Her mother was right. She shouldn't have stormed out the way she had. "Thanks, Mom. I love you."

She kissed her mother goodbye and hurried home to Kurt.

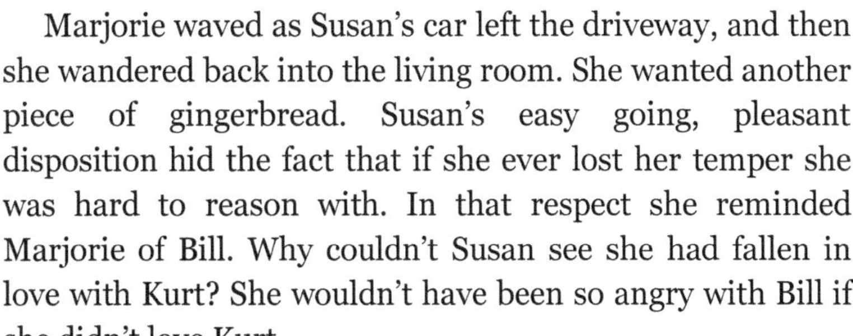

Marjorie waved as Susan's car left the driveway, and then she wandered back into the living room. She wanted another piece of gingerbread. Susan's easy going, pleasant disposition hid the fact that if she ever lost her temper she was hard to reason with. In that respect she reminded Marjorie of Bill. Why couldn't Susan see she had fallen in love with Kurt? She wouldn't have been so angry with Bill if she didn't love Kurt.

She probably couldn't see it because of the way they were forced into marriage. Susan hadn't been ready to get married, and she doubted Kurt had either. Nevertheless, they were married, and they had a baby on the way. Maybe a little granddaughter who'd enjoy tea parties with grandma. That baby would change their lives in so many ways, and most of them were wonderful.

It would take something really big to make Susan see the truth, simply because she had gotten stubborn. Marjorie sighed. *I don't know what form the revelation will take, but I hope it hits them soon. The sooner they realize their true feelings, the sooner both of them can be happy.*

What was going on at the English house? Kurt sighed and checked his watch for the third time in five minutes. He should have gone out there instead of calling, but like a fool he had been afraid to go because he didn't think he could resist punching Bill English in the nose.

Of course Bill wasn't the only one at fault. Tommy Price had to assume part of the blame. He hoped he didn't see Tommy again for a very long time; it would feel so good to knock that rich home-wrecker on his butt, but that wouldn't solve anything.

Okay, what would make things better? Susan had made it plain she meant to stay with him, but how could a man live with a woman knowing she didn't love him?

Maybe he should give Susan her freedom. He didn't think she'd keep the baby away from him, and he'd gladly support his child. Good old Tommy Price would love to take care of Susan, and finally Bill would have the son-in-law he wanted. Funny, but he didn't like this plan at all. His stomach churned at the thought of losing Susan and his child.

He heard Susan's car outside and breathed a sigh of relief. She'd been way too upset to drive. His nerves had been torn up ever since she shot out of the driveway. His shoulders tensed as he watched her get out of the car. What would he do if she hadn't calmed down?

She shut the door this time instead of slamming it and greeted him with an apology. "I'm sorry I ran out of here and worried you. I won't do it again. I'm sorry about Tommy too. He had no right to come here."

Kurt drew a deep breath. *So far so good.* "Did you see your father?"

"No, Dad wasn't home, but I did talk to Mother. She's going to make him see that he can't interfere with our lives like he did."

His shoulders finally relaxed. She might have hurt herself or the baby tearing out of here like a bat out of hell. Too bad he didn't have the nerve to tell her so, but he didn't, and that was all there was to it.

Susan slipped her arms around him and snuggled close. "Let's go to bed. I'm totally worn out."

Kurt hesitated. He hadn't expected her to come home in this mood. "Ah, Susan, I've had a lot of time to think since you left, and maybe it would be better if I slept in the guest room until we get things straightened out between us."

Susan lifted her eyes to his and begged, "Please, don't do that. I want you to share a bed with me; I like being close to you. Don't move out of our room. Please, don't."

Really it would be for the best, but...was she about to cry? "Sure, forget I said anything about it."

Susan stood on tiptoe and kissed his cheek. "I meant what I said before. I don't want a divorce, and I don't want Tommy either. You're my husband, Kurt Deveraux. You're the only man I want. You're handsome, kind, talented, and wonderful." She gave him a big hug. "I like being married to you."

He doubted it, but why make an issue of it? Even though she hadn't really meant it, it did feel good to hear the words. If that made him seem needy and foolish, so be it.

Susan sighed and punched her pillow. Apologies had been given and accepted, but emotions still ran high anyway. Who could sleep after an evening like they'd had?

Around three she got up for the second time to go to the bathroom. She reached for a tissue on her way back to bed, but the box on the bathroom shelf was empty. "In the linen closet," she muttered, but as she opened the closet door, a cardboard box clattered down from the top shelf and hit her squarely in the face. A tremendous noise reverberated around the room as the box and its contents crashed to the floor.

Oh, gosh, that hurt! She grabbed her eye and sank down onto the bench in front of her makeup mirror just as Kurt charged into the bathroom. "What happened? Are you okay?"

"I'm sorry to wake you," she moaned, "but a box fell off the shelf and hit me in the eye."

"Let's see it. This has been our night for trouble, hasn't it?"

He raised her face to the light. "Baby, I'm sorry, but you're going to have one heck of a shiner tomorrow."

As he bent to pick up the box and its spilled contents, he frowned. "Susan, I'm sorry. I put this box on the shelf yesterday. I guess I didn't slide it back far enough."

She shrugged. "It's just one of those things."

Kurt cleared the floor and put the box back on the shelf. "Let's see if we can sleep. Pregnant women need their rest, and we have to work tomorrow."

This disaster didn't especially surprise her. After the day they'd had, she would have been surprised if anything good had happened. She obediently followed Kurt into the bedroom, and when they got into bed, she snuggled close and put her arm around him. It made her feel so much better.

Eighteen

Melissa swung into Susan's room and stopped short when she saw Susan's face. "What happened to you?" she cried.

Susan laughed. "You're about the one hundredth person to ask me that." It was better to laugh about her poor eye than to cry, so she'd made jokes about it all morning. "It's Kurt's fault. I mouthed off to him last night and he…"

The squawk of the intercom interrupted Susan before she finished her sentence. "Miss Taylor, please report to the office for a parent conference," Mr. Dennis called.

"You've got to finish this later, Susan," Melissa insisted. "I want to hear the rest of the story."

"Later," Susan agreed, but in the rush of the day she didn't see Melissa again until after Melissa's lunch date with Jason.

Jason and Melissa had begun to spend more and more time together, and it looked as if it might turn out to be serious between them. They always had lunch in Melissa's room, but on this particular day Melissa's angry eyes and stiff posture made Jason's heart burn. Had he done something to offend her? He couldn't think of anything, but…oh, why not just ask her?

He cleared his throat and shifted in his desk. "Ah, Melissa, is anything wrong? Are you mad at me about something?"

"Is it so obvious something is wrong?"

He nodded. "To me it is, so tell me. What's put you in such a bad mood?"

Melissa set her salad fork down and wiped her mouth as though eating were the last thing on her mind. "I wanted to tell you about it, Jason, but I didn't know how to start or even if I should. Kurt is your best friend, so I didn't want you to think I was bad-mouthing him."

Jason frowned. "Well, that isn't what I expected. What does Kurt have to do with your bad mood? Did he say something that upset you?"

"I haven't seen him today, but I did see Susan."

Was she about to cry? Her mouth had puckered and her eyes looked damp. "Okay, and what did Susan say to upset you? Did it have something to do with Kurt?"

Her eyes flashed now and filled with more anger than he'd dreamed her capable of. "Oh, it certainly does have something to do with Kurt. According to Susan, he's responsible for her black eye."

"What!"

"She tried to cover it with makeup, but it's too bruised."

Jason dropped his own fork. "Did I understand you correctly? Susan has a black eye, and she actually said Kurt hit her?"

Melissa's lip quivered. "She told me it was Kurt's fault, and those are her exact words. She said she mouthed off to him last night. I suppose that's when he did it."

Acid boiled in Jason's stomach. Kurt had been his best friend since they were in the first grade, and it cut to the quick to think that he'd hit any woman, much less his pregnant wife. He'd always looked up to Kurt, but ever since he got involved with Susan, his behavior had changed. First drinking and premarital sex and now abuse. He suddenly remembered that Benjy had accused Kurt of treating Susan too roughly. Could Benjy have been right all along?

It would be so easy to blame Susan for everything, but Kurt had to assume some of the blame. Susan didn't force him to sleep with her, and no matter how she provoked him, he should never have lost control and hit her; no man had the right to hit a woman. As anger mingled with shock, he vowed to get to the bottom of this thing.

"I'm not making excuses for him, Melissa," he said. He heard the cold note in his own voice and felt like cringing. "His father needs to be told. Mr. Deveraux has a lot of influence with Kurt, so he might be able to do something." Jason shook his head. "I still can't believe it. I'm so... well I...I don't know what to say."

Her eyes filled with sympathy. "I'm sorry. I know how close the two of you are. Maybe there were extenuating circumstances."

He appreciated her efforts, but... "No, I don't think so, but I'll find out what happened before this day is over."

⸺ ❧ ⸺

"Did you see your sister-in-law today?" Randy asked Sheila as they rode the bus home that afternoon.

Sheila sniffed. "And why would you suppose I want to see her?"

"Oh, you should have seen her. She has a black eye."

"So? I don't care."

"Rumor has it your brother popped her one."

Sheila's stomach lurched. "No, he wouldn't do that."

Randy shrugged. "All I know is what I heard. You know Leah McKinley? She's an office assistant, right? When she took some packages to the faculty lounge she heard Miss English say her husband hit her."

"Well, I don't believe it." On the other hand, she still couldn't believe Kurt had gotten Miss English pregnant either. Guess she didn't know him as well as she'd thought she did. Maybe he had done this awful thing, but she wouldn't say so to Randy.

"I don't want to talk about my brother or his wife. If you want to sit with me, you'll have to change the subject."

"All right," Randy muttered. "Gee, I thought you'd thank me for telling you about your big brother."

Her mother was waiting for her when she got off the bus. "Hey, baby. How was your day?"

"It was okay."

"How does chicken sound for dinner?"

Who cared one way or the other? Since her little conversation with Randy she didn't have much of an appetite. Should she tell her mother what Randy had said? No, Helen would just take Kurt's side the way she always did.

She dashed upstairs and curled up on her bed. It was almost impossible to imagine Kurt hitting Miss English. Would he have hit her with his fist? Tears oozed from her eyes as she wiped sweat from her forehead. She hated Miss English, but she hated Kurt more because he was the one who had fooled her about his character.

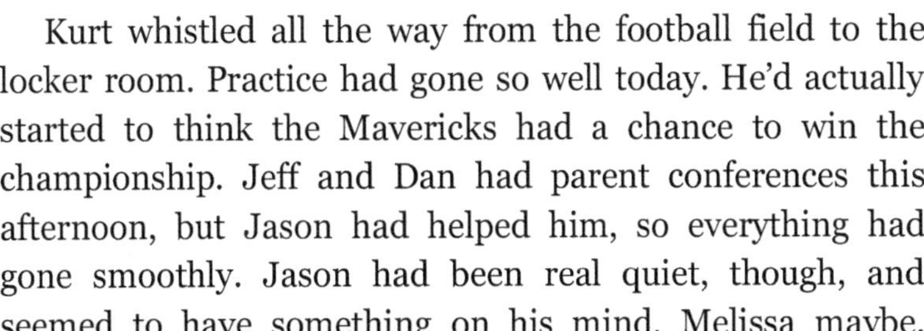

Kurt whistled all the way from the football field to the locker room. Practice had gone so well today. He'd actually started to think the Mavericks had a chance to win the championship. Jeff and Dan had parent conferences this afternoon, but Jason had helped him, so everything had gone smoothly. Jason had been real quiet, though, and seemed to have something on his mind. Melissa maybe. Those two were spending a lot of time together.

As they walked into the gym, he bent over to tie his shoe, and Jason said, "I need to talk to you about something."

"What's up? Didn't the practice go well today? I've actually started to think the Mavericks have a chance of winning the playoff."

He stood up and got a look at Jason's face. "What's wrong? You look sorta sick or maybe mad."

Jason nodded. "I guess I feel both ways. When I had lunch with Melissa today, she told me Susan has a black eye."

Kurt's smile faded. "Yeah, she does, and I hate it because it's my fault."

"I had hoped Melissa misunderstood," Jason said, his voice cold and stiff. "What's wrong with you? She's your wife, and she's pregnant. Don't you know you could hurt her?"

Kurt shrugged. "Getting a black eye hurts, but it isn't the end of the world. I'll be more careful in the future." Wow, Jason's face had turned beet red.

"You might as well have raped Susan by sleeping with her after she had too much to drink, and in the process you disappointed your family and all of your friends. That's bad enough, but you've hit a new low this time. Susan may have had to take crap off you last night, but if I had been there she wouldn't have. This is for Susan."

Jason threw a punch and hit Kurt a solid blow to the face. Taken totally unaware, he went sprawling on the floor just as Jeff and Dan opened the gym door. Through the haze of pain radiating from his eye, he heard Jeff cry, "Jason hit him!"

Kurt sprang from the floor and took the fight to Jason. He got in a couple of good licks before Jason punched him again. He lunged forward, but someone grabbed his arms and pulled them behind his back. Dan.

"What the hell is the matter with you?" he snarled as he struggled to free himself from Dan's tight grip.

"Like you don't know! I told you why." Jason tried to break Jeff's grip, but he couldn't.

"Both of you shut up," Dan snapped. "Jason, are you hurt?"

"No."

"Jeff, take him outside, and put him in his car. Jason, go home. I'm taking care of Kurt's face, and then I'm sending him home. The two of you owe each other apologies."

Jason threw Dan a sullen look and accompanied Jeff, leaving Kurt humming with tension and frustration. Dan tightened his arms around Kurt's. "If I let you go, are you gonna behave? I've never seen you so angry, and I don't want you taking it out on me."

Kurt forced himself to relax. "I don't want to fight."

Dan let him go. "Let me look at your face," he said. He conducted an inspection of Kurt's face and gave his conclusions. "You really need a stitch or two under your eye. You've got a deep cut there."

"It'll be okay. Just put a band aid on it."

"What's wrong with him? I saw him hit you first."

Kurt shrugged. "I don't think what I did was so awful. I put a box on the top shelf in the bathroom at home the other day. I guess I didn't slide it back far enough because when Susan opened the closet door, the box fell off the shelf and hit her in the face. It gave her a black eye, but was that any reason for him to try to take my head off?"

"There has to be something else."

"Not that I know of."

Dan thought for a moment. "Well, I don't get it either. What happened was an accident. Was Susan mad about it?"

"No, not at all. She said accidents happen."

"You can talk to him tomorrow. Maybe he misunderstood the situation, but right now let me fix your face."

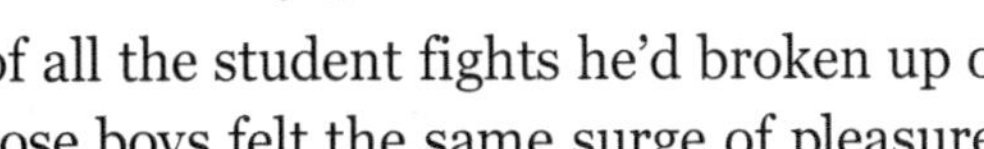

Kurt thought of all the student fights he'd broken up over the years. Had those boys felt the same surge of pleasure he did when he hit Jason? He'd had to be so good with Susan and her hateful father; it had been such a relief to finally hit back.

Residual anger flared when he thought of Jason. Yeah, they'd been friends for a long time, but nothing gave Jason the right to slug him that way. He hadn't hurt Susan on purpose, but even if he had, it wasn't any of Jason's business. And where did that dirty comment about raping Susan come from? He hadn't raped her. Could the two of them ever be friends after this?

Susan was putting dinner on the table when he got home. She turned around to greet him and exclaimed, "Kurt! What happened to you?"

She rushed across the room to look at his eye. "Don't touch it," Kurt grumpily said as she reached for his face. "It hurts."

"Tell me what happened."

"Jason and I had a fight."

Her eyes widened as she worried her lower lip. "It must have been some fight. Has this ever happened before?"

"No."

Susan touched his arm this time. "Why were you two fighting?"

"I don't want to talk about it." His jaw clenched. "I have a headache, and I'd like to soak in the bathtub for a while."

She nodded. "Well, go ahead. I'll put your dinner away, and after you get out of the tub, I'll warm it for you in the microwave."

She was being so good to him even though he'd been grumpy with her. He pulled her against him and kissed the top of her head. "If I ask you something, will you promise to tell me the truth and not try to spare my feelings?"

"Yes, if you like."

Kurt drew a deep breath. "Okay, when we spent the night with Mendoza, you were drunk and so was I. You don't think I ..."

Susan stepped out of his arms. "Don't think you what?"

"Took advantage... Oh, hell, might as well say it. Do you think I raped you that night?"

The look of shock and horror on her face reassured him before she even spoke. "Why would you think such a thing?" she demanded. "I wanted you as much as you wanted me."

"You weren't really able to say no because of the tequila."

She stepped back against him and hugged him close. "Don't think that, okay? Both of us wanted sex; you didn't force me to do anything I didn't want to do." She paused and stroked his back for a few moments. "Who said something to you? It better not be my father or Tommy."

"No, nothing like that." He forced himself to smile at her. "I'm going to clean up."

"You believe me, right?"

Her reassurance had melted some of the coldness lodged in his chest. "Yes, I believe you."

He kissed her again and went to soak in the tub. How could Jason have thought he'd hurt his wife?

Nineteen

Jason didn't go straight home even though he wanted to. He turned his car toward the outskirts of town where George Deveraux's store was located. George made a good living operating the little store. A lot of students stopped by after school to pick up drinks and snacks, and since several new housing developments had been constructed nearby, lots of people stopped in to buy the milk or bread they remembered needing.

He stopped in front of the store and turned off the ignition. He had to do this, but he wasn't looking forward to it. Mr. Deveraux would be upset, but he had no choice in the matter. Susan could never defend herself against Kurt, and once a man started hitting a woman, it was hard for him to stop. A brief flare of anger threatened to break through, but sorrow quickly replaced it. What could have happened to Kurt? He had been a leader both at school and church. The kids under his care had learned a lot from him.

Mr. Deveraux called a cheerful greeting to Jason as he entered the store, but the welcoming look on his face morphed into apprehension. George saw that something bad had happened.

He finished serving his customer in record time, and the minute the woman left the store he said, "How bad is it?"

"Pretty bad." Jason grimaced. "Nobody died or anything, but it's bad."

Mr. Deveraux hurried around the counter and turned the open sign on the door to the closed side. "If it's that bad, I don't want interruptions. Tell me."

Jason took a deep breath. "I hate to tell you this, but I think you have to know." He drew another deep breath and got it over with. "I had a fight with Kurt a while ago. I mean a real fight. I think he probably needs stitches under his eye."

Mr. Deveraux looked astonished. "Why? What was the fight about?"

"He hit Susan last night and blacked her eye."

"No! Jason, are you *sure*?"

"He admitted it to me," Jason answered. His shoulders slumped. "I know fighting with him probably made things worse, but he didn't seem too upset about it, and when I thought about Susan being pregnant, I just lost it. Before I knew it, I decked him. He came up fighting, and I guess we'd still be slugging it out if Dan and Jeff hadn't come in and broken it up."

"I just can't believe it! I can't believe Kurt would do such a thing." George shook his head. "No, something terrible must have happened last night. I know nothing justifies his hitting Susan, but there must be a reason for him to lose control of himself. Kurt isn't like that."

Jason shrugged. He wouldn't say so to George, but the way things had happened, he wondered if either of them knew Kurt as well as they thought they did. "I know they had a fight over the weekend, but Kurt sent her flowers and planned to take her out to dinner last night to make up for it," he said.

A determined look came to rest on George's face. "That doesn't sound like he was angry with her, does it? Something happened last night, and I intend to find out what it was. Don't worry about Susan. I'm going to see Kurt right now. I think I'll try to get him to take Father Duncan's class on anger management. If he won't cooperate, he may have to be separated from Susan. He can't be allowed to hurt her."

Jason sighed. How would Mr. Deveraux go about removing Kurt if he didn't want to go? Sometimes he seemed to forget that Kurt wasn't a child anymore. "I'm sick about it all," he said. "I got mad at Kurt because he had no business hitting a woman, but he's like a brother to me. It kills me to think of him abusing Susan. What happened to him? Do you think it's Susan's fault? Kurt didn't start this bad behavior until he started going out with her."

For a moment, George looked hopeful, but sorrow replaced hope almost immediately. "I don't think we can blame Susan for this, Jason. It's killing me too, but Kurt needs us now. I know he's done something wrong, but he needs help. Don't turn your back on him."

Jason rubbed his face. "Kurt may not see it that way. He may not want to be my friend anymore. I mean, I sucker-punched him and hurt him pretty bad."

George gave his shoulder a compassionate pat. "Hopefully, you're wrong. Now go on home and let me call Father Duncan. I think he should go with me to talk to Kurt."

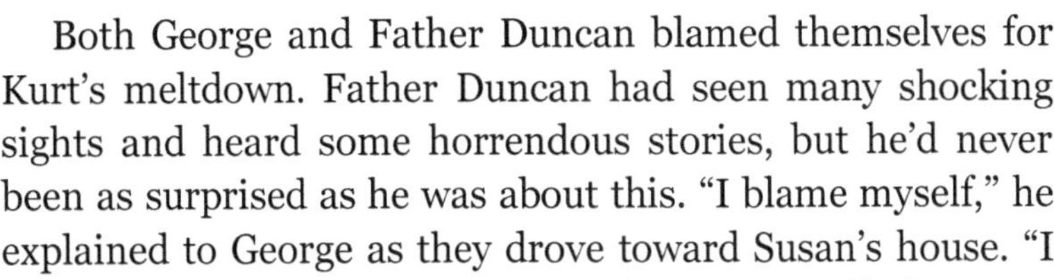

Both George and Father Duncan blamed themselves for Kurt's meltdown. Father Duncan had seen many shocking sights and heard some horrendous stories, but he'd never been as surprised as he was about this. "I blame myself," he explained to George as they drove toward Susan's house. "I should have known Kurt was in trouble emotionally."

Mr. Deveraux signaled and turned left. "How could you have known? He hid it well. I thought everything was okay between them. I'm not much of a father if I didn't realize Kurt was so close to the edge."

"I should have known because I asked him yesterday if he intended to organize the youth Christmas fair this year. You know he always does, but he turned me down." Father Duncan sighed. "He said he didn't think the parents would want somebody like him in charge of their kids in a church setting. Obviously, he still feels a lot of guilt over getting Susan pregnant."

"*Somebody like him!* They don't come any better than Kurt. I had hoped if Susan and he were happy he'd get over feeling guilty. Guilt can make people do strange things."

Father Duncan nodded. "I think you're right. Kurt's always been a role model for so many young people. I suppose not living up to everyone else's expectations, much less his own, was more than he could take. He certainly isn't himself if he blackened Susan's eye."

Conversation ceased as the car turned into the driveway. "This is the trouble with being a father; you worry about your kids until the day you die," George muttered.

Father Duncan squeezed George's shoulder. "We'll help him, George. Kurt's one of the good guys. True, he made a mistake, but that doesn't make him a bad person."

George drew a deep breath. "Okay, let's get it over with."

Kurt sighed when he heard the doorbell ring. His eye throbbed like a toothache, and he wasn't in the mood for company. A sudden thought struck him. Jason had better not be the one bothering him. Even if he came to apologize, who wanted to see him?

Susan's front door had a little window in it, so he saw his dad and Father Duncan standing on the porch. Bet the farm they knew about him and Jason. "Dad, Father Duncan, won't you come in?"

They stopped inside, and Father Duncan shook his hand. "I hope we didn't interrupt anything."

"No, I was just watching TV."

His father put a hand on his chin and turned his eye toward the light. "That looks bad."

"It's nothing. Come and sit down."

"It looks like something to me," he heard his dad mutter as they all took a seat in the living room.

"Who told you?" Kurt asked.

George clasped his hands together and leaned forward. "Jason did. He's real upset."

Kurt struggled to get a grip on his temper. "*He's* upset? I don't give a...er, I don't care if he's upset or not. What did he tell you?"

"He said you were responsible for Susan's black eye, and he lost his temper and hit you."

"I guess that's about right," sighed Kurt.

For some reason, both his dad and Father Duncan looked shocked. Did they expect him to wail and wring his hands over things? Yeah, the box hurt Susan. Yeah, Jason slugged him one, but it wasn't the worst thing that ever happened. Why the long faces?

Mr. Deveraux cleared his throat the way he always did when he was trying to find the right words to say and was afraid he couldn't. "Kurt, you do know, don't you, that something like this can't happen again? What if you had seriously hurt Susan? What if you injured your baby?"

Kurt frowned. "Is that likely? I never thought about taking her to the doctor."

Susan, who had been taking a shower, chose that moment to wander into the living room. Her hair was wet, and her face was free of makeup which gave Kurt a good look at her eye. It had to hurt. His did.

"I'm sorry. I didn't know we had company," she apologized. "Let me get dressed."

She was only gone a couple of minutes before she rejoined them. "May I get you some coffee or tea?" she asked with a smile.

Everyone declined, so she sat down beside him. He'd like to hold her hand, but they had company so he didn't.

Father Duncan gave Susan an encouraging smile, the one he used at church to relax nervous people. "Susan, Kurt said he gave you that black eye. Is that true?"

She shrugged. "I guess so, but it was an accident. He didn't mean to do it."

"That's very generous of you, but I don't see how this could be an accident."

Susan blinked. "Surely, you don't think he did it on purpose."

Father Duncan looked absolutely beatific now. "You have a kind heart, Susan, and I don't want you to worry. We're going to get everything straightened out. One mistake doesn't change your husband's good character."

Susan was slightly frowning now, but Father Duncan had finished with her. "I conduct a class on anger management, and, Kurt, I think you need to take it. You obviously feel a lot of anger and guilt, and I'd like to help you deal with it."

"Son, please do what he asks," Mr. Deveraux said. "I love you, but I don't want you to hurt Susan or your baby."

"The class meets every Thursday night at seven," Father Duncan continued. "I'll expect you this Thursday." He paused for a moment to study Kurt's face. "I really think you need to go to the hospital for stitches. You'll have a bad scar if you don't."

Scowling, Susan butted into the conversation. "I'm getting the impression you both think Kurt hit me. Is that right?"

Nobody answered.

"Yesterday Kurt put a box on the top shelf of the closet. Last night I opened the door, and since he didn't slide the box back far enough on the shelf, it fell off and hit me in the face. That's how I got the black eye. He didn't hit me."

Air rushed from Kurt's lungs as if someone had punched him in the stomach this time. "Good G..., Dad, is that true? Did you really think I hit her?"

Mr. Deveraux literally wrung his hands. "Well, yes, I did. It sounded like you were admitting to it when you said it was your fault."

Defeat ran through Kurt's veins and pooled in a big knot in his chest. "I've never struck a woman, and I didn't hurt my wife," he said. He got up and leaned on the fireplace mantle with his head on his arm. Nobody said a word.

Susan resisted the urge to throw herself on the sofa and cry. She couldn't bear it. This was all her fault! Why had she made jokes about her eye at school? As usual in her dealings with Kurt, she had hurt him without meaning to. Springing from the sofa, she hurried to his side. Oh, why did things always have to go wrong? He hadn't done anything to make his father think something so bad. Yes, she was definitely the one to blame. Hadn't she started things by making that stupid bet with Robin? Kurt hadn't been anything but honorable and good since the whole mess started.

In that moment she knew the truth. She had fallen in love with Kurt. Why else would she be so unhappy about Mr. Deveraux's assumption? Why else didn't she want Kurt to see Tommy's divorce papers?

Such a revelation demanded expression. She hugged him tight, and even though it might not be proper in front of other people, she kissed him on his shoulder. He resisted the comfort that she offered for the space of a few heartbeats, but his need was probably too great. With a sigh, he relaxed against her and put his arms around her.

"I'm sorry, sweetheart," she murmured. "I'm so sorry. Are you okay?"

Kurt didn't answer, but when he nodded, she took charge. This useless, embarrassing confrontation needed to end right now. "You need stitches in your face, and I intend to see you get them whether you want to or not. Put your shoes on. I'm taking you to the hospital."

Both their guests looked stricken and seemed at a loss for words, but Kurt let them off the hook. "Dad, I know the two of you meant well. I'm not mad at either one of you. I feel bad you'd think I'd be abusive, but from what I said I can see how you might have thought what you did. It's okay."

"I'm sorry," Mr. Deveraux croaked.

Oh, she felt sorry for George because he looked so pitiful. It was good of Kurt to forgive him. Father Duncan too.

Father Duncan's reaction somewhat surprised her, though. He appeared cheerful and upbeat in spite of thinking so poorly of Kurt. "Thanks be to God we were mistaken," he said, "but Kurt, you still have some guilt you need to work through. Why don't you call me tomorrow and set up a counseling session? I've been told I do a pretty good job."

Kurt made no promises, but as he and Susan left for the hospital he said, "We never get a break, do we?"

Susan reached for his hand. "Don't think about it. They apologized, and you accepted their apologies, so let it go."

Personally, she felt like they'd gotten a wonderful break tonight. Tonight was the night she realized that she loved him.

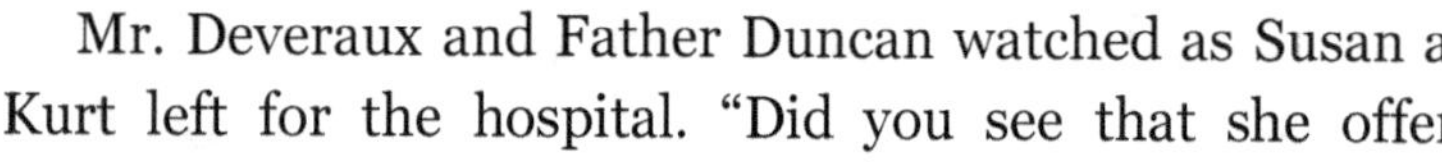

Mr. Deveraux and Father Duncan watched as Susan and Kurt left for the hospital. "Did you see that she offered comfort to him, and he accepted it?" Father Duncan asked. "I think they may be able to work this thing out after all."

Sheila carefully tiptoed down the hall, avoiding one certain board that always creaked if you stepped on it. It was so easy to listen at her parents' door. Sometimes they even left the door cracked while they talked. Maybe it showed a lack of character for her to eavesdrop on them, but she had found out some interesting things that way.

Tonight, for instance, she had found out that Kurt didn't give Miss English her black eye. A box had fallen off a shelf and hit her. She was still angry with him, but it was good that he hadn't hit her awful sister-in-law. Kurt wasn't the nice guy she had taken him for, but he wasn't abusive either, which was a relief.

She eased her own door shut. Really, her parents should be more careful. One day she might overhear more than they wanted her to.

Twenty

Kurt sighed as Susan squeezed his hand again. "They won't hurt you," she said. "They'll give you something before they sew you up."

He nodded. "Yeah, maybe a shot."

She paled and took deep, uneven breaths. What was wrong with her? This wasn't major surgery. Oh, wait. Susan must be afraid of hospitals and needles. "Honey, I'm fine, and it won't hurt. Honestly. Please don't worry."

"Oh, I'm not," she quavered.

When the doctor told them he really would need stitches, she looked so washed out and scared that the doctor saw and insisted she wait outside while he did his work.

When he finished, Kurt went to find Susan. She was pacing the floor wearing out the carpet. When she saw him, she swiftly crossed the room to examine his face. "Are you all right?" she demanded with a catch in her voice.

"Baby, it's fine. Don't get so worked up about it."

At home, Susan insisted on treating him as if a cut under his eye had turned him into an invalid. She refused to let him get off the couch, covered him with an afghan, and made him drink hot tea. She brought him some Tylenol even though he told her he didn't need it. She even offered to call Mr. Dennis and tell him Kurt couldn't come to school the next day. Why did she seem so much more concerned now than she had been before his father and Father Duncan arrived? Never mind. He wouldn't ask for the world.

At first it felt funny to be the recipient of such attention, but if she wanted to boss him around and pamper him, let her. He didn't complain when she came out of the bedroom with additional orders for him. "I've filled the bathtub with warm water. You go and have a bath. I'll find you some clean underwear to put on."

He minded her, even though he'd already had one bath that evening, but he dropped the soap into the tub when Susan opened the door and came in without knocking. "Susan, I'm kind of undressed here."

Giggling, she said, "I hope so. You're in the bathtub, after all."

"I... don't know that I'm comfortable with you in here."

"Get over it," she answered with a smile. "I'm going to help you take a bath whether you like it or not."

She sat down on the edge of the bathtub and took the washcloth from him. After lathering it, she started on his face, taking great care to be gentle. He relaxed as her hands moved across his shoulders and back.

"Does that feel good?" Susan asked.

Something in her voice made Kurt sit up and take notice. "Yes, I like it a lot."

"Good. I want you to relax enough to sleep tonight." She took her time, and before she finished he felt too distracted to think of his stitches.

She rinsed a stray patch of soap from his shoulder. "Wait one minute while I get your towel."

"You don't have to do that. I've got one on the towel bar."

"Just wait."

Susan returned in a moment with a towel warm from the dryer. "Here you go," she said, and she held out the towel so that Kurt could stand up and wrap it around himself. "I think I'll buy one of those heated towel racks. That would sure make the towels feel good."

"Ah, Susan, I think I can do this part by myself, if you don't mind."

"Oh, but..."

"No, ma'am. I can dry myself and put on my clothes just fine. Wait for me in the bedroom."

He saw that she didn't want to leave him, but with a sigh she gave in and went into the bedroom.

The warm towel felt wonderful, so he hoped she would buy that towel rack. He put on his pajama pants and joined her in the bedroom. "You were right about the towel."

"I thought you'd enjoy it, but never mind about the towel. I want you to come to bed. If you insist on going to work tomorrow, you need to rest."

Susan turned back his side of the bed and covered him after he lay down. Then she turned off his lamp and got into her own pajamas. Once in bed, she slid over next to him and put an arm across his stomach.

"If you need me in the night, don't hesitate to wake me up," she said.

What if I need you now? What would you say if I asked you to make love to me? Would you cringe like you did before?

He might have tried to find out, but he had had an awful day and felt worn out. Before the thought could do much more than cross his mind, he fell asleep.

Yeah, she knew she had overreacted. He wasn't dying, for goodness sake! He had a stitched up cut, but the extent of his injuries didn't seem to make any difference. She wanted to do something, anything, to make him feel better because she loved him. How could she not have known? Her mother had seen it and recognized it. Why hadn't she?

It didn't matter. She knew the truth now and blessed Jason for fighting with Kurt. After all, if not for Kurt's eye, his dad and Father Duncan wouldn't have visited, and if they hadn't, she might never have realized just how much she loved him.

Fingers running softly through his hair woke Kurt. Susan whispered something he didn't catch and kissed his forehead.

"Kurt, are you awake?" she asked. "It's time to get up if you feel like it. Are you sure you don't want me to call Mr. Dennis?"

He cleared his throat. "No, I'm fine. I have a headache, but I'll take something for it."

"Well, you get up and see how you feel. I can call him later if moving around hurts your head too much."

She threw back the covers, and moments later Kurt heard the water running in the bathtub. He got out of bed, wincing slightly as he bent his head.

"Kurt?"

"What?" he answered.

"Come and hand me a razor."

When Kurt opened the bathroom door, a shaft of desire shot through him pretty much at light speed. Susan was covered with bubbles and had one leg propped up on the edge of the tub. She had pinned her hair on the top of her head, and the bubbles barely covered the tips of her breasts. He realized he was holding his breath, wondering if movement would part the bubbles and allow a better look.

"I'm being lazy and didn't want to get up," Susan said. "Hand me a razor so I can do my legs."

Kurt found a disposable and handed it to her. She made no effort to put her leg back under the water.

"I think my ankle might be swollen this morning. See what you think."

"It looks okay," mumbled Kurt. If he touched her ankle, he'd want to do much, much more to her.

"No, you need to feel it. Go on, it won't hurt you."

He began to examine her ankle in the same way he would that of a football player, but his hand had a mind of its own. It moved up Susan's leg, touching and caressing all the way.

With a start, he broke the sensual reverie into which he had fallen. He prayed Susan hadn't noticed anything out of the ordinary. "It's okay. I don't feel any swelling."

"Thank you," she said, honey dripping from her voice.

She lazily drew her washcloth up her arm and across her shoulder. She trailed it across the front of her neck as her head tilted back to expose her throat. When her hand approached her breasts, Kurt mumbled something about the paper and hurried away.

He was absolutely adorable, and she was crazy about him. As the door shut behind him, Susan laughed silently at the expression on his face and wondered how long it would take before he broke down and asked her to make love to him.

"I'm going to your office with you the first thing this morning," Susan said as they left for school. "I want to be there when Jason comes in."

"Why? I promise I'm not going to fight with him."

"I want to thank him."

Kurt snorted. "Why? For beating the hell out of me?"

"No, silly. I want to thank him for taking up for me even if it was against his best friend. It took a lot of courage to do that."

Kurt shrugged. "I guess, even though as long as we've been friends, he should have known better."

She took his hand and gave it a squeeze. "Please, don't let this ruin your friendship. He did the right thing. If you really had been hitting me, you could have hurt the baby and me. It's good he didn't want that to happen."

Kurt flushed. "I hope you know I'd never hurt you. You don't ever have to be afraid of me."

Susan touched his face. "I know."

They drove to school, and true to her word, she accompanied Kurt to his office in the gym. "It looks like you're the first one here," she said, "but the light's on, and the door's unlocked."

"Sometimes the janitors do it for me." Kurt was standing by his desk thumbing through his mail, so Susan stared at him until he noticed her. "What?"

"Coach, you look awfully sexy standing there in those tight pants. I think you need a hug and a kiss," she purred.

Kurt dropped his mail on his desk and shook his head. "Remember what happened the last time I kissed you at school."

"The last time was in the cafeteria, not in my room. Anyway, there's nobody around but us."

Kurt sat on his desk as Susan moved purposefully toward him. She hugged him as she moved between his legs, her lips gently finding his. For the second time that morning, she wanted him. She and Tommy had hurt him so much, and she prayed her mother's advice would help her convince Kurt that she loved him. Their bodies melded together when he slid off the desk.

"We're acting like a couple of kids," Kurt whispered. He pulled out of her arms and put some distance between them.

Susan followed him. "What were you like as a teenager? I'll bet you were the captain of the football team."

"Well, I was. Were you a cheerleader?"

"Head cheerleader, thank you."

Kurt laughed; his eyes twinkled. "We're walking clichés. Think about it. The captain of the football team gets drunk at a party and gets the head cheerleader pregnant because he forgot to use a condom."

"The head cheerleader didn't stop him because she was smashed too."

He grinned. "At least the captain of the football team took the head cheerleader in a bed and not in the backseat of a car."

"And then the captain of the football team had to marry the head cheerleader."

The smile on Kurt's face melted away. "How much did the head cheerleader resent being pregnant by the captain of the football team?"

"The head cheerleader was knocked on her butt by it," Susan answered, "but after she got used to the idea, she found that she liked the thought of having a baby with the captain of the football team."

His eyes dropped. "The captain of the football team was afraid the head cheerleader wouldn't want *his* baby."

"The captain of the football team was wrong. His baby is the only baby the head cheerleader would want."

Color spread across Kurt's face. "Did the captain of the football team ever tell the head cheerleader how special that night was to him?"

"The captain of the football team told her the next day, but then he got his feelings hurt, and it was six weeks before he would speak to the head cheerleader again."

"The captain of the football team really regrets that."

The head cheerleader smiled and moved into the captain's arms. The captain had just begun to kiss her when the gym door opened with a screech. By the time Jason and Dan reached the office, the captain of the football team was sitting behind his desk while the head cheerleader sat demurely in the chair beside the desk.

Jason had dreaded this first meeting so much he couldn't sleep. When he saw Kurt, he came to an abrupt halt just inside the door. Kurt looked horrible! His face had turned an alarming shade of red and purple around the stitches; it looked painful.

"How bad is it?" he asked.

Before Kurt could answer, Susan jumped up and threw her arms around him, almost giving him heart failure. Then, to make a bad situation worse, she kissed him. Jason felt hot blood color his face. Kurt would probably kill him this time for sure. Kurt didn't strike him as a man who'd overlook his wife kissing another guy, especially a man who'd beaten him up the day before.

To his great relief, Susan soon moved away from him. "Thank you, Jason," she said. "I know you were standing up for me yesterday, and you don't know how much I appreciate it. If Kurt had really done what you thought he did, I would have needed the help, but he didn't. I want to tell you what happened."

Susan told her story, leaving Jason unable to lift his eyes to the desk where Kurt sat. "Kurt, I…" He broke off and hung his head. He had probably ruined his lifelong friendship with Kurt because of his impulsive action, and he'd never regretted anything so much in his life. How could he have believed such a thing about the best friend he'd ever had?

The creaking of the desk chair alerted him that Kurt had gotten up. He raised his face. If Kurt wanted to use him as a punching bag, he deserved it.

"Jason, it's okay. Forget about it. The way I answered you yesterday was sure to make you think I hurt Susan. We've been friends too long to let a black eye and a couple of stitches get in the way."

Kurt stuck out his hand. What? Was it really going to be this easy? Jason laughed aloud for sheer relief and gave Kurt a quick, guy type of hug. He had no right to expect Kurt to forgive him, but he wouldn't argue about it.

Susan smiled and gave both of them another kiss. "I'll see you guys later. I have to talk to Melissa and straighten her out too."

———

Kurt stood beside the volleyball net and watched as the coed game heated up. The boys were all showing off for the girls who were flirting with them nonstop. Sometimes he reminded himself of a teenage boy. He constantly ogled Susan, and he had tried to show off for her during regular football season.

He had wanted her so much this morning, and she almost acted like she wanted him too. She knew darn good and well there was nothing wrong with her ankle, so why did she ask him to check it? Why had she behaved so seductively when he saw her in the bathtub?

It would be nice if she'd leave him alone. Every time they tried to get close something bad happened, and he'd had enough hurt feelings and emotional upsets. Could they remain in a platonic marriage forever? Guess he'd find out.

———

Jason shut the door of Melissa's room behind him and struggled to fit himself into a desk made for skinny teenagers, not grown men. Then, he unwrapped the sandwich he'd made that morning. The cafeteria always served fish sandwiches on Thursday, but he didn't like them. Melissa did, though. She was eating hers with obvious enjoyment.

She was so adorable! Everything about Melissa pleased him, even the way she enjoyed a fish sandwich. They had such fun together. He'd never met a woman he had more in common with. At times it almost seemed like they could read each other's minds because they always knew exactly what the other one was thinking.

"I love you," he blurted out. He had wanted to say so for weeks, but he'd always lacked the courage. He didn't know why he had found the nerve to tell her now, but he thought it had something to do with her fish sandwich.

Melissa's head snapped up. To Jason's chagrin, she started to laugh. "Jason Cooper that's the most wonderful and unromantic thing you've ever said to me. We're crammed into desks meant for teenagers, and I'm eating a fish sandwich."

Melissa paused to laugh her fill. "I love you too, Jason."

Jason felt light-headed with relief. She loved him too. It didn't get any better than this.

Susan yawned and scowled. Why did she have to get up this morning? The last couple of days had been so emotionally exhausting she would rather have slept in, but she didn't think she should use her sick days now. Once the baby came, she'd probably need them more. At least it was Friday.

She flung the covers aside and forced herself to sit up. Oh, how funny. She had covered Samson up. Only the tip of his tail stuck out from under the blanket.

"Kurt, you're going to be late," she warned. She gave his shoulder a shake and pulled the covers off of Samson. "Come with me, kitty," she crooned. "You get some tuna for breakfast."

Samson didn't move. "Samson, aren't you hungry?" Susan demanded. She touched the old cat's head and started to cry. One touch had told her that her old friend was gone.

"What's wrong?" Kurt muttered. "Why are you crying?"

"It's Samson," Susan choked. "He…he's dead."

Kurt rolled over and looked at Samson. "I'm sorry, baby." He snuggled Susan against him and patted her back. "Don't feel bad. He had a great life."

Yes, but it didn't help much. Samson had lived with her for a long time. She couldn't imagine what she'd do without him.

Kurt got out of bed and slipped his pants on. "Would you like me to bury him?"

Her throat closed up and she nodded because she couldn't speak. She found a pretty enamel box her father had given her for Christmas one year and lined it with a soft, fluffy towel. It wasn't good enough for Samson, but of course nothing would be.

Kurt finished dressing and went to find a shovel. He came back and asked, "Where do you want to put him?"

"Underneath the oak tree in the back yard. He loved to nap there."

They took Samson outside where Kurt dug a hole for the enamel box. "I think it's big enough now," he said.

Susan stroked Samson for the last time; her eyes blurred with tears. "Sleep tight," she whispered. She put the lid on the box and fell mute as Kurt covered her friend's grave.

"I'm sorry, Susan. He was a fine cat."

Susan nodded and put her arms around Kurt. Why couldn't pets live longer? It wasn't fair they had to die so young.

Kurt kissed the top of her head and walked her back into the house.

Susan dragged through the entire day and left school as quickly as she could. Losing Samson on top of everything else had knocked her for a loop. She wanted to go to bed and sleep. When she slept, she could forget about her troubles for a while.

She'd visit Samson before she lay down for a nap. He had greeted her when she came home for quite a few years; the least she could do was greet him today.

She walked around the side of the house and came to an abrupt stop. An angel stood on Samson's grave. She ran toward the grave and sank down beside a concrete angel. "Where'd you come from?"

The angel held a big sword in his hand and looked as if he stood guard over Samson. Her lip quivered. Kurt must have done this at lunchtime.

Susan fixed a stern look on the angel. "You take care of him." After patting the earth on top of Samson, she went into the house to take her nap. The angel had helped, but when had she had a worse day?

She cried a little bit before she went to sleep and didn't wake up until Kurt got home at six. He sat down on the side of the bed and rubbed her shoulder. "Susan, wake up and tell me what you want for dinner."

She turned over and smiled at him. "You bought me an angel."

"Yeah, well, he can watch over Samson while he's asleep."

She bit her lip and managed not to cry. "I'll get dinner in a minute."

"No way. You stay right here. I'm in charge of dinner tonight."

Why argue about it? She felt too bad to argue tonight. Anyway, she had plenty of quick and easy things Kurt could find. "Thank you for the angel," she said. She put her arms around Kurt and pulled him close. "It's the nicest thing anyone's done for me in a long time."

"I'm glad you like it. I feel bad enough about him. I can only imagine how you must feel." He gave her a little kiss on her forehead. "You rest. I'll get dinner."

Twenty-one

Bill slammed the door behind him, causing Marjorie to wince as several pictures danced on the wall. He had taken her criticism better than she had expected. She had left him in no doubt he had to apologize to both Susan and Kurt, and naturally he didn't want to.

She absently started to clear the table, her mind wandering back to the time she first saw Bill. They were both sophomores at a small community college, and neither of them had any money. She met Bill in a literature class. He was a bit late, which ticked off the professor, but Bill had taken it all in stride.

He had stared at her the entire time, but it hadn't made her nervous. If she did say so, she was a beauty in her younger days. Men always stared at her.

Bill had walked her back to her car that afternoon with her heartfelt approval, and by the time they reached the parking lot, she had fallen hopelessly in love with him. She smiled. He'd been so handsome with his athletic build and beautiful, expressive eyes. He made an adventure out of every little thing they did, although she'd have to admit he could be absolutely infuriating. Bill had been and still was a male chauvinist, but he got away with it because he knew what he was and jokingly accepted it. And because he knew better than to try it out with her.

He was crazy about teaching and football and dreamed of being a high school football coach. She didn't care a thing about teaching or football, but she learned to like them because of Bill.

She had majored in home economics, a really useless major in her father's opinion, but she loved it. Her parents had made their displeasure felt in countless ways when she fell in love with a man who wanted to be a teacher. She wouldn't make any money, so they thought she should marry a man who probably would. It was uncanny how Bill had felt the same way a generation later when Susan married Kurt.

Bill's dream had come true; he had become a high school football coach while she had started working in a bakery. They never did have much money, but they were rich in love anyway, and they had two beautiful children. She had suspected for some time that Bill felt like a failure because of their finances, but until his outbursts following Susan's announcement of her pregnancy, she hadn't known how deep the scars went.

She prayed Susan would find happiness because she loved her daughter, but she also wanted Susan to be happy because she loved Bill. If Susan was happy, maybe Bill could feel better about himself.

Personally, she liked Kurt. He seemed like a decent man who'd take care of Susan. Oh, his salary wouldn't allow her to live in the lap of luxury, but she wouldn't starve either. He'd probably be a fine father too.

If only Bill would make an effort to forgive him. The two of them had so much in common. Too bad you couldn't make people like each other. She'd just have to hope that when Bill saw his grandchild, he'd be willing to forgive Kurt.

Bill got to make his apologies the following Saturday. He still didn't want any part of apologizing, but Marjorie hadn't given him much choice. "We'll go right after lunch on Saturday," she'd said. "That way you can get it over with. You were wrong to do what you did, Bill. You owe them an apology."

Bill had resisted, but in his heart of hearts the consequences of his rash statement to Tommy appalled him. Of course, he still resented Kurt, but he also believed Susan's marriage was valid. It had the seal of God and man on it, so he didn't expect Susan to divorce Kurt simply because he taught school and coached football for a living.

He grumbled during the entire drive to Susan's house, but he cheered up when nobody answered the door. "I don't think they're home. Let's go, Marge."

"Oh, please. You aren't getting out of it this way. Both of their cars are here, so they haven't gone too far."

He sighed. "Then let's check around back." Sure enough they found Kurt and Susan in the back yard.

Susan and Kurt had lined up to play a game of football. As he and Marjorie watched, Susan took the ball and ran toward the side of the yard. Kurt easily overtook her. He put his arm around her waist and pulled her backward against him. Then he fell to the ground with Susan on top of him.

"He's going to hurt her!" Bill hissed. "I'm going to beat the crap out of him!"

"You stand still," Marjorie ordered. When she used that tone most people paused to listen, and so did he. "He's not hurting her. They're only playing, and you know it. He's being very careful of her."

The same thing happened several more times, but then as Kurt went down, Susan jerked from his arms, grabbed the ball, and struggled to her feet. Kurt grabbed her leg and hauled her back. He and Susan were laughing which somewhat hindered Susan's efforts, but she valiantly struggled against him until Kurt finally rolled her over on her back and straddled her. Susan tried to tickle him, so Kurt pinned her arms above her head.

"He's too heavy to sit on her like that," an outraged father cried.

Marjorie smacked his arm. "Bill, shut up. Most of his weight is on his knees."

They heard Kurt's voice across the cold air. "Now what?"

"I guess I lose the game. You wouldn't let me score at all."

Kurt's head dropped lower. "What if I should try to kiss you while you're helpless?"

Susan, who still halfway struggled beneath him, went still as an impish grin split her face. "If you want a kiss, you'll have to make me."

Kurt burst into laughter. "And that would cause me a lot of trouble?"

"Yes, and you'd better be careful. I'm getting my second wind."

Unwilling to stand and watch Kurt kiss his daughter, Bill called, "Hey, Susan, you let him get through your defenses."

Susan's laugh rang out and made Marjorie smile. "I couldn't help it. He's too big for me to handle."

Kurt took her hand and pulled her up, and they joined Bill and Marjorie. Bill did a double take when he got a good look at their faces. "What the hell happened?" he demanded.

"Long story, Daddy. Let's go in, and I'll tell you all about it."

Susan produced hot tea and lemon cookies for them, and over refreshments she explained what had happened to cause two black eyes.

Even though he hadn't expected to, Bill felt a stirring of sympathy for his son-in-law and shame for his own behavior. Kurt had been treated pretty badly the last few days, even though there didn't seem to be anything wrong with him except that his job didn't pay much. He blinked. Was he really thinking of forgiving Kurt? With a start, he realized he was. *After all, Susan could have said no if she'd wanted to.*

He interrupted Marjorie who was speaking and said, "Susan, you might have hit his eye again falling on him like you were doing in the yard. Be careful."

All conversation came to a halt. Everyone looked confused, confused and shocked. Bet nobody expected that. *Kurt probably expected me to throw a fit about something. I've done a lot of that lately.*

"I will, Dad," Susan said.

Marjorie gave him a warm smile before resuming her conversation with Kurt. "I hope what happened won't ruin your friendship with Jason. The two of you have been friends for so long."

"I'm not going to let it ruin anything. Susan and I saw Jason yesterday morning, and we all made up."

Susan laughed. "I kissed him to thank him for standing up for me, but I think I embarrassed him."

"Well, I guess so," Bill growled. "You're a married woman, so you've got no business kissing other men. I imagine Jason thought Kurt might not like it, and frankly, I don't guess he did. Your husband is the only man you should be kissing. Find some other way to thank Jason."

Susan didn't seem as shocked this time. "I will, Daddy."

"And while I've got the floor," he continued, "I want to apologize for what I said to Tommy the other day. I'm sure he drew up those damn divorce papers because of me, but as far as I'm concerned, this marriage is permanent. I caused trouble between the two of you, and that was wrong."

Kurt immediately accepted his apology. "It's okay. I appreciate your saying so, especially since I know you don't like me."

"You know I appreciate it too, Daddy," Susan said with a suspicious quiver in her voice, "but I want you to like Kurt. He's my husband and the father of your grandchild."

Kurt cut her off before she could say anything else. "Let it go, Susan. He isn't required to like me, and I don't want to talk any more about it."

Bill saw the look of surprise on Susan's face. She too must have heard the steel in Kurt's voice because she did as he said and changed the subject.

As their car pulled away, Bill voiced his observations first. "I wondered who was wearing the pants in the family. It looks like Kurt is. When he told her to be quiet, she did."

Marjorie frowned at that. "You make him sound like a tyrant, and I don't think he is. Susan is too independent for that."

"Yes, but he does have a mind of his own, and he won't let Susan run all over him. Tommy let her do just that, so she didn't respect him."

Marjorie nodded. "Yeah, I think so too. Do you still dislike Kurt so much? He believes you do."

They paused at a stop sign. "There's not much wrong with him that I can see, except that he won't make any money, but Susan will just have to deal with it. If she wanted a richer man, she should have kept him at arm's length. I doubt he would have made her do anything she didn't want to do."

"His playoff game is in three weeks. Are you going?"

"Wouldn't miss it for the world. I want to see if he wins."

Later that evening Kurt and Susan drove over to the Deverauxes' house for dinner. It was nice that Susan didn't mind spending time with his family. He had heard of wives who refused to get along with their husband's parents, but Susan didn't act that way. She had even offered to bring dessert.

He heard Sheila screaming the minute they got out of the car. "Something's wrong!" Kurt yelled. He raced into the house with Susan right behind him.

They found Sheila and his mother in the foyer at the bottom of the steps. Sheila wore her jacket, but Kurt could see his mom didn't want her to leave the house. "I could hear you screaming outside," he reproached. "What's wrong?"

"Nothing," Helen answered with a fierce scowl for Sheila. "Sheila, take their coats, please. I need to get to the kitchen."

"Yeah, right. I told you I'm not sitting through a meal with them."

"You go to your room," Helen snapped. "Your father will speak to you later."

Sheila tossed her head. "I'll be glad to. At least I can have a little privacy in my room."

As she clattered up the stairs, Helen tried to smooth things over. "Teenagers. I don't know how you two deal with them every day."

Kurt let it go because he didn't want to upset Susan, but maybe he'd have a little talk with his sister before he went home.

They heard George's car pull into the driveway. "I'd better get in the kitchen," Helen cried. Susan went with her, leaving Kurt to meet his father.

"Hey, Kurt, how's it going?" Mr. Deveraux asked. He slapped Kurt's shoulder and gave him a quick hug.

"Not too well. Sheila and Mom were fighting when we got here. I think it was because Sheila didn't want me and Susan to come to dinner."

"Oh, she probably wanted to go out with her friends, and your mother wouldn't let her. She's been spending a lot of time with them."

Kurt nodded. That made sense. Teenagers were awfully moody, and their families weren't as important to them as their peers. He and Sheila had always had a good relationship, and he'd hate for his marriage to ruin it, but with just a little bit of luck, she'd fall in love with the baby once she saw it and forgive him for disappointing her.

He had a nice time with his parents. After dinner they all played Phase Ten, a game he loved. He didn't win, though.

That honor went to his father, who crowed and acted awfully proud of himself.

"How about a cup of coffee?" Helen offered as she replaced the cards in their box at the conclusion of the game.

"Sounds good," Kurt agreed. "You make great coffee, Mom." Susan and his mother went to the kitchen to get the coffee, and George went to the bathroom, so Kurt sneaked upstairs to talk to Sheila.

He knocked softly on her door, but she didn't answer, so he pushed it open and called, "Sheila? May I come in?"

"I'd rather you didn't," Sheila answered, her tone snarky and hateful. "Didn't you take a hint when I wouldn't answer you?"

Kurt went in anyway. "What's wrong? You're acting like an old sore-tailed bear."

"What's it to you if I am?" Sheila challenged. "Leave me alone, Kurt. I don't have anything to say to you."

"Are you angry because Mom wouldn't let you go out tonight?"

Her eyes glittered with what he thought was amusement. "Is that what they told you?"

"Yes."

"Well, it was kind of a lie."

He sat down on the cedar chest that stood at the foot of her bed. "Why don't you tell me the truth then?"

"Okay, since you ask I will. I wanted to go out tonight because I didn't want to see you and Miss English. Oh, excuse me. I mean Mrs. Deveraux."

Sheila's hateful attitude had started to take a toll on his patience. "Why are you mad at me and Susan?"

Sheila shot him a look of pure disdain. "You figure it out, smart guy."

"Neither Susan nor I have done anything to you, Sheila, so knock it off."

She laughed. "What are you going to do? Whine to Mom and Dad?"

"Sheila…"

"Just shut up, Kurt. Randy was right about you. You don't know your ass from a hole in the ground."

"Hey, watch your mouth."

"Or what?" She tilted her head to the side and waited to see what he had to say.

He refused to pick up the gauntlet she'd just thrown down. "Susan told me she saw you and Randy Poser together."

"She's a little tattle tale, isn't she?"

Kurt's blood ran cold. She could get into major trouble if she continued to see this boy. "Stay away from him, Sheila. He's trouble waiting to happen. I turned him in a couple of weeks ago for drinking on the school grounds. That's why he got suspended this last time. You're asking for trouble if you hang around with him. Think how it would hurt Mom and Dad if something happened to you."

"Something like what happened to you, maybe?"

Guilt washed over him. His mistake had affected so many people. "What happened to me doesn't matter," he said. "I'm older than you are, and I'm a guy. Girls have to be careful."

"Your wife wasn't careful, was she?"

"Sheila…"

"This conversation is over," Sheila spat. "You're a hypocrite. You got Miss English pregnant and have the nerve to say it doesn't matter, but then you lecture me and tell me to stay away from Randy because I might get into trouble." She made a gesture of repugnance. "Get out."

"I did make a mistake, but I learned from it. I don't want you to have to go through what I've gone through."

"You're so noble," Sheila mocked. "Get out."

Mr. Deveraux appeared in the doorway. "Your coffee's ready, son."

"Thanks." He stood up and appealed one final time to Sheila. "Think about what I said, okay? Randy's bad news."

"Randy Poser?" George questioned. "Isn't he the young man you went out with, Sheila?"

Sheila's face turned brick red. Thanks, Kurt," she screamed. "I hate you! Get out of my room."

His father's lips thinned. "Go on downstairs, Kurt. Sheila and I need to have a talk."

His feet felt almost as heavy as his heart as he left Sheila's room. How could he have messed up so badly? He'd hurt Susan and himself, but he'd hurt Sheila too. If something happened to her because of him, he'd never forgive himself.

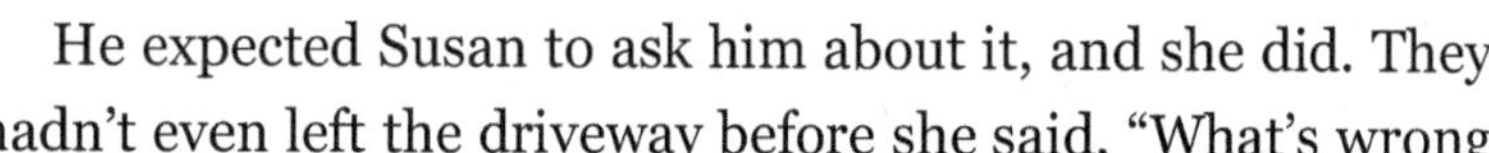

He expected Susan to ask him about it, and she did. They hadn't even left the driveway before she said, "What's wrong with the drama queen now?"

"Aw, she's still mad because she thinks I let her down by getting you pregnant."

"That isn't really her business, is it?" Susan's voice was so chilly he winced. "She's been nothing but rude and horrible to me ever since we got married. I've about had enough of her little theatrics."

Ouch, she sounded really ticked off. "Give her a little time to get used to things," Kurt begged. "Sheila's a good kid. She's just upset by this."

"Yes, you know I will," Susan said, but Kurt doubted she really meant it. Truly, he didn't much blame Sheila for disliking him. He didn't like himself too much either.

Twenty-two

Having finally admitted to herself that she had fallen in love with her own husband, Susan embarked on a crusade to get Kurt's attention both in and out of bed. She was far more successful than she would have believed, because after her rejection following the consummation of their marriage, Kurt was too gun shy to want a repeat performance. He flirted with Susan and enjoyed her kisses and touch, but remembering how the previous intimacy had turned out, he was afraid to take the steps necessary to move their relationship to a deeper level.

His attitude frustrated and worried Susan. She had begun to wonder if maybe Kurt didn't want her, a fear that goaded her to constantly plot new strategies to get his attention. Since most of her strategies created a great deal of sexual tension that found no outlet, both she and Kurt constantly felt frustrated and on edge.

Kurt's frustration finally erupted at school after a particularly trying morning. He and Susan had gotten up as usual, and Susan had gone to take a shower. She had come out of the bathroom wearing a thin, silk robe that showed her curves all too well.

"Kurt, the skin on my back is awfully dry. Will you rub this lotion on for me?"

He hadn't wanted to. Touching her only deepened his frustration, but he couldn't think of any logical reason to say no. So he had taken the small tube from her. "Turn around."

She had done so, but she had untied the sash and slid the robe off her shoulders in the most seductive way imaginable. Her shoulders had moved sensuously under his hand. She had shut her eyes and dropped her head while saying in a throaty, breathless voice, "Oh, Kurt, that feels so good."

A blind fool could see she wants more than just lotion, he'd thought.

Thank goodness he had stopped himself before things could go any further. On the night they had seen that awful movie, it had seemed so easy to ask her if she wanted more than just a kiss from him; but now there was so much between them, most of it bad, that taking her up on her invitation seemed impossible.

Heat flooded his face. Would he ever get over feeling inferior after he caught Susan crying on Tommy Price's shoulder? No matter how hard he tried to forget it he couldn't. And there was the little matter of how Susan couldn't even touch him after the love making that consummated their marriage.

He stood and walked over to the window. As usual, he had come to school edgy and tense, and today he had taken his frustration out on one of his students. His reaction had shocked the boy, but if the look on Jason's face was anything to go by, he had horrified his best friend.

His hands fisted. After the way he'd behaved, even the coaching staff felt leery of making him angry. They avoided him whenever possible and said very little when they couldn't.

The office phone rang just as he finished checking his last set of tests. He saw his father's number pop up. "Hey, Kurt, I wondered if you could stop by the store on your way home."

"Sure. See you in a minute."

He found his father alone when he got there. "Hey, Dad. What'd you want to see me about?"

His father smiled. "Your face looks better. Are you sure you're not mad at me for thinking you hit Susan?"

Kurt shook his head. "No, I told you I can see why you thought what you did."

George clapped him on the back. "What'll you have to drink?"

"Oh, a Coke I guess."

Mr. Deveraux got Kurt's drink and opened one for himself too. He sat beside Kurt and took a long swallow. "Ah, that's good. I hope this won't upset you, but Jason called me today. He said something was wrong, and you were taking it out on the students." He laughed. "Jason's afraid to talk to you, but he wanted me to do it. After what happened with your eye, I hesitated to agree, but if there's a problem I want you to know I'm here for you." He paused. "Is there anything you'd like to talk about?"

Kurt drank nearly a third of his soft drink in one long swallow before answering. "Nothing can be done about it anyway. It's pretty embarrassing, so there's no sense talking about it."

"Might make you feel better."

Kurt took another long swallow. "I'm just frustrated is all."

"About what?"

"Well, you know, about sex."

"Susan won't sleep with you?" His father frowned. "I'd imagined that by now the two of you had a normal marital relationship."

Kurt felt the pink stain that spread across his face. "No, she acts like she wants to be with me in that way."

"You don't want to sleep with her then."

Kurt gave a short laugh. "Oh, I want to," he answered as he drained the last of his drink.

"Then you'll have to tell me what the problem is, because I don't get it."

He tried to keep his mouth shut, but the floodgates opened wide anyway. It was such a relief to have someone to talk to. "Dad, it's awful at home. Susan goes out of her way to tease me, and I get so hot and bothered that half the time I don't know what I'm doing. The other day she walked out of the bathroom in a little skimpy thing and walked around in the bedroom like I'm a two-year-old child that wouldn't notice, but I did notice. Susan's got great, uh that is, she looks good.

"All the time she calls to me and wants me to do something that involves touching her. At night she snuggles against me and hugs me. She isn't careful where her hands go either. I want her all the time, and the more I see her, the more I want her. I'm starting to have dreams about... well, it doesn't matter what. I don't know where it's all going to end."

George blinked. "I still don't get it. You want her, she wants you. Why not make love to her? It's okay to do it, you know. She's your wife. Part of your obligation to her and hers to you is to be available for sex. I just don't see the problem."

"It's hard to explain." He shifted in his chair, unable to find a comfortable position. "I know she acts like she wants me, but I don't know if she really does or if it's all just something she's doing to try to make me feel better about everything."

"You mean about your eye?"

"Partly, but about Tommy Price too."

Mr. Deveraux frowned. "What about Tommy Price? Has Susan been seeing another man?"

"No, it's nothing like that." Kurt told his father the story. "Every time we start to get close, something bad happens, and the one time we did make love it didn't go well."

His dad's eyes sharpened. "She didn't want you?"

"Oh, she wanted me; it was only afterwards she couldn't get away from me fast enough. She started talking about being tied down and not having any choices in her life."

His father squeezed his shoulder. "I'm sorry, son. I'm sure it was a demeaning experience. We men are creatures of ego whether we want to admit it or not." He sighed. "I imagine your ego is probably on the floor."

"Yeah, I guess so."

Mr. Deveraux thought for a moment. "It sounds to me like Susan knows she was in the wrong and is trying to make it up to you; let her. To me, her attitude indicates that she cares about you on some level or she wouldn't make the effort she's making. If you sleep with her and try to get your relationship on a more normal footing, you'll feel better, and I think she will too."

Kurt tossed his Coke can into the trash. "I want to but right now, except for being tied in knots all the time, everything is good between us. She flirts with me and teases me, and we have a good time together. I'm too scared to do anything that might mess things up again."

"It doesn't look to me like you have any choice in the matter." Mr. Deveraux spread his hands. "Do you plan on spending the rest of your life in a platonic relationship? At this point, the longer you wait, the harder it'll be. You say Susan's willing, so go ahead."

"I can't." Kurt took a deep breath and blew out hard. "If something went wrong this time, I think our marriage would be over, and I'm not ready for that to happen."

"I'm at a loss here," his dad said. He stood up and reached for an apple in a bowl beside the cash register. "I think you could solve your problems if you'd take a little initiative. Let her persuade you to have sex. I know you've taken some pretty bad emotional beatings, but you can make things a lot better if you give her what she wants."

Kurt passed over his father's opinion. "I know I've been short at school. That's probably why Jason was afraid to talk to me. I've bitten off a few heads this week, but I'll work on it."

"Sleep with your wife and get rid of all that frustration, and your temper will return to normal," Mr. Deveraux shot back.

They dropped the subject, but Kurt didn't sleep well that night either. It was time for him and Susan to resolve matters, but he'd be damned if he had the guts to try.

"Hey, we going out tonight?" Randy demanded as he dropped into the seat beside Sheila on the bus.

"I guess so."

"When do you want me to pick you up?"

"I'll have to meet you somewhere. Kurt told Daddy he didn't approve of you, and of course Daddy listened to him. He said I can't see you anymore."

Randy smiled. "Coach Deveraux must be really ticked off. Where do you want to meet?"

"How about in front of Marie's Diner? It's only a few blocks from our house."

"I'll be there."

Sheila ran down the street. She was ten minutes late, which she knew would irritate Randy. In fact, he might not wait for her, and she'd die before she went back home tonight.

"You're late," he accused when Sheila finally joined him.

"Yeah, well, you tell my mother that. I practically had to break out of the house to get here."

"Let's go," he ordered.

He didn't bother to open the car door for Sheila who had given up expecting him to. Her father opened the door for her mother, and she had seen Kurt do it for Miss English, but Randy didn't seem to find it necessary.

Truthfully, she didn't much like his car. It was old and rusty and didn't smell good, but Randy boasted about the car's speed and power. In fact, he was going a little too fast as they went through the town square.

"You'll get a ticket if you don't slow down," she warned.

Randy treated her to one of the black looks that she hated. "Shut up. You sound like your brother."

Sheila did shut up. God forbid she should sound like Kurt. "Where are we going?"

"To Baker State Park."

"Why? It's cold tonight."

Randy sneered at her. "You really are an idiot. Why do I have to spell it out for you? Don't you know that people go to the park to...be alone?"

No, she didn't. When she went to the park it was either to have a picnic or swim.

The park looked deserted and dark when they drove by. "Aren't we stopping?" Sheila asked.

"There's a turnoff just up ahead."

The road Randy indicated wasn't really inside the park; it ran parallel to it. He turned and a few minutes later he pulled off the road into the woods.

Sheila stared out the window and into the gloomy darkness. "I don't like this place. It's scary."

Randy didn't bother to argue. He jerked her across the seat and kissed her. "Your brother really won't like this," he whispered.

Very true, so Sheila kissed him back. Kissing Randy in a place that looked like the setting of a horror movie didn't do much for her, but if it would hurt Kurt, she'd kiss him all night. They were in the middle of a deep kiss when a flashlight suddenly illuminated the front seat.

Sheila screamed but she saw a flashing blue light in the background and realized the flashlight belonged to a policeman.

Her heart sank when she identified Sheriff Kincaid, who sometimes stopped by her father's store. He motioned Randy to roll down the window. "You kids don't need to be out here," he said. "It isn't safe. We're had reports of a guy hanging around the lake after dark."

Randy, who'd had dealings with the law before, knew better than to argue, but Sheila didn't mind speaking up. "Oh, please," she scoffed. "Why are you trying to scare us? You just don't want us to have any fun."

The sheriff's eyebrows shot up. "Fun? That isn't exactly what I'd call it. I'd call it dangerous and stupid."

"I guess you'd know about stupid."

"Shut up," Randy ordered, but the damage had already been done.

"What's your name, young lady?" the sheriff asked.

"Sheila Deveraux. Why?"

The cop pushed back his hat and smirked at her. "Well, Sheila, it's like this. I intend to take you home and tell your parents what you were up to tonight."

Sheila went from anger to fear in a heartbeat. If her parents found out about this, they'd be livid. Who knew what they might do?

"Get out," the sheriff ordered and turned to Randy. "Go home, son. This is no place you need to be."

Randy cranked the car and left Sheila without a word, probably scared to spend his evening in the police station.

"Chivalrous, isn't he?" Sheriff Kincaid muttered. "Give me your address, Sheila."

Sheila remembered she'd like Kurt to know what had happened tonight. "I live at One-twelve Oak Street."

"Let's go."

She didn't mind if she did.

Susan greeted Kurt with a kiss when he got home that evening. "Hey, sweetie, where have you been? I was getting worried about you."

"I went by to see Dad. Something smells good."

She beamed at him as if he'd given her a hundred dollars instead of a small compliment. "I made roast beef for you and used my secret recipe to season it. I've got something special for dessert too, but I believe we'll have it later, in front of the fire maybe."

Dinner tasted as good as it smelled. Why was she going to so much trouble on a school night? Everything she cooked was good, but this was more elaborate than usual.

After they finished their dinner and washed the dishes, Susan pulled a DVD box out of her book bag and showed it to him. "I bought us a movie on the way home."

Kurt reached for the box and read, "*Saturday Surprise.* What's it about?"

"Wait and see." Susan left the room and came back minutes later dressed in thin, flimsy lounging pajamas. Good grief! He could almost see through them. She also had a bowl of strawberries and hot fudge.

"Go get the champagne, Kurt."

Kurt shook his head. "I don't want you to drink champagne. Pregnant women shouldn't drink at all because it damages the baby."

"Oh, I'm not, but you can. I'm having sparkling grape juice."

Kurt went to the kitchen, but he returned with only the sparkling grape juice.

Susan stared at the bottle in his hand. "Don't you want champagne? I got it just for you."

The episode at Mendoza's house flashed through his mind. "I'd rather have grape juice." He had vowed never to drink again, a vow he intended to keep.

"Okay, you can have the grape juice too."

The movie turned out to be a steamy romance complete with vivid love scenes. Susan dipped a strawberry in the hot fudge and fed it to Kurt as they sat on the rug in front of the television. "Look at his hands, Kurt. I don't think there's an inch of her body he hasn't touched."

Okay, no use to answer her.

Undeterred, Susan continued her commentary. "Look how submissive she is. Do men really enjoy it when women act that way?"

"Sometimes," Kurt said, trying not to stare at the television screen.

Susan leaned against him, allowing him to feel some delicious curves. "How does it make a man feel?"

"Powerful, in control, masculine," he mumbled.

If possible she moved even closer. "Do *you* like it when your woman submits to you?"

"Yeah, Susan. I'm a man. I do."

"Like this?" Susan lay back on the rug with her arms around his neck and pulled him down beside her.

Logic told him to get off the floor immediately, but his body had other ideas. Flesh and blood could only stand so much. He stretched out beside her and kissed her as if he were starving for her. He cupped her bottom to pull her closer, and that was when the doorbell rang.

Kurt cursed, and rolled away from her. Uh oh. The look on her face told him his language had shocked her. "Kurt, please!" she exclaimed.

"Sorry," he muttered, "but why now? For once why can't things go right?"

She grabbed his arm and hung on tight. "If we don't answer, they may go away."

The bell rang again. Susan jumped up and made a run for the bedroom, and with a groan of frustration, Kurt heaved himself off the rug and answered the door.

Fairfield's sheriff, Bill Kincaid, stood on the porch, and so did Sheila. "Mr. Deveraux?" the sheriff asked.

Crap. What could have gone wrong now? "Yes, sir. I'm Kurt Deveraux. What's going on?"

"This young lady says you're her father."

"I'm her brother, not her father."

"Well, Mr. Deveraux, we've got a little problem."

Kurt's heart sank. He saw Sheila shiver in the night air and realized his own feet were cold. "Come in."

They all went inside where Sheriff Kincaid told him why he had come. He concluded by saying, "I was going to send them on their way, but your sister got a little mouthy, so I decided to take her home myself. I'm sorry I bothered you. She led me to believe her parents lived here."

Did she lie to the sheriff because she feared what their parents would say, or was it was because she wanted to hurt him? Could be either one, but in the long run, it didn't much matter. "I appreciate your looking out for her," he said. "I'll see to it she gets home okay."

"Fine by me," Sheriff Kincaid said. "Take care now." He excused himself, leaving Kurt to deal with Sheila.

"Would you like to tell me what's going on?" Kurt asked.

Sheila tossed her hair and flung herself down on the sofa. "You know exactly what's going on. You aren't the only one who enjoys spending time with the opposite sex."

His ears burned, but he managed to keep his cool anyway. "I understand your behavior isn't safe."

She smirked at him, crossed her legs, and by golly if she didn't pull a cigarette out of her jeans!

"Safe? In what way, Kurt? Do you mean safe from the lurker person Sheriff Kincaid told me about, or are you talking about safe sex? If it's safe sex, you don't know much about it."

"What's a crack like that supposed to mean? And give me that cigarette right now."

He held out his hand, and Sheila tossed the cigarette at him. She glared as if he were her worst enemy. "If I'm remembering this right, you and Susan did have to get married, didn't you? She is pregnant, isn't she? At least Randy and I weren't drunk."

"And you're very lucky you weren't," Susan said as she walked into the living room. "Are you saying since Kurt messed up, it's okay for you to do it too? If you are, I've got a few things to share with you."

Kurt flinched. *Oh good grief. What would Sheila say?* "Ah, Susan, maybe I'd better handle this."

Susan turned a cool gaze on Sheila. "No, you let me talk to Sheila. Woman to woman, you know."

"Well, if you're sure."

Susan nodded, and Kurt escaped to the kitchen. Maybe it was cowardly, but he was so relieved to turn this problem over to someone else. She was his sister, so he should deal with her, but after all, Susan really could give Sheila a woman's point of view. And yeah, he knew that was a bunch of crap.

Sheila sneered at Susan as Kurt left the room. "If you think I'm talking to you, you'd better think again."

"Oh, I don't want you to talk. All you have to do is listen."

Hot, red anger burned Sheila. "You don't intimidate me. I almost feel sorry for Kurt living with a slut like you. Almost, but not quite. He deserves anything you can dish out."

Susan laughed. "I guess it takes a slut to know one."

"Don't you dare say that about me!" Sheila cried. "I've never done the disgusting things you and Kurt did."

"Isn't that why you went to the park with Randy?"

Sheila made no answer and tried not to cringe when her awful sister-in-law sat beside her.

"Premarital sex probably isn't what you think it is. When I woke up and found Kurt in the bed beside me, I wanted to die, but it was too late to take it back. What we've done can never be undone. We have to live with the consequences of our actions until the day we die.

"And if you think it was easy to tell my parents I'm pregnant, you're an idiot. How would you like to tell your parents you're having a baby? That was pretty bad because I hated to disappoint them, but you know what? It was worse when I told Kurt."

"I don't see how," Sheila cried, startled into answering.

"Really? Do you have any idea how it makes me feel to know my husband only married me because I'm pregnant? I don't know if he cares for me or not. If it weren't for the baby, he might move out tomorrow. If you remember, you're the one who pointed out those facts for me at Super Mart. Right?"

Yeah, she'd said that and took a lot of pleasure in it. She and Randy had laughed over telling Susan off.

Susan stuffed one of the sofa pillows behind her back and said, "What's more, I'd planned on doing a lot of wonderful things before I settled down, but I won't be doing them now. Can you imagine how you'd feel if some young man asked you out and you had to turn him down because you couldn't get a baby sitter? Or maybe the guy you liked wasn't interested in you because you already had a child. Lots of men don't want to raise another man's child.

"Kurt married me because he's a grown man with a good job. He's a very special, wonderful person. If you get pregnant, your boyfriend will probably run away. I doubt you'll ever see him again because most teenage boys aren't interested in being fathers. Look at all the young girls with fatherless babies, and you'll see I'm telling the truth."

Sheila's face burned like it did the time she had such a dreadful sunburn she had to go to the doctor. It was all she could do not to jump up and run home. "Stop trying to pull me down to your level! I'm nothing like you, and I never will be."

"Tell me something, Sheila." Susan's eyes bored into hers with such intensity that she had to look away. "Are you really willing to cut your brother out of your life? He told me the two of you have always been close. Maybe he didn't mean as much to you as he thought he did. It looks that way to me. If you really loved him, you couldn't reject him and his child."

Close to tears, Sheila snapped, "Just shut up and leave me alone!"

Susan stood. "You think about it, baby girl. You've got a lot of pride and freedom to lose."

Sheila stared at the wall and refused to speak, and Susan called Kurt. "We're finished in here. Why don't you take Sheila home now?"

Kurt grabbed his shoes and coat and Sheila followed him out the door. She slammed the car door almost hard enough to tear it off, but she didn't say a word. Ordinarily, she didn't mind telling Kurt what she thought, kinda liked it, in fact, but tonight the words stuck in her throat and refused to come out.

Kurt turned into their parents' driveway and stopped his car. "I won't tell Mom and Dad if you'll promise me you won't go parking again."

Jerk. He is trying to bribe me. But the idea of her parents knowing..."Aren't you afraid I'll lie to you?"

"No. You've never been a liar."

She set her jaw. "You have my word."

Kurt watched as Sheila slammed the car door and ran for the front porch. She had started this nasty, dangerous behavior when she found out about him and Susan, so he had to answer for this too.

With a sigh, he backed out of the driveway and turned toward home. For a minute there he'd thought he and Susan might actually resolve the impasse between them, but Sheila's visit had killed that hope in a hurry. The jinx was still on.

Twenty-three

The rest of the workweek went more smoothly. While still in the grip of a deep frustration, Kurt kept his temper under control. As a result, his staff breathed a little easier.

Fortunately, the playoff game took place in a week's time, forcing Kurt to focus on work, not his situation at home. Also, since Susan realized a lot was at stake for him professionally, she had temporarily suspended her campaign to make him notice her. Kurt slept a little better at night, and that too helped his temper.

Two days before the playoff, Melissa stopped by Susan's room before she left school for the day. "Do you have to go home right away, Susan?"

"No, Kurt said he'd be late tonight, so I'm not in a hurry. Why?"

"I want you to go shopping with me. Jason's mother invited me to lunch on Sunday, and I want something new to wear."

"This is looking pretty serious," teased Susan as she shut down her computer and slid it into a cabinet. "Your birthday is just around the corner. Are you getting an engagement ring from Jason?"

Melissa's smile gave Susan her answer.

"I'm so happy for you both." She gave Melissa a big hug, "Of course I'll help you find something to wear."

Melissa beamed at her. "Thanks. You have uber-style you know."

"Why, thank you."

"I've been afraid to tell you," Melissa said. "I'm glad you finally know."

"That's odd. Why were you afraid for me to know?"

Melissa blushed. "Well, you had to get married, and you told me how awful it was to have a baby with Kurt. I just thought you might feel bad hearing about my romance."

"You're my best friend." Tears filled Susan's eyes. She cried over anything lately. "You have to know I wouldn't resent your happiness. You can always talk to me, and you can forget what I said about Kurt. Things have changed. I like being married, and I already love the baby."

"But do you love him?" persisted Melissa as she methodically stripped a pencil of its decorative wrapping. "I can't forget the look on your face when you told me about the baby. I'm still afraid Kurt can't make you happy."

Susan laughed. "You can put your mind at rest. I love him, and he's made me deliriously happy."

Melissa hugged her. "That's what I wanted to hear. Hurry and get your coat. We have to go shopping."

Melissa found exactly the outfit she wanted, and with Susan's advice she selected shoes and accessories to match. "If I weren't pregnant, I'd buy that blue sweater." Susan pointed toward the sweater. "Since I am, I think I'll get this little maternity blouse." She held up a blouse with vertical blue and pink stripes and the word Baby printed on the front. "Most of my things are getting a little tight, so before long I'll need it."

Melissa nodded. "I like it, and I bet Kurt will too."

They emerged from the mall into the falling dusk and paused on the sidewalk to say goodbye. Susan stepped off the curb just as a small minivan careened around the corner. She had no time to get out of its way. The car stopped when it crashed into the curb, but Susan lay on the pavement where she had fallen.

"Susan! Oh God, Susan! Help me, somebody help me!"

Melissa's screams alerted security who phoned for an ambulance. After what seemed like forever to Melissa, Susan was en route to the hospital.

Kurt turned around when the gym door opened. Why, it was his father. Crap. *Something has to be wrong.* That air of grim purpose on his dad's face was scary. The coaches had stayed behind after football practice to drink coffee and talk, and it forcibly struck Kurt that he had forgotten to turn his cell phone on.

"What's wrong?" he demanded as he sprinted across the gym to meet his father.

"Don't panic, but come with me quickly. Susan's had an accident, and they want you at the hospital."

At that moment Kurt found out what people meant when they said their blood ran cold. A chill swept through him and froze him in place. "How b...b...bad is it?" he stammered.

"I don't know! Don't waste time on questions! Move!"

His father's sharp exclamation broke Kurt's paralysis. "Jason," he yelled. "Susan's had an accident. Lock up."

Kurt and his father rushed from the gym and began the seemingly endless drive to the hospital. Mr. Deveraux filled Kurt in as well as he was able. "I don't know too much about it," he said. "Melissa called me when she couldn't reach you, and I volunteered to go find you. She's looking for Bill and Marjorie. All she said was that she and Susan went shopping, and a car hit Susan. They took her by ambulance to the hospital, and Melissa went with her."

Kurt groaned aloud. "Dad, she can't be hurt too bad, she just can't! She's been driving me totally crazy, but I don't know what I'd do without her. I've even gotten used to the idea of being a father. Sometimes I think about what our baby might look like, and I wonder if it'll be a boy or a girl. I want both of them to be okay. Can't you hurry?"

"I'm going as fast as I can. We don't want another accident."

The car had scarcely come to a stop at the emergency room door before Kurt jumped out and ran for the door. The receptionist told him where to go, and as he tore into the waiting room he saw Bill, Marjorie, Melissa, and his mother huddled together, their faces tight with worry.

"Do we know anything yet?" he demanded.

Bill shook his head. "Where were you?"

"In the gym. We had our phones turned off."

Mr. Deveraux, accompanied by Jason, Jeff, and Dan whom he had met in the parking lot, arrived at the waiting room. "How is she?" Mr. Deveraux asked.

Nobody answered him, though, because at that moment the doctor finally came out to talk to them. "Which one of you is Mrs. Deveraux's husband?" he asked as he looked around the room at all the eligible young men.

Kurt stepped forward. "I am. How is she?"

"Is your name Kurt?"

"Yes. Why?"

"I'd like to speak to you in private, Mr. Deveraux. Come with me, please." The doctor pointed the way to a small room at the end of the waiting area. Kurt followed and took the seat that he indicated.

"Mr. Deveraux, my name is Gerald Davis, and I have good news for you. Your wife must be the luckiest woman in the world. The car hit her, but as far as we can tell, it only made contact in one place on her body, and that was her head."

Kurt gasped. "Oh, God. How bad is it?"

"Not bad at all. It was enough of a blow to knock her unconscious, but that's about it. We don't see any swelling, internal bleeding, or any other trauma. She's going to have a headache and may have a very mild concussion, but she's fine."

"What about the baby? She's pregnant."

"She's still pregnant, Mr. Deveraux. No harm came to the baby."

"Are you sure?" Kurt demanded. Upon receiving an affirmative answer, he relaxed a little. "When can I see her?"

"In just a moment, but first I wanted to ask if you and your wife have been having marital problems."

Kurt hesitated. "Yes, we've had a few problems. Why do you ask?"

"Simply because when your wife was recovering consciousness in the exam room she talked a lot. Over and over she said, 'I love you, Kurt. Please don't leave me.' If your problems are that bad, Mr. Deveraux, I'd seek counseling if I were you. You've got a baby on the way, and that baby needs a mother *and a father.*

"If you absolutely can't work it out, you should wait until after the baby is born to separate. The mind and the body are connected, you know. For the sake of her health, you need to wait."

Kurt shook his head. "I have no intention of leaving her. Not ever. I had no idea she was worried about that."

"I'm relieved to hear it. I'm an old fashioned man who believes marriage should be forever." He smiled at Kurt. "You work it out, and give Mrs. Deveraux a little reassurance. She doesn't need to worry about losing you if you aren't going anywhere."

Kurt shook the doctor's hand. "Does she need to spend the night in the hospital?"

"We'll keep her one night. Why don't you go and tell her parents she's okay, and then the nurse will take you to her room. Do you want to spend the night with her?"

"Yes, I do."

"I'll arrange it."

Bill and Marjorie were probably desperate to hear the doctor's report, so Kurt hustled back to the waiting area. Everyone crowded around him to hear what the doctor had to day. Face beaming, he gave the good news.

"She's going to be fine, and so is the baby. She has to stay here tonight, but I can take her home tomorrow."

Exclamations of relief flew around the room, but Mrs. English's voice rose over the rest. "When can we see her?"

Nurse Whitaker, who had just bustled into the room, answered the question. "Right now, but you can only see her for a minute so she'll know you're here. Then everybody except Mr. Deveraux will have to leave. I'm sorry, but only her parents and Mr. Deveraux's parents can go in."

Kurt passed his keys to Jason, who promised to take Susan's car home. Then the nurse handed Kurt a small bag that contained Susan's jewelry and clothes. "If you'll follow me, I'll take you to Mrs. Deveraux's room," she said.

Susan looked so still and white it scared Kurt. "Why is she still unconscious?" he begged Nurse Whitaker.

"She recovered consciousness a while ago. She's sleeping now. She had quite a shock, you know."

The Deverauxes didn't try to wake Susan. After satisfying themselves that Kurt didn't need them for anything, they decided to go on home. "We'll check on you tomorrow," they promised.

Mr. and Mrs. English stayed a bit longer, but since Susan still showed no signs of waking, Bill said they should go too. Marjorie started to cry, so Bill put his arm around her and handed her his handkerchief. "You call us if there's any change," he said, his voice gruff and strained, and Kurt promised he would.

Left alone with Susan, Kurt sat in the bedside chair. *I love you, Kurt. Please don't leave me.* Susan's words ran through his mind over and over. *I love you, Kurt. Please don't leave me.*

She must mean it. Susan must really have fallen in love with me. When did it happen? I knew she was trying to get me into bed, but I didn't know it was because she loved me.

And what about his own reaction to the news of the accident? *I was scared to death that something really awful had happened to her. When did I fall in love with her? I don't remember doing it, but when Dad told me she was hurt, I knew it was true.*

He deliberated for a long time as he sat beside Susan's bed waiting for her to wake, but he never could decide when he had fallen in love with her. What finally seemed clear, and really it was all that counted, was that no matter how their marriage had come about, he and Susan loved each other. *Thank God I found out in time. From now on things are going to be different. Since I know she loves me, our relationship is going to be a lot more intimate, and maybe I can finally get over being jealous of Tommy Price.*

A sound from the bed caught Kurt's attention. Susan stirred and called, "Kurt? Where are you?"

In a twinkling, Kurt stood by her side. He took her hand in his and answered with a catch in his voice, "I'm right here."

Susan's eyes fluttered open. "What happened? Where am I?"

"A car hit you while you were shopping with Melissa. You're in the hospital, but you're fine. You can go home tomorrow."

"The baby! Kurt! What about the baby? Is the baby okay?"

"Shh, don't worry about the baby," Kurt soothed her. "The baby is okay too."

Susan started to cry. "Are you telling me the truth? Don't try to spare my feelings. If I lost the baby, tell me."

"You didn't, sweetheart. You're still pregnant, and our baby is fine." Kurt's heart burned with gratitude for this miracle.

Susan sighed and relaxed. As her eyes closed, she raised Kurt's hand to her lips and kissed it. "I love you," he was almost sure he heard her whisper in the moment before she fell asleep.

Sheila wiped her eyes and blew her nose. What a horrible evening! She had been babysitting for one of their neighbors, but when she got home the house was empty. She couldn't find a note to tell her where everyone had gone either.

After a while she had started to worry, but before she had time to get too worked up her mother and father had come home to tell her what happened to Susan.

She didn't like Susan, but she didn't want anything to happen to her either. Oh, and what about the baby? Nothing that had happened was the baby's fault. For the first time Sheila realized that in a few months, a little person would arrive to be a part of their family. Amazingly, she would be the small person's aunt. No, she didn't want anything to happen to the baby.

And she didn't want something so bad to happen to Kurt either. He had let her down and disappointed her, but he didn't deserve to have his child die. Of course, it wasn't going to die. The doctor had said both Susan and the baby were okay.

She thought about what Susan had said to her the night the sheriff dropped her off at their house. It probably did hurt to know your husband only married you because you were pregnant.

Did Kurt really care about Susan? From his point of view, it probably wasn't fun to marry a woman just because you made a mistake and got her pregnant.

Maybe her mother and father had been right. Maybe Kurt and Susan needed a lot of support right now, and of course there was that innocent baby to consider. It certainly gave her something to think about.

Twenty-four

The rest of the night passed uneventfully. Susan didn't wake again, even though nurses came in several times to check her blood pressure or take her temperature. It did, however, wake Kurt, so by the time morning finally arrived, he was eager to leave the hospital and take Susan home.

Around seven Susan stirred and called, "Kurt?"

He rushed to her side. "Good morning, beautiful. I don't think I've ever seen a more wonderful sight than those pretty blue eyes. How's your head?"

Susan smiled. "It felt worse after a night of tequila at Mendoza's house."

It was the first time either of them had mentioned Mendoza, and been able to joke about it. Taken by surprise, it took him a minute to realize that the embarrassment, anger, and shame he had felt for so long had vanished.

"I never asked you this," Susan continued as she fumbled for his hand, "but did you throw up after you went home? I heaved myself silly, remember?"

"No, but I would have felt better if I had." He took her hand and pressed it to his face. "You know what? If I had the choice to make, I'd do it all over again."

"All of it?"

"Yes, baby. Every bit of it. I wouldn't change a thing."

Her eyes filled with tears. "Kurt, I…"

Susan never finished what she'd started to say because Jason called, "May I come in?"

Kurt straightened up and sighed. "Come in." As usual something had prevented him and Susan from having any meaningful communication.

His face broke into a smile, though, as Jason handed him a cup of steaming hot coffee. "I thought you might need it."

"Oh, yeah, you have no idea how much."

Jason walked over to Susan's bed when he saw she was awake. "How do you feel this morning?"

"Better, but I want to go home. Is Melissa okay?"

"Yes. She'll be by in a few minutes."

As if on cue, Melissa tapped on the door and joined them. "Susan, you scared me to death. I've been so worried about you."

"I'm fine, Melissa. Even my headache is gone, and the baby is fine too."

"Oh, I know. I stayed at the hospital yesterday until they told us you and the baby were okay."

Susan took her hand and squeezed. "Thank goodness you weren't hurt."

The girls continued their conversation while Jason pulled Kurt into the hall to talk football. "Are you having a practice today?"

Kurt considered it. "Do an abbreviated practice, but don't let anybody get hurt or anything. Tell the kids I'll be there tomorrow."

Both sets of parents arrived, so they had no more time for private conversation. The doctor looked in on Susan as he made his rounds. He chased everyone out into the hall while he examined her. Before long he called Kurt into her room.

"She's fine, Mr. Deveraux. I'm signing her release papers, so you can get out of here anytime."

"Should she take it easy for a while? Does she need to stay out of work?"

Dr. Davis smiled. "She can rest for a day or so if she needs it, but she can do whatever she wants. She's fine. Oh, and by the way, there's no reason for the two of you to limit sexual activity. You won't hurt her or the baby."

The doctor waved goodbye while Kurt and Susan each spared a fleeting glance for the other. The doctor's words had touched on a subject about which both of them had thought long and hard.

Nurse Whitaker called Kurt to sign some papers, and Mrs. English helped Susan dress. Jason and Melissa left for school, and Kurt returned shortly to take Susan home. He hoped it was a long time before he had to come there again.

"Do you think Kurt's in love with her?" Melissa asked as she and Jason rode down to the hospital lobby on the elevator.

"I'm pretty sure he is," Jason said. "He's never told me that in so many words, but it's obvious he's got it bad for her. I'm glad you told me she feels the same way about him."

"She was crystal clear about it. She said she was crazy about him, that she loved him and wanted to have his child, but I know in the beginning she didn't feel that way at all. She told me it was awful to have a baby with Kurt."

Jason nodded. "He looked pretty grim when he told us about it too, but it looks like they've both come to terms with it. I guess they decided not to let it ruin their lives."

Melissa's voice dropped as her cheeks flushed. "To tell you the truth, I've been angry at both of them, especially Susan."

"Me too," Jason agreed, "but I was madder at Kurt."

"Lately, though, I've started to understand how they could want each other so much they gave in to their need and slept together."

Jason understood perfectly what Melissa was trying to say. "I want you too, honey, but we're waiting. I'm not taking any chances with you."

They paused for a kiss and continued on their way to school in perfect accord.

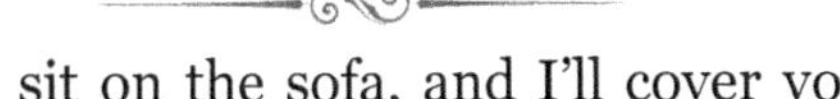

"Here, baby, sit on the sofa, and I'll cover you with this afghan," Kurt said. "It's almost lunch time. What can I get you?"

"I've been craving eggs and toast."

Kurt smiled. "Coming up."

He looked at her beautiful face, sat beside her, and pulled her into his arms. "If anything had happened to you and the baby, I don't know what I would've done. I still can't believe you're okay."

Susan rubbed his back. "I'm fine, Kurt. Relax." She grinned at him. "You can relax...*after* you scramble my eggs."

As the time approached for the dismissal of school, Susan glanced at her watch. "Aren't you going to practice today? It's time for you to leave."

He shook his head. "No, I'm staying with you. Don't you know you're more important to me than any football team in the world?"

Susan blushed. Her eyes were so warm and full of happiness he had to kiss her again. After a time, she pushed him away. "Why don't you go on? I feel fine, and you know the boys want to see you."

Kurt stroked her shining hair, marveling that it felt like warm, living silk. "I won't leave you. I'm afraid for you to be by yourself."

The doorbell rang before they could argue about it. "I'll get it," Kurt said. "You stay put."

When he opened the door, his jaw dropped. "Sheila. I didn't expect to see you here."

"I guess not. Can I come in?"

"Yes, of course." Kurt stood aside and Sheila entered the house. "I thought I'd stay with Susan if you want to go to practice this afternoon," she mumbled.

Kurt smiled from ear to ear as he grabbed her and gave her a big hug. "You're cracking my ribs," she complained, but he knew she didn't really care. He had prayed for this moment, and with no warning she had worked through her anger and wanted to make amends for her behavior. Now if Susan would only cooperate...

They went into the living room where Susan lay curled up on the sofa. "Sheila came to stay with you while I go to practice," Kurt said.

He didn't think she really wanted to see Sheila, not that he could blame her. Sheila had treated her pretty badly. He held his breath awaiting Susan's answer.

"Good. Now we won't have to argue about whether you're going or not."

Kurt made a mental note to kiss her as soon as possible.

He grabbed his jacket and hurried away, leaving Susan and Sheila alone. "I owe you an apology," Sheila blurted out. "I treated you like crap, and I'm sorry."

Wasn't that just like a teenager? They thought saying they were sorry made all the bad stuff go away. Well, it didn't. She could still remember how hurt she had felt when Sheila told her she would never be a member of the family.

The thought of Kurt stayed her tongue. He loved Sheila and wanted his family to like his wife, and for Kurt's sake she'd put up with a lot more than Sheila. "I accept your apology, Sheila. I think I have some peanut butter cookies in the kitchen. Why don't you bring us some and maybe a glass of milk?"

Kurt arrived shortly after practice began. Benjy saw him and raced from his place on the field. "Hey, Coach. How's Mrs. Deveraux?" he yelled.

"She's doing fine. The doctor said she could come back to school next week."

"Can she come see us play tomorrow?"

"She wouldn't miss it for the world."

Benjy thrust a fist skyward and raced back to the field.

After assuring Jason and the other coaches that Susan was fine, they made a few last minute adjustments to their game plan, and Kurt dismissed everyone. As he unlocked his car, he caught of glimpse of something small and gray as it ran under the front of the car. He hadn't seen what it was, so he bent over to look and came face to face with a small, scared kitten.

"Here, kitty," he called, but the kitten meowed piteously and refused to budge. Kurt sat patiently for a few minutes until finally the kitten moved into reach. He grabbed the little animal and pulled it toward him. It spit and hissed, but it was so small and thin he didn't have any trouble hanging on to it.

When the little creature meowed again, it sounded for all the world like it had started to cry. Its fur looked dirty too. As that little body went limp in his arms, Kurt was a goner. If the kitten had a home, they sure weren't taking care of it. Guess he'd take it with him.

The poor little thing shook the whole way home. It had started to rain, so when he got out of his car he stuck the kitten inside his jacket to keep it dry. "Susan," he yelled as he came in the door. "Where are you?"

Sheila came running from the kitchen, and Susan bolted from the living room. "What's wrong?" they both cried.

"Nothing. Susan, why aren't you resting?"

"You yelled for me, remember? What's wrong?"

Kurt unzipped his jacket and took the kitten out. "Look what I found."

"Oh, the poor little thing!" Susan exclaimed. "Where did you find him?"

"In the parking lot at school. He looks half starved."

Susan stroked the kitten's tiny head. "We still have some cat food in the cabinet. Let's feed him."

They fed the kitten, who gobbled down the food as if it had been a long time since he had eaten a meal. He finished his dinner, stretched, and sat down to wash his face.

"What will you do with him?" Susan asked.

Kurt smiled when the kitten tried to climb up his pants leg. Oww, it had sharp little claws. "I brought him for you. You've lost Samson, and this kitten needs someone. I thought the two of you might be good for each other."

"Oh, Kurt, I don't know." Susan bit her lip. "Just thinking about it makes me feel guilty, as if I'm being disloyal to Samson."

"He's a spunky little cat, and he needs a home. I don't think Samson would mind, so what do you say?"

Susan stared at the kitten, who steadily met her gaze and tried to meow, but not much more than a little squeak came out. "He's so bedraggled! He has to have a bath right away to get rid of any fleas."

"I'll help," Sheila said. "What's his name?"

Susan thought a moment. "Lucky. His name is Lucky because it was lucky for him when your brother found him."

"Lucky it is, then."

Susan scooped Lucky up and cuddled him close. "Let's bathe him now."

Kurt smiled as he and Sheila both followed her to the bathroom. This was one animal that would live up to his name. Susan would love him, and he'd have a life of cat luxury.

Kurt turned over again, but it didn't help. He hadn't slept well even though he'd spent the previous evening at the hospital. Might as well get up so he didn't wake Susan with his tossing and turning.

While he waited for some coffee to brew, he brought in the morning paper and thumbed through the sports pages where he saw an article about the playoff game. The Mavericks, it seemed, were going to lose. With a snort of disgust, he threw the paper onto the table.

"Don't believe everything you read," Susan said as she pushed open the kitchen door. She yawned and rubbed her face. "What did it say?"

"We're going to lose."

Susan laughed as she poured herself a cup of coffee. "We'll see, won't we? I know how hard you've worked on strategy, and the boys would walk through fire for you. I'd bet on you any day, Coach."

Kurt laughed. "You already bet on me, remember?"

"You're sure you're not still mad about that?"

He shook his head. "I'm sure. Do you remember the first week we were married? The team invited you to dinner, and you promised me a kiss whether I won or lost."

"I remember. Why do you ask?"

He reached for her hand. "If I win a playoff, what do I get?"

"Let's just say it's more than a kiss," purred Susan. "I can think of some things I think you'll like, and if you lose, which you won't, I believe I can make you feel a whole lot better about it."

I just bet she can. Maybe I should ask for a preview of coming attractions, but no, I'm so nervous I'd rather wait.

———— ❧ ————

Randy called Sheila right after lunch. "Hey, I haven't seen you in forever. Why don't I come over while everybody's at the football game?"

"I'm going to the game too."

"Why? You don't care about football."

"But I do care about Kurt. I've been wrong to act like a baby. Everything I've done was to hurt him because he disappointed me. Anybody can make a mistake, even Kurt, so I'm going to his game, and I hope he wins."

"I guess that means you won't be seeing me anymore," Randy snarled.

Sheila drew a deep breath and blew it out. "That depends."

"That depends?"

"Yes, it depends on you. If you want to see me again, there are certain rules you'll have to follow."

She heard Randy sputter, and in the background someone yelled for him to let the dog out. "Who do you think you're talking to!" he cried.

Sheila rolled her eyes. And people said girls were drama queens. "I know who I'm talking to. If you want to keep seeing me, the first thing that has to change is the drinking. I'm not drinking anything else, and if you're with me, you can't do it either."

"How did big brother get to you?"

"Second, I'm not going parking with you either, and until Mama and Daddy give me permission to go out with you, we'll have to stay at our house and watch videos or something."

Randy made a gagging noise. "Excuse me while I go throw up."

"You think about it. In spite of everything, I like you, and maybe you like me too, but we didn't start seeing each other for the right reasons. If you can play by the new rules, give me a call."

She sighed as Randy slammed down the phone. Time would tell if he came back or not.

"Susan, do you feel all right?" Marjorie crossed her arms across her chest, a sure sign she was nervous. "You're getting awfully excited about this game."

"I feel wonderful now that the Mavericks are ahead! It's so exciting, Mother! I want Kurt to win so badly!"

Susan and Melissa sat on the fifty-yard line with Mr. and Mrs. English and Mr. and Mrs. Deveraux. Both fathers smiled at Susan, who leaned over to give her father a hug. "You know what I mean, don't you? It looks good, right?"

Bill hesitated. "It could be better. There's another quarter to go, but it looks to me like the defense is getting tired."

"But they're a touchdown ahead!"

Bill shrugged. "That doesn't leave much room for error. If they make a mistake this late in the game, it could cost them the championship."

"Don't worry, Susan," Melissa answered with an empathic bob of her head. "Jason and Kurt won't let them lose."

"I sure hope you're right."

However, as the minutes of the fourth quarter ticked by, it began to look as though Bill might be right. The Mavericks lost two chances to score, and even though everyone could see Kurt was concentrating on boosting his defense, the Mavericks were slowly being pushed toward their own goal line. With three minutes left on the clock, the opposing team scored a touchdown. The extra point was good, putting the Mavericks in a tie ball game.

Susan swiped angry tears from her eyes when the other team won the extra point. "He's got to win! He needs this so much. I can't stand it if he loses."

"It's a game," her father remonstrated as everyone turned to stare at her. "Some you win, and some you lose. He knows that and can live with it, or he wouldn't be coaching."

Susan sprang to her feet. "I'm going down to the field."

Bill grabbed her arm and pulled her back down. "No, you aren't going down to the field. Do you want to make sure he loses? If you go down there, he'll be thinking about you, not about what he needs to do. Now sit still."

A sense of urgency overcame Susan. Something had to be done! "Then you go, Daddy. Go and help him. I know you can think of something."

"Go on, Bill," George urged.

Bill laughed. "Okay, I'll go, but don't be surprised if he chases me off the field. I doubt he's a member of my fan club."

As Bill made his way toward the field, the kickoff gave the Mavericks possession of the ball. Ken Banks did a brilliant job of gaining yardage. The opposing team finally brought him down at the forty-yard line. The next play gained a first down, but that seemed to be as far as the Mavericks could go.

Kurt called a time out. From the stands Susan saw him put his arm around Ken Bank's shoulders and talk earnestly to him. Ken nodded, turned, and sprinted back to the field where he gave directions to the team. Everyone held their breath as the team lined up. In an unexpected, bold play that relied on the element of surprise, they gained another first down, and Kurt called his final time out.

The coaches huddled together on the field. "Kurt, we're running out of time! We can only get off one more play," cried Jason. "Let's use Susan's play. It might win us a championship."

Kurt shook his head. "No, let's run the same play again."

"Won't work," Dan chimed in. "They'll be expecting it. Go with Susan's play."

"I said no."

"Use it if you want to," replied a new voice.

Kurt swung around to face Bill. "It's your play, not mine."

"And you're my son-in-law. It's yours if you want it."

"Come on, Kurt," Jason pleaded. He gave a loud yell as Kurt, with a long look at Bill, nodded his okay.

Ken Banks received his instructions; the crowd held its breath as the Mavericks lined up. In the stands, people rose to their feet. The team snapped the ball, and just as it did before, the play totally confused the opposition. Before they could figure out what had happened, the end carried the ball over the goal line.

The Maverick fans went wild as the band played a rousing fight song, and the cheerleaders led the crowd in a cheer. Susan burst into tears while on the field Kurt had a large bucket of cold water dumped over his head right before Ken Banks tackled him and wrestled him to the ground. The season ended in a championship as the final horn sounded.

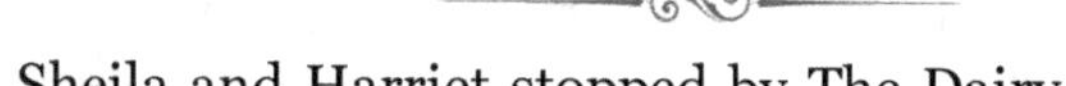

Sheila and Harriet stopped by The Dairy Queen to get a shake after the game. "Do you want to drink it here?" Sheila asked.

"Yeah, I'm not in a hurry to get home."

They were sipping their shakes and talking about the game when Randy strolled in. He spotted Sheila and Harriet, and they saw his shoulders go stiff. "What's his problem?" Harriet muttered.

Randy scowled at them, but he didn't speak; he got in line to buy his food.

"Let's go, Sheila."

"Not yet. I want to see what Randy does."

Harriet sighed. "I thought you said you weren't seeing him anymore."

"I'm not, at least I don't think so."

"Well, that makes no sense."

Randy finished paying and sauntered into the dining room. Did he intend to ignore her? No, he didn't. With the air of a man who was doing a hard, maybe unpleasant, thing, he strolled over to their table. "Hey," he mumbled.

"Hey yourself."

He took a deep breath. "Can I sit with you?"

"No," Harriet answered.

"Yes," Sheila said.

Harriet scowled at Randy. "You'll have to sit beside her."

Sheila slid over so Randy could sit down. "Want a French fry?" he asked.

Sheila shook her head. "No, I don't. Want part of my shake?"

"What kind is it?"

"Chocolate."

"Yeah, give me a drink."

Sheila passed the cup to him. "Did you go to the game?"

He nodded as he set the shake down on the table. "Yeah, I went."

"I didn't see you."

"You weren't looking for me either, were you?"

A strange feeling of compassion filled her heart, but Randy didn't need babying. He needed someone to help him with his behavior so she told him the truth. "No, I wasn't looking for you. Harriet and I were sitting with our friends."

"I guess I'm not in that group, huh?" he sneered.

"I told you, Randy; it's up to you."

He refused to meet her eyes. "I..uh...I wanted to ask if I could come over tonight. We could watch a video or something."

Sheila didn't care if the whole world was watching her. She put her arm around Randy's shoulders and kissed his cheek. "No, you can't. Dad's taking us out to dinner to celebrate, but I'm not busy tomorrow."

"What time?"

"What's good for you?"

"I don't know. How about six?"

"Six is perfect."

Randy hurriedly finished his burger and fries. "See you later."

"Later," Sheila agreed with a smile.

Now came the hard part. Now she had to convince her parents Randy was turning over a new leaf.

Twenty-five

"Where is he, Lucky?" Susan demanded for at least the tenth time. She absently stroked the kitten's soft fur. "He's had plenty of time to get here. Where could he be? Oh, wait. I hear his car now."

Susan dropped Lucky on the sofa and raced to meet Kurt. When he opened the door, she threw her arms around him and almost bowled him over like Ken Banks had done. "Kurt! You won! I just can't believe it! You won the championship! I'm so proud of you I can't stand it!"

Kurt smiled from ear to ear. "It was awfully close."

Susan took his hand and led him over to the sofa. "You used Daddy's play."

Kurt told her what had happened on the field between him and her father.

"I don't think Daddy dislikes you anymore, Kurt. In fact, he seemed glad of a chance to help you out, and he and your dad are taking everyone out to dinner tonight to celebrate."

"Who's everyone?"

"The coaches and their dates and both of our families. We're supposed to be there at six thirty, and it's already five. What took you so long?"

"I have to talk to you about that, but I guess I need to shower and shave first. Do we have to dress up?"

"Yes. We're going to The Brass Lantern."

Kurt whistled. "Pretty expensive."

"Nothing is too good for you, Coach."

Kurt laughed. "Yeah, right. I'll go and get dressed."

While he showered, Susan tried to find something to wear. She was still staring into her closet when Kurt came into the bedroom. "Better hurry," he said. He glanced at his watch. "We need to leave in a minute."

He went into the living room and Susan picked her black silk suit to wear. She slipped into a pink lace teddy and fastened a string of pearls around her neck. She frowned. They weren't going to look right with the suit. Dang it, she couldn't get them off. Kurt would have to help her.

She bustled into the living room and called, "I can't get the pearls off, and I've decided not to wear them. Help me with the catch."

She turned her back to Kurt who unfastened the necklace for her. "Thanks, Coach, I'll hurry."

She hadn't taken two steps before Kurt grabbed her arm. "Not this time. This time we aren't walking away from it."

Susan tried to pull her arm away. "This is no time for what you have in mind. We'll be late for your celebration."

"I don't care. If we wait something will happen, just like it always does. I'm not leaving here until I make love to you. I refuse to sit through dinner with my insides tied in knots because I want you so much."

In an instant she made her choice. With a little sound of submission, she moved into the circle of his arms. Kurt hugged her and bent his head to kiss her. His kiss both seared and dazzled and made her slightly dizzy.

He raised his mouth from hers and ripped the knot of his tie with one hand and threw it to the floor. She tugged on the buttons of his shirt as he unbuckled his belt. It was getting awfully warm in the house.

Kurt fumbled at the bottom of her teddy. "Get that thing off."

He didn't wait for her to do it. He scooped her into his arms and carried her to their room where he placed her on the bed and removed the lace teddy himself.

Susan gasped and slid her arms around his shoulders. "This is lots better than going to a dinner, Coach. Sometimes you do get good ideas."

Helen tugged on George's arm. "George, I think you should call them. We've been waiting for twenty minutes now."

Everyone at the table looked at him. "Okay, I'll call."

It was a little noisy at the table, so he went into the lobby to call Kurt. Kurt didn't answer until the fourth or fifth ring.

"Hello?" he mumbled.

"Kurt, where are you? Everyone's here and waiting for you."

"Dad, I'm sorry," exclaimed Kurt who suddenly sounded much wider-awake to his father. "We were taking a nap, and I guess we overslept. Have an appetizer, and we'll be there in thirty minutes."

"Okay, see you then," Mr. Deveraux answered. If Kurt hadn't been in such a hurry, he would have heard the smile in his father's voice. *I believe they had their own private celebration*, thought Mr. Deveraux. *It's about time.*

He returned to the dining room to order the appetizers while Susan and Kurt madly scrambled to get dressed. As they dashed out the door, Kurt stopped and pulled Susan against him. "This time you cuddled me after we were finished. Didn't you think about lost opportunities and choices this time?"

Susan flushed and hid her face on his chest. "No, all I could think about was you."

He'd love to kiss her again but he didn't dare. "Let's go. We're late as it is."

Susan raised her face to his. "I need a kiss before we leave."

Kurt laughed and shook his head. "I know better than to kiss you now."

"Now seems like a good time to me."

He pulled her against him even though it really was anything but a good idea. "If I start kissing you now, I won't want to leave at all, and we have to go."

"I guess." Her little frown smoothed out. "We don't have to be gone long, though."

Kurt kissed her anyway. "Promise we'll continue this later?"

"Yes, Coach. I promise."

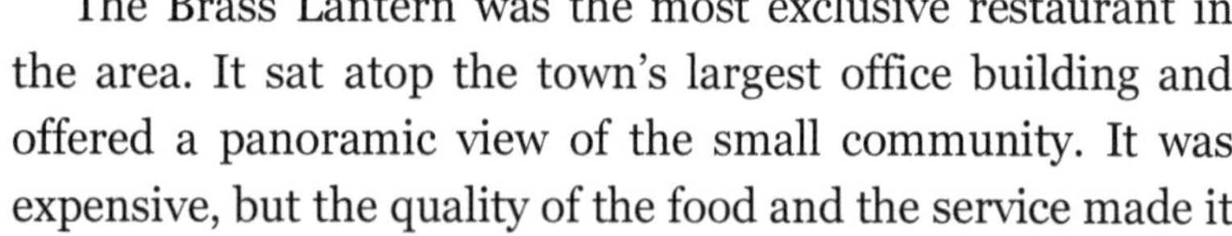

The Brass Lantern was the most exclusive restaurant in the area. It sat atop the town's largest office building and offered a panoramic view of the small community. It was expensive, but the quality of the food and the service made it a popular attraction. Many of the townspeople celebrated special occasions there, so the staff tried to recognize and compliment the honorees.

When Kurt and Susan arrived the hostess beamed at them. "Congratulations, Coach Deveraux. You sure made us proud today."

"Thank you," Kurt said. He tried not to grin like some laughing hyena, but he smiled from ear to ear anyway.

"If you'll follow me, your party is waiting for you."

To Kurt's surprise, the entire table burst into applause as he and Susan approached. Everyone got out of their seats and besieged him with backslapping, hugging, and cries of congratulations.

They finally sat in the two vacant seats beside Bill and Marjorie. Bill extended his hand to Kurt. "You did a good job today. Congratulations."

Kurt took his father-in-law's hand and marveled that this day had ever come. Who would ever have believed he and Bill would be friends? "Thanks for the use of the play."

"Not a problem. You're family."

Over dessert, Kurt reached into his pocket and took out an envelope, which he handed to Bill. "This is why I was so late getting home today. What do you think I should do about it?"

Bill looked a bit apprehensive. "You haven't gotten into trouble have you?"

"No, it's nothing like that."

Bill opened the envelope and read while around the table conversation petered out as everyone watched him. He handed the papers back to Kurt. "Have you talked to Susan about it?"

Kurt shook his head as he passed the envelope to Susan. "I haven't had a chance yet."

Bill grinned. "I can't help you with this one. You'll have to do what you think is best for you, Susan, and the baby."

Susan finished reading and looked at him with stars in her eyes. "This is why you were late?"

Kurt nodded. "They caught me coming out of the locker room. We went to my office, and they laid it all out for me."

"What's this all about?" asked George.

Kurt passed the papers to his father. "Tri State Tech offered me a job."

"Offered a job nothing!" exclaimed Susan. "They've offered him the head coach's job, and he gets to pick his own support staff."

Kurt took advantage of the buzz of conversation that broke out around the table, and said to Bill, "The money is a whole lot better. I don't think it would match what Tommy Price makes, but it's a whole lot better than what I make now."

Bill fiddled with his water glass and refused to meet Kurt's gaze. "I'm ashamed of myself for making you think money is all that's important in life. You may not get rich as a high school football coach, but you won't starve either. Don't take the job at Tech just for the money. Do it because it's what you want, or don't do it at all."

Susan touched his hand. "Don't do it unless it would make you happy. I'm proud of you either way."

"Are you, Susan? Are you really proud of me? I'm not a lawyer like Tommy Price."

Susan smiled as she pulled him close enough for a kiss on the cheek. "Yes, Coach, I'm proud of you. I don't care what you do for a living. I'm proud to be your wife."

"Oh, he likes hearing that," Bill whispered to Marjorie as Kurt raised Susan's hand to his lips and kissed it. "Well, what man wouldn't want his wife to be proud of him? Kurt's no exception, and I guess the way they got together, he might need to hear it more than most men, especially after that mess with Tommy."

"Have you made up your mind yet?" Jason called to Kurt.

Kurt shook his head. "Not yet. I've got a week to give them an answer, so I'm thinking long and hard before I say anything. If I do say yes, are you coming with me?"

"Probably, but I'd need to talk it over with Melissa."

Kurt nodded his understanding, and the conversation became general.

The group lingered a long time over coffee and dessert. Nobody really felt like going home, but they finally noticed the staff would like to clean up. Susan leaned over and whispered to Kurt, "I'm going to stop by the powder room on the way out." Kurt, who was talking to his father, nodded and squeezed her hand as Susan left the table.

Susan rounded a sharp corner and crashed into another person on the other side of the wall. He extended his arms to balance himself, and when she looked up, Susan saw Tommy Price.

"Tom...Tommy," she stammered. Her heart sank at the thought of Kurt on the other side of the wall. Things had been going so well! She prayed she could get rid of Tommy before Kurt saw him. "How are you? I'm sorry I charged into you like that."

"Oh, that's okay. No harm done." Tommy looked searchingly at Susan. "Is everything okay with you, Susan? I thought you might call me. I didn't know if it was a good sign or a bad sign when you didn't."

"I'm fine, Tommy. I told you when I last saw you that Kurt was a good guy."

"Was he upset about finding me with you?"

"Yes, he was, but we worked it out, and to tell you the truth, it started a chain of events that brought us much closer together."

Tommy almost smiled. "Are you trying to tell me you've fallen in love with him?"

"Yes, I guess so."

"Does he feel the same way about you?"

"He does."

An attractive blonde came out of the powder room and took Tommy's arm. "Susan, let me introduce Mimi Rogers. She's new to Fairfield, so I'm showing her the sights."

Susan understood why Tommy had seemed a little nervous. She took the hand that Mimi offered. "I'm delighted to meet you."

"Where's Kurt?" Tommy asked. "You aren't here by yourself, are you?"

He got his answer as he spoke. Kurt and his father came around the corner and bumped into Susan much as she had bumped into Tommy. "They really need to fix that corner," laughed Susan. She held out her hand to Kurt and drew him close to her side. Since he had seen her with Tommy, she decided to pretend as though nothing could possibly be wrong.

Tommy hesitated, then smiled. "I saw you on the news tonight. That quarterback hit you pretty hard."

Kurt laughed. "Yeah, he sure did. He was really excited."

"Do you coach?" Mimi inquired.

"Yes, I'm the football coach at the local high school."

Susan squeezed his hand. "He won a championship today."

"Yeah, it was a good game," contributed Tommy.

They took their leave of each other and Susan finally went to the powder room.

"So that's Tommy Price," observed Mr. Deveraux as he and Kurt watched Tommy and his date at their table. "Seems like a nice guy."

"Yeah, that's Tommy Price. Handsome and rich as ever."

"He's got a new girlfriend."

"Good."

Mr. Deveraux touched Kurt's shoulder. "You aren't going to get upset about this and start a fight with Susan, are you? She had no control over his being here, and it would have been ridiculous not to speak to him."

"No," Kurt said. "I'm not going to start a fight or get bent out of shape about it. I'm the man in Susan's life, not Tommy. I'm the father of her baby too. I have an important decision to make about our future, and I just don't have the time to be jealous of him anymore."

Mr. Deveraux looked pleased. "See to it that you remember it," he said with a laugh.

Susan came out of the powder room, and after exchanging good nights with the Deverauxses, the celebration ended.

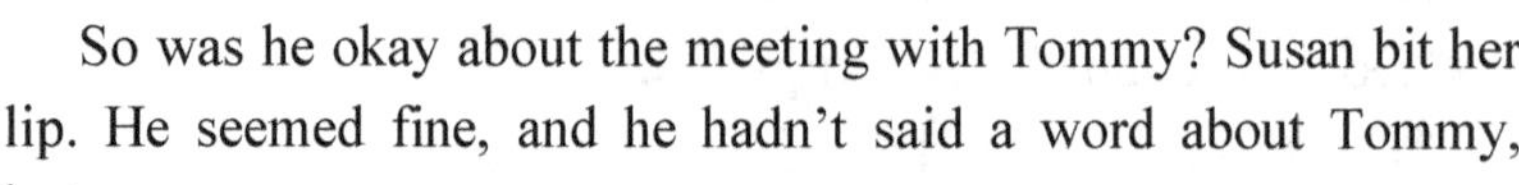

So was he okay about the meeting with Tommy? Susan bit her lip. He seemed fine, and he hadn't said a word about Tommy, but…

They stopped for a red light, and he unbuckled his seat belt and leaned over to kiss her.

"I can't seem to get enough touching and kissing, Mrs. Deveraux."

Susan smiled as Kurt reached for her hand.

"What are you smiling about?" he asked.

"Because I think you need a lot more loving, Coach. I'll be glad to help you out."

Kurt grinned. "Well, okay, but I don't want to wait too long."

"You don't have to wait." She gently ran her fingernails around his neck. "Is the minute we walk in the door soon enough?"

"I'm having a hard time controlling myself, but I guess I can wait that long."

Their car pulled into the drive, and almost before it came to a stop, Susan unfastened her seat belt and darted away. "If you want me, you'll have to catch me," she cried.

Kurt lunged for her but missed. He jumped from the car to give chase. Susan was trying to unlock the front door when he grabbed her shoulders. He nuzzled her hair to the side and gently kissed her below her ear.

"Do you still want to run away from me, Susan?" he muttered.

"What?" sighed Susan. She leaned back against him. "Kurt Deveraux, you feel so good."

Kurt turned Susan around to face him and took her in his arms. For several moments they stood there with their arms around each other, their bodies pressed together. Then Susan looked into his eyes. "I love you, Kurt."

Kurt put her hand on his heart. "Can you feel my heart pounding? I've waited weeks to hear those words." He cupped her cheek. I love you, Susan Deveraux."

Susan gave a big sigh and rested her head on his shoulder. "What a long, convoluted road we've followed to get to this point."

"Uh huh. What do you want me to do about the job?"

"I don't care, Coach. Whatever you decide is right. I'm still your biggest fan and I'll be your head cheerleader for the rest of my life."

The captain of the football team bent his head and kissed the head cheerleader, who responded with all the enthusiasm the captain could have hoped for. "It's cold out here," he said. "Let's go inside where it's warm."

He opened the door, and the two of them hurried inside, eager to begin the rest of their lives together.

Meet Elaine Cantrell

Elaine Cantrell was born and raised in South Carolina. She holds a master's degree in personnel services from Clemson University. She is a member of Alpha Delta Kappa, an international honorary society for women educators and is also a member of Romance Writers of America. Her first novel, A New Leaf, was the 2003 winner of the Timeless Love Contest. When she isn't writing or teaching, she enjoys reading, traveling, and collecting vintage Christmas ornaments.

Works From The Pen Of Elaine Cantrell

The Welcome Inn - Julianna can't stand Buck Abercrombie! He's rude, chauvinistic, and exasperating, and he's her new boss. Why wouldn't the bank loan her the money to buy The Welcome Inn? As manager she has proved her worth.

Worse yet, Buck's criminal brother Travis works for him, and her friend Melanie likes him!

The Captain and the Cheerleader - Susan English can't stand Robin Lanford! She's so full of herself she irritates everyone on the faculty of Fairfield High. When Robin bets Susan fifty dollars that she can't get a date with Kurt Deveraux, the head football coach, Susan jumps at the chance to put the little heifer in her place. She had no idea that teaching Robin a lesson would irrevocably change her life, strain treasured friendships, and throw two families into chaos.

Flood - Drawn together by their love of animals, Aria De Luca and Caleb Hawkins burn for each other. They never suspected that malignant forces around them were successfully plotting Caleb's ruin from the moment he entered her life. When the flood of a century strikes Aria's hometown, an alienated Caleb is all that stands between her and catastrophic loss

Turnaround Farm - Dedicated career girl Holly Grant has no time for romance. She doesn't need a man to complete her, thank you very much. Building Grant Realty takes all of her time and attention. If she can close a deal for Turnaround Farm, her business will take off like a rocket. Her first problem is that Jeb Wakefield doesn't want to sell his farm, and her second problem is Jeb's grandson Dan, the finest looking man Holly's ever seen.

Letter to Our Readers

Enjoy this book?

You can make a difference.

As an independent publisher, Wings ePress, Inc. does not have the financial clout of the large New York publishers. We can't afford large magazine spreads or subway posters to tell people about our quality books.

But we do have something much more effective and powerful than ads. We have a large base of loyal readers.

Honest reviews help bring the attention of new readers to our books.

If you enjoyed this book, we would appreciate it if you would spend a few minutes posting a review on the site where you purchased this book or on the Wings ePress, Inc. webpages at:

https://wingsepress.com/

Thank You

Visit Our Website

For The Full Inventory
Of Quality Books:

Wings ePress, Inc

Quality trade paperbacks and downloads
in multiple formats,
in genres ranging from light romantic comedy to
general fiction and horror.
Wings has something for every reader's taste.
Visit the website, then bookmark it.
We add new titles each month!

Wings ePress Inc.
3000 N. Rock Road
Newton, KS 67114